Praise for Joan Smith
and her Loretta Lawson mysteries

"A charming combination of sophistication, wit and unpretentious learning."

The Washington Post Book World

"Ms. Smith is a literate writer who manages to both educate and to entertain, which is no mean achievement."

The New York Times Book Review

"Smashing . . . Resembles Amanda Cross's urbane whodunits."

The San Diego Union

"Smith brings much-needed freshness to the academic mystery. . . . [She] is a tidy, streamlined, and clever prose stylist. She also manages to use sexuality in ways English writers seldom do: as both a weapon and a source of salvation."

Booklist

DON'T LEAVE ME THIS WAY

Joan Smith

FAWCETT CREST • NEW YORK

A Fawcett Crest Book
Published by Ballantine Books
Copyright © 1990 by Joan Smith

Library of Congress Catalog Card Number: 90-43897

ISBN 0-449-21964-X

This edition published by arrangement with Charles Scribner's Sons, an imprint of Macmillan Publishing Company.

Manufactured in the United States of America

First Ballantine Books Edition: November 1991

for Rosemary Goad

Acknowledgements

Grateful thanks to Carol Baker, Heather Barrington-Ward, Kay Brand, Susan Campbell, Lee Chester, John Mullan, Imogen Parker, Francis Wheen, and the late Dolly Adams.

1

LORETTA GENTLY UNROLLED THE STOCKING over her left knee, taking care not to snag the fragile fabric, then stood up to make sure it wasn't twisted before fastening the suspender. She stretched each leg in front of her admiringly, deciding it had been worth paying for real silk, and turned to the bed. The dress, an early Christmas present from Robert, lay neatly on the quilt where she had left it before her bath. There was no denying it was a beautiful garment, very much the sort of thing she would have chosen herself, but she felt a faint twinge of reluctance as she picked it up. She eased it gently over her head and down over her plain black slip, anxious not to damage the antique gold lace. It was a perfect fit, the dropped waist resting lightly on her hips, and she crossed the room eagerly to stand in front of the dressing-table mirror. She turned from side to side, enjoying the dramatic effect, but her uneasiness persisted. In the drawing-room a recording of Vivaldi drew to a close and she left the room to change it, puzzling over her feelings as she went downstairs. Perhaps it wasn't the dress that was making her uncomfortable, but the fact that it was a Christmas present from Robert? She remembered the casual way he had handed it to her the previous Sunday evening, saying he was giving it to her early because she needed something to wear for the party they were going to on Christmas Eve. And now here she was, dressed up in one of the most beau-

1

tiful outfits she had ever owned, and feeling—well, as if she, like the dress, was simply a possession. It wasn't a good start to the evening, and she made an effort to shake off her awkward mood. She put the Vivaldi cassette back in its box and rummaged in her collection for something energetic and cheerful, settling on the Communards, whom she knew Robert loathed. She turned up the volume as the first song started and began to sing along, then let out a yelp.

"Bertie!" she exclaimed. "Look what you've done!" She bent down to disentangle the cat's claws from the hem of her dress, picking him up and giving him a quick stroke before returning him to his favourite place on the sofa. Then she surveyed the damage, of which there was fortunately very little; she was engrossed in pushing a stray gold thread through to the underside of the material when the phone rang. Loretta gave the dress a gentle shake, hoping its fragile seams would survive the evening without further mishap, and reached for the phone.

"Hello?" she called, raising her voice above the music. "Sorry, can you hold on a minute? I can't quite hear—" She put down the receiver, went over to the stereo system and turned down the volume. "That's better." She paused, waiting for the person at the other end of the line to reveal his or her identity.

"It's a bit early in the evening for a party, isn't it?" asked a woman's voice, faintly quizzical. There was something familiar about it, although Loretta couldn't immediately come up with a name. "Or are you just getting into the Christmas spirit?"

"Um—" Loretta hesitated, still no wiser. The caller, whose voice was low for a woman, gave a deep chuckle.

"You haven't a clue who I am, have you? Well, it has been a long time. This is Sandra—Sandra Neil."

"Sandra? Good God, you're the last person I expected—" The words were out before Loretta had time to reflect that her reaction had hardly been civil. "I mean—gosh, I *am* sorry, I didn't recognize your voice."

2

Sandra chuckled. "I obviously have caught you on the hop! How are you?"

"I'm—I'm very well," Loretta said distractedly. How long was it since she had spoke to Sandra Neil? It couldn't be less than four years, it might even be five. "What about you?"

Sandra gave a heavy sigh. "Frankly, I'm in a bit of a spot. That's why I'm ringing you—I can't tell you how relieved I was when you answered the phone. Everyone else I know in London seems to be out or has moved. I suppose I ought to have expected it on Christmas Eve. So—I've phoned to throw myself on your mercy."

"On my mercy?" Loretta was immediately wary. She had not forgotten Sandra's skill in extracting what she wanted, even from people who, like Loretta, didn't like her very much.

"Yes. To be honest, I'm in an absolutely bloody mess. My flat's flooded, I can't find a plumber, and the landlord's away on holiday. I really am desperate."

"Where are you—where are you living these days?" Loretta asked cautiously, wondering what was coming next. "Have you still got that flat in—Blackheath, is it?"

"Good God, no, I haven't lived there for *years*. I've been working away from London, as a matter of fact. I only came back a couple of weeks ago. I've got a new job, and I've rented a flat in Notting Hill—"

"Oh dear, I don't know any plumbers over that side of London. There's quite a good one in Holloway Road, but I think he only does Islington. I can ask him, if you like? As it's an emergency . . ."

"Heavens, Loretta, I wasn't expecting you to find me a plumber. Even If I could find one who was willing to come out, which I doubt, the place is going to take days to dry out. And he'd no doubt charge the earth, you know what they're like. No, I rang to ask if you could put me up for a few days."

"Stay here, you mean?" Loretta was aghast. "But—I've only got one bedroom. And I've got someone staying over

3

Christmas," she added awkwardly, reluctant to mention Robert to Sandra.

"God, you're not back with that creepy husband of yours?" Sandra demanded. "What's his name—Lacey?"

"Tracey," Loretta said sharply, "John Tracey. No, I'm not. He's in the Middle East, as it happens, Cyprus. He isn't coming back for Christmas. No, it's—a friend."

"I'm glad to hear it. But even so, you must have a floor I can sleep on? Look, Loretta, put yourself in my position. How would you like it, Christmas Eve and up to your ankles in water?"

"What about your husband?" Loretta asked, suddenly bold. If Sandra could ask personal questions, so could she. "Can't you stay with him?"

"Hardly," Sandra said frostily. "He's gone off skiing."

"But what about your children? Surely—I mean, aren't you going to see them over Christmas?"

"They've gone with him. We are *separated*, you know." Sandra scarcely bothered to hide the irritation in her tone. "Really, Loretta, I've been through all the alternatives. I've even tried a few hotels. But as I keep saying, it's Christmas Eve."

Loretta stifled a sigh. "You'd have to sleep on the sofa," she pointed out. "It's a sofa-bed, actually, but—"

"A sofa would be bliss," Sandra said feelingly, sensing that Loretta was giving way. "You won't even know I'm there—really."

Loretta doubted the truth of this promise, but was too polite to say so. "When do you want to come over?" she asked in a resigned voice. "The thing is, I'm—we're going out in about an hour, as soon as Robert gets here. Can you be here by then?"

"What's it now? Ten past seven. No problem, I'll set off as soon as I've thrown a few things into a bag. What's he like, by the way?"

"Who?"

"This Robert."

4

"He's—well, you'll meet him when you get here. Have you got the address?"

"Yes, I found it in an old address book. Unless you've moved and taken your phone number with you."

"No, I'm still in Liverpool Road. Do you remember how to get here?"

"I've got an A to Z. See you soon."

There was a click as Sandra put the phone down. Loretta moved across the room, sitting down heavily on the sofa next to the grey cat. He immediately opened his yellow eyes, regarding her questioningly, and she began to stroke his head.

"Bertie," she said ruefully, "what have I let myself in for?" She remembered all the things she disliked about Sandra, trying and failing to convince herself that it was all a long time ago and the woman had probably changed for the better. Then there was Robert to be considered; the more Loretta thought about it, the more unlikely it seemed that he and Sandra would get on. Nor would they be able to avoid each other since Loretta's flat, while spacious for one person and a cat, certainly hadn't been designed for three human beings.

"Some Christmas this is going to be," Loretta told the cat, who had rolled over on his back and was purring loudly as she stroked his tummy. The scene with her mother, silent and tearful by turns on hearing that her elder daughter would not be arriving at the family home in Gillingham until the evening of Christmas Day, had been bad enough; now there was the imminent arrival of Sandra to contend with as well . . . Loretta curled her legs under her, careful not to put any strain on the material of her dress, and stared gloomily into space.

"You look terr-ific," Robert said, putting his arm proprietorially around Loretta's waist. He had a way of drawing out words as though he had discerned an extra syllable invisible to other people. "Those twenties things suit you, they go with your hair. That colour's very good—gold and blonde. I knew that dress was you. It took me forever to find it. I was

5

sure it was there somewhere, but I had to turn out half the loft.''

"The loft?" Loretta stopped just inside the drawing-room. Robert had arrived a few minutes before, and they were carrying their drinks through from the kitchen.

"Yes. It belonged to my grandmother. I was looking through some old photos the other day and I suddenly remembered there was a trunk of her stuff up there. You should have a look through it some time."

"I'm afraid I haven't got you anything so exotic," Loretta said, thinking of the Fair Isle pullover she had wrapped up earlier in the day. "Or so historic. How was the traffic?" she asked, changing the subject. Robert lived in a village in Oxfordshire, and his arrival in London was usually accompanied by stories of roadworks and traffic jams. She wanted time to absorb his revelation about her Christmas present: at least he hadn't, as she feared, spent a small fortune on it; on the other hand, there was something peculiarly *intimate* about wearing a dress which had belonged to one of his closest female relatives.

"The road was empty." Robert took a seat to one side of the smouldering fire. "Does this need more wood? I suppose it isn't worth it, we won't be here long. We-ell, here's to Christmas."

He raised his glass and Loretta did the same, smiling across the room at him. She noticed he was wearing a new tie, one with a vivid pattern of green and blue swirls. Loretta was still surprised, she didn't know why, by the care with which Robert dressed. He was tall and thin, his features rather bony, and although she hadn't been attracted to him at their first meeting she was now aware of a powerful physical reaction to his presence. She realized she had been staring at him and looked away, her face reddening, trying to conceal her embarrassment by paying extravagant attention to the cat.

"Sorry?" She looked up blankly.

"Penny for them." Robert was smiling. "I was only remarking we ought to keep an eye on the time. When do we need to set off?"

Loretta looked at her watch. "Oh, we've got another ten minutes or so. I booked the table for half past eight. In fact— um, I'm expecting a friend to arrive any minute."

"A friend?" Robert raised his eyebrows.

"Well, someone I used to know a few years ago. She's not exactly a friend—I've told you about the women's group I used to be in?"

"Ye-es." Robert looked at her quizzically, but Loretta refused to be drawn. At times like this he reminded her of her estranged husband, who routinely referred to the women's group as "the coven" and blamed it, unfairly, for the breakup of his marriage to Loretta.

"Sandra was in the group," she explained. "I haven't spoken to her since—till an hour ago, that is. She seems to be in rather a mess, she rang and said her flat's flooded and she's got nowhere to sleep. So I said she could stay here . . ." Loretta's voice trailed off as she saw Robert frown. "Look, I'm sorry, *I* don't want her here either—to be absolutely honest, I don't even like her. I didn't get on with her, right from the start . . . But what else could I do? It is Christmas Eve."

Robert shrugged lightly. "You don't have to apologize. It's your flat. How long is she going to be here?"

"Well, realistically, it's only Thursday today . . . I don't suppose she'll be able to get anything done till Monday at the earliest. But it needn't affect us. I mean, I'm going to my mother's tomorrow evening, so it's only really a day—"

"Just as well I brought two pheasants," Robert said. "I take it she'll be here for lunch tomorrow?"

"I don't know," Loretta said. "We didn't go into that. She may already have something arranged . . . But don't worry, I can do the cooking. Another drink? She should be here any minute."

"I hope so," said Robert. "All right, I suppose I might as well—don't get up. Can I get you something?"

He took Loretta's glass and went into the kitchen, leaving her to reflect that he hadn't taken the news of her unwanted guest too badly. She sighed, and looked at her watch again:

7

almost twenty past eight. Where had Sandra got to? She looked up as Robert came back into the room.

"Do you think one of us should ring the restaurant?" he asked, echoing her thoughts. "If she doesn't arrive soon . . . It's only fair to warn them."

"I can't understand it," Loretta said, taking her gin and tonic from his outstretched hand. "It was just after seven when she rang, ten past in fact. She should have been here ages ago."

"Where did you say she was coming from?" Robert sat down beside her, draping his arm along the back of the sofa.

"Notting Hill. She's just moved there, apparently. She lived in Blackheath when I knew her."

"In that case, she really should be here by now. I came in on the Euston Road and it was clear all the way. Have you got a number for her?"

"No. I didn't think—it didn't occur to me that she'd be late."

"You don't think she's changed her mind?"

"It doesn't seem very likely," Loretta said sharply, irritated by Robert's question. "I mean, she's not going to think, oh, I might as well stay here after all, the water's quite pleasant when you get used to it."

Immediately regretting the way she had spoken, Loretta glanced at Robert and carried on in a more conversational tone. "Especially not Sandra. She wasn't very happy with where she was living when I met her—she'd just qualified, it was her first job as a social worker, and she didn't have much money. She hated her flat, she said she couldn't get used to living in such—such *inferior accommodation*." Loretta smiled weakly. "The rest of us couldn't understand why she didn't move to a cheaper area, somewhere with more space. I don't think she'd ever been short of money before."

"She's younger than you, then?" Robert asked. "I must have the wrong impression—from what you've said I thought you were all about the same age. You don't talk about it—the women's group—much, do you? But if she'd only just started work—"

8

"Oh, she didn't start her training till her children were—I don't know how old they were, but she seemed to feel she could leave them. I think they may have been away at school or something. She did her training in London, I don't know why—I don't know much about how you train for social work. I can't remember how old she is exactly, but I know she's older than me. Thirty-six, thirty-seven—something like that."

"What about her husband? I presume she had one?"

"Oh yes. He lives in the country somewhere—Hampshire, I think. Where on earth can she have got to? Typical Sandra—" Loretta stopped, deciding not to reveal any more of her prejudices to Robert. "You're quite right, I'd better ring the restaurant."

She got up and went to the phone, picking up the receiver with one hand while opening the E to K telephone directory with the other. She found the number she wanted, dialled it, and warned the waiter who answered that they might be late, assuring him that they would arrive by nine at the very latest.

"If she isn't here by then," Loretta said worriedly, putting down the phone, "I suppose I could leave a note on the front door . . . It's a pity Shahin's away, or she could have let her in—she's got a key." Shahin was an Iranian exile who had recently bought the flat downstairs. "I really am—"

She was interrupted by the welcome sound of the buzzer in the hall. She went to the entryphone, picked it up, and heard Sandra's voice at the street door two floors below. Loretta pressed a button to release the lock.

"It's her," she called ungrammatically to Robert, opening the front door of the flat. She was immediately assailed by the sound of someone struggling through the street door, slamming it, and coming noisily up the stairs. A second later Sandra appeared round the bend.

"My God, I'd forgotten your stairs." She was out of breath, weighed down by a suitcase in one hand and a holdall in the other.

"Here, let me help you," Loretta offered, going down a few steps to meet her guest and taking the holdall. The bag

9

was heavier than she expected, and part of a nightdress was trailing out of one end where the zip had not been fully fastened.

"Did you get lost?" she asked, grumpily leading the way into her flat.

"That's better." Behind her Sandra dumped her suitcase on the floor and looked around. "No, I didn't have any trouble . . . Well, this all looks pretty much as I remember it."

"Really? It was redecorated last year . . . I was sure you'd got lost."

"Why, am I late?" Sandra made a great show of looking at her watch. "Oh well, if you're going to call *that* late—" She broke off, peering over Loretta's shoulder into the drawing-room. "Hello, you must be Robert." She skirted Loretta and advanced, hand outstretched. "I'm Sandra, Sandra Neil."

"Loretta's told me about you." Robert's tone was neutral as he came forward and took Sandra's right hand. "Robert Herrin."

"Oh!" Sandra turned to Loretta, a broad grin on her face. "You didn't tell me, Loretta!" She turned back to Robert. "My husband's an admirer of yours. He took me to one of your concerts once—your music, I mean, I can't remember whether you were there. You conduct as well, don't you? Well, well!" She looked back at Loretta, obviously delighted by her discovery.

Loretta felt, absurdly, as though Sandra had caught her out in some guilty secret. She pretended to study Sandra's luggage, then looked up again.

"Let me take your coat," she offered, and Sandra began unbuttoning her Burberry. She was considerably changed, Loretta thought, watching Sandra covertly; she was not sure she would have recognized her if she'd passed her in the street. Sandra's hair was cut differently, with a heavy fringe and the rest of it in a sort of page-boy—it occurred briefly to Loretta that she resembled an ancient Egyptian queen. The illusion was emphasized by Sandra's naturally olive complexion, though Loretta had never seen an Egyptian queen

10

in heavy horn-rimmed spectacles. They were definitely a mistake, she thought, observing the way in which they magnified the fine lines round Sandra's brown eyes. Loretta suddenly felt sorry for Sandra, and spoke to her over her shoulder as she hung up the damp raincoat.

"Would you like some tea or coffee? We're in rather a hurry but I've just got time—"

"I'd rather have something alcoholic," Sandra said, glancing at the empty glass in Robert's hand. "Was that a g and t? Heavenly. I've had an absolute stinker of a day—it wasn't going all that well even before the pipes burst. Where are you two off to?"

"We're going to a restaurant on Islington Green, and then to a party," Loretta said, leading the way into the kitchen. "Some friends of Robert's."

"Lucky old you," Sandra said, frankly envious. "So that's why you look like a silent film star. You look good, Loretta, that dress does a lot for you. While Cinderella here will have to spend Christmas Eve by the fire with a good book."

"I'm sorry, Sandra, but I had no idea you were coming," Loretta said guiltily, wondering whether Robert would mind if she invited Sandra along—yes, of course he would. "There's lots of food in the fridge. Help yourself to anything you fancy—"

"Don't *worry*," Sandra told her, apparently amused by Loretta's discomfort. "I'll be perfectly all right on my own. I'm used to it by now."

"I'd better just show you where everything is," Loretta said anxiously. "Is there enough gin in that? You're welcome to more if you—oh, OK. The bathroom's upstairs, next to the bedroom, and this is how you control the central heating . . ."

Five minutes later, to Loretta's relief, she and Robert were finally able to wrap themselves up in coats and scarves and leave the flat. They were ushered out of the front door by Sandra who, to Loretta's consternation, had already assumed the air of a hostess seeing a couple of unwanted guests off the premises.

11

"Bye. Don't do anything I wouldn't do!" Sandra's voice floated down the stairs after them as Loretta reached the street door. Robert looked at her, eyebrows raised, and she gave him a forced smile as she stepped out of the house into the unusually quiet street.

2

"But. Don't do anything, I woron't. No." Sandra's voice floated down the stairs after them as Loretta reached the street door. Robert looked at her as bronze ripped, amused

"MORNING LORETTA. YOU'RE UP BRIGHT AND early." It was the Tuesday after Christmas; Sandra yawned widely, pushed the kitchen door half shut with her bare heel, and pulled a chair out from under the table. "Come on, puss, you'll have to move," she added, addressing the cat who was sleeping peacefully on its seat.

Loretta watched, astonished, as Sandra tipped Bertie on to the floor and sat down in his place. The cat walked majestically from the room, weaving through the small gap left by Sandra's half-hearted attempt to close the door, his tail high in the air to signal indignation.

"And after such a late night, too," Sandra went on archly, grinning across the table at Loretta. "I wish I had your stamina."

Loretta met her gaze neutrally, determined not to be provoked. "Oh dear, did I wake you? I did try to be quiet."

"Actually I'd only just got to sleep. Anyway, it's your flat. No Robert this morning?"

"Robert? No, he's in Oxford. I'm not seeing him till New Year's Eve. Why d'you ask?"

"I wasn't sure whether I heard two sets of footsteps or one last night. Are you going to eat that?" Sandra's hand hovered over an uneaten slice of bread in the toast-rack.

"Help yourself." Loretta put down the *Guardian*, resigning herself to a conversation across the breakfast table—one

13

of the many drawbacks, she thought, of this enforced flat-sharing.

"Thanks." Sandra reached for Loretta's crumb-strewn plate and drew it towards her, picking up the sticky knife which lay on it and using it to butter her toast.

"You can have a clean one," Loretta protested, starting to get up.

"Nn-n." Sandra shook her head violently, gesturing Loretta back into her seat. There was a moment's peace while she crunched her toast.

"Any luck with a plumber?" Loretta asked hopefully.

"A plumber?" Sandra looked blank.

"Yes—I thought you might have found one yesterday. With Christmas being over, more or less . . ."

"Oh—I didn't even try. You know what it's like, people take so much time off these days—I don't suppose I'll have any joy till the New Year." Sandra finished and pushed her plate away.

Loretta frowned, alarmed by her guest's attitude. She had assumed that Sandra would want to get her flat sorted out at the earliest opportunity, and here she was—

"You know, you surprise me, Loretta," Sandra said suddenly, putting her head on one side. "You really do."

Loretta returned her look nervously, wondering what was coming. A complaint about her lack of hospitality? It would be just like Sandra to take offence at Loretta's mild suggestion that it was time to start ringing plumbers. "Why don't I make some more toast?" she asked brightly, hoping to head off whatever observation Sandra had been about to offer.

"No thanks—I'm not like you, I have to watch my weight."

Loretta said nothing, unable to help herself glancing across at the lilac kimono Sandra was wearing in lieu of a dressing-gown. It did nothing to hide her wide hips, and it occurred to Loretta that Sandra was made up of two triangles: a small inverted one for the head, ending in her pointy chin, and a larger one, right way up, for her body.

"So do I, these days," she said quickly, afraid that Sandra

14

had intercepted her look. "It was all right till I got to thirty, then—" she shrugged.

"Come on, Loretta, you're irritatingly slender and you know it," Sandra said disbelievingly. "How old *are* you, by the way?"

"Thirty-four."

"Lucky you. Still the right side of thirty-five. I wish I was."

"But presumably you'll have to . . ." Loretta paused, searching for a tactful way of expressing herself. "I mean, now that you've got this job at the health club—won't they expect you to, um, set an example?"

During Christmas lunch, Loretta had made the surprising discovery that Sandra had recently abandoned social work; the new job she had mentioned on the phone was, apparently, manageress ("Don't you mean manager?" Robert had asked Sandra innocently, his eyes on Loretta) of a health club in South London.

"They haven't employed me to prance around in a leotard, if that's what you mean, Loretta," Sandra snapped. "I'm management. All I've got to do is show people round, make sure everything's running smoothly. A doddle after what I've been doing, I can tell you." Her brow had darkened and she stopped speaking, her eyes roving round the small kitchen and its fittings as though she had been asked to make an inventory. It was a habit she had indulged right through Christmas Day, and it was beginning to annoy Loretta.

"What did you mean?" she asked, suddenly combative.

"What did I mean when?" Sandra's face swivelled back to Loretta as though she had just been reminded of her existence.

"You said I surprised you."

"Did I?" Sandra's eyes narrowed with the effort of recall. "Oh yes—this business with Robert, that's what I was talking about. It just struck me—do you know, I think I will have some more toast. Don't get up, I'll make it myself. God, the amount I've eaten these last few days." Sandra put a hand on her stomach and pulled a face as she went over to the

15

breadbin. "I'll say this for you, Loretta, you're a damn good cook. I was picking at that pheasant right through Boxing Day. Want any more? Toast, I mean." She sawed clumsily at the remaining half of a brown loaf, crumbs flying off the breadboard and landing on the kitchen floor.

"No thanks. What about—what about Robert?" Loretta had a tight feeling in her chest, and a strong sense that she wasn't going to like whatever Sandra was about to say.

"Well, I wouldn't have thought he was your type, that's all. He's a bit straight—a bit conventional for you."

"Oh, I don't know—"

"I mean, there's nothing I can put my finger on, but—to tell you the truth, he reminds me of your husband." Sandra turned her back on Loretta, attempting inexpertly to light the grill with a match which flickered and went out. "Damn."

"John? I didn't know you'd met him."

"Oh yes, a couple of times. I can't remember where. He was very much as you—what's wrong with this wretched thing? Oh, I see—described him." The grill dealt with successfully, Sandra turned and leaned back against a waist-high cupboard so she could watch Loretta's reaction. "Bossy."

"I don't think I ever said he was bossy!"

"Not in so many words. But that was the gist of it, wasn't it? Not treating you like an adult. Why don't you do this, Loretta, do you have to do that, Loretta. You know what I mean. That's what Robert reminds me of. Buying you that dress, for instance. That little gold number you were wearing on Christmas Eve."

"He didn't buy it."

"Didn't he? That's not the point, is it? I'm not going to argue about where he got it from. The thing is, I said something about it on Christmas morning when he was peeling the potatoes. You were upstairs, I think. And he said, 'I'm glad you like it—Loretta has this idea she should wear black all the time, because of being blonde, but I want her to be a bit more adventurous.' What I mean is—well, *come on*. You're thirty-four, you said so yourself. Aren't you old enough to choose your own clothes?" She gave Loretta a

16

frank, open look, then reached across to pull out the grill-pan and turn over her toast, which was beginning to take on a dark brown colour.

"It's only happened once," Loretta said awkwardly.

"Yes, but it's not just that," Sandra said over her shoulder, her attention now firmly fixed on the grill. "God, this thing's fierce when it gets going." She hooked the bread out, whirled round and dropped it on the table. "Ouch, that was hot." She sucked her fingers thoughtfully, then transferred the piece of toast to Loretta's dirty place. "It's the effect he has on you. I could be wrong, I haven't seen you for a long time, but when he's around you seem—subdued."

Loretta's heart sank even further. "You haven't seen us together very much," she protested weakly.

"All of Christmas Day," Sandra pointed out, not looking up from loading marmalade on to her second piece of toast. "You didn't go off to your mother's till—what, sevenish? I mean, I don't want to be rude, but it's not what I expected of you. I remember in the women's group, I was terrified of you and Bridget. You were always so . . . *pure*."

"Pure?"

"Come on, you know what I mean. You'd read everything, all those books I'd hardly even heard of. I didn't dare admit it, but I went off and tried reading one of them, Andrea what's her name? You know who I mean."

"Dworkin?"

"That's her. And I thought, my God, is this woman serious? But let's face it, I always was the odd one out, wasn't I?" She paused from eating, one hand poised in the air.

"I don't know what you mean," Loretta began, aware that the statement was half true but irritated by the self-pity in Sandra's voice. "You always got on very well with Sally. She saw more of you outside the group than she did the rest of us."

"That was just because we happened to have the same job," Sandra said, shaking her head. "It didn't last long after the group broke up. But the rest of you—frankly, I always

17

felt if I arrived late you'd been talking about me behind my back.''

"Oh, for heaven's sake," Loretta said impatiently. "The group didn't work like that. If you felt left out, it was because the rest of us had more in common to start with. You'd only just come to London, remember, and the rest of us had been here for ages. And you had children, which the rest of us didn't.''

"All right, all right, I don't want an argument—I can't cope with it over breakfast. Let's change the subject—you were telling me about Robert.'' Sandra picked up her knife, licked it, and smiled knowingly at Loretta. "How long have you two—known each other?''

"A while,'' Loretta said evasively. She didn't feel like discussing the relationship with Sandra.

"And?''

"And what?''

"How did you meet, when did you first—you know.''

Loretta sighed audibly and hoped Sandra would take the hint. Instead, the other woman went on looking at her expectantly.

"We, um, we saw a bit of each other eighteen months ago,'' Loretta said awkwardly. "Then it all went wrong and—as a matter of face, I didn't even see him again till six weeks ago. I'd been to something at Convent Garden and he was waiting for a taxi when I came out . . . We got talking, and he asked me to a party . . . That's all there is to it. He isn't the great love of my life, you know.''

"Hmm. Is he good in bed?''

Loretta felt her cheeks grow hot. Before she could answer, Sandra laughed.

"I thought that must be it, I couldn't see why you stuck with him otherwise. I know he's quite famous, but I didn't think it was quite your scene. All right, you don't have to tell me if you don't want to.'' She shrugged and reached for the paper. "What's been happening in the world?''

"Nothing much. Everything seems to shut down over Christmas. Even wars and things. What about you? What

18

about your love life?'' The last words had no sooner left her lips than Loretta regretted them; she had allowed Sandra to annoy her into unaccustomed rudeness. Not to mention her unfortunate phrasing—she sounded like a fifteen-year-old schoolgirl exchanging confidences behind the bike sheds.

"Oh, I live the life of a nun, these days," Sandra said airily, opening the paper wide. "Nothing to report on that score."

"But your—" Loretta stopped in mid-sentence. She had been on the verge of inquiring after Sandra's husband and children, who had not been mentioned in the course of Christmas Day, but decided against it. Sandra's life was really none of her business; the woman would move out soon, and Loretta thought it highly unlikely that they would keep in touch. "I must get on," she said, standing up and starting to pile the dishes next to the sink.

"What you need is a dish-washer," Sandra's voice observed from the depths of the *Guardian*. "Leave them, I'll do them when I've finished this."

"Thanks," said Loretta, glad of any sign on Sandra's part that she was willing to share the household chores. "I'll go and run my bath. By the way—" She stopped at the door, choosing her words carefully. "You're welcome to stay as long as you like, I'm not trying to get rid of you . . . But the Yellow Pages are underneath the phone books if you did want to try some plumbers . . . You never know, you might be lucky . . ."

Sandra put down the paper, an exasperated expression on her face. "Look, Loretta, I realize this is putting a strain on you—I'll be out of here as quickly as I can. But it's not easy for me, either. This has come at the worst possible time, what with the new job and all these bank holidays . . . What are your plans for today?" she added in a less hostile tone. "I can do some ringing round but I don't want to get in your way . . ."

"Oh, I'm going to be out all day. I'm finishing a book." Loretta cheered up at the thought. "I've promised it to Vixen, that's my publisher, by the beginning of January, and I've

19

still got quite a lot to do. It's all on the department computer, so I have to go into the office . . ."

She paused, giving Sandra a chance to inquire about the subject of the book. She didn't.

"OK. Have a good day." Sandra waved her hand, picking up the paper again.

Loretta waited a second, raised her eyes to the ceiling, then made her way upstairs to the bathroom.

The day's work got off to a good start. Loretta let herself into the silent English department with her key, unlocked her room and sat down at her desk. It was not a particularly attractive place to work, the college being a relatively recent addition to the University of London and housed in a functional nineteen-sixties block, but the office was at least spacious and well-equipped. Loretta opened a drawer, took out the discs on which her book was stored, and slotted one of them into her computer terminal. The main body of the much delayed work, a literary biography of Edith Wharton, was now complete; all that remained was to annotate the text and attach a list of sources to each chapter. Loretta had been halfway through when she broke off for Christmas, and she took up the task again at chapter eight with a light heart. Another couple of days, she thought, and it would be finished—just in time to meet the deadline agreed with Vixen Press, a small but lively feminist imprint. She still had to think of a title, but she was confident that something suitable would occur to her once she had the manuscript printed out and in her hands. She worked with a mounting sense of excitement, Edith Wharton's novels stacked neatly on the desk beside her, and it was after three when her aching back told her it was time to take a break.

Returning from the vending machine in the corridor with a cup of scummy tea in one hand, Loretta realized she was hungry and wondered what to do about supper. There wasn't much food left in the flat, although it was just possible that Sandra had gone out and stocked up. Possible but unlikely, Loretta thought, reaching for the phone. She dialled her own

20

number and to her annoyance listened to it ring unanswered. Sandra *had* gone out; moreover she had failed to switch on Loretta's answering-machine, in spite of being shown how to do it on Christmas Day.

"God, that woman," Loretta said impatiently. Then she brightened. It had seemed to her that morning that Sandra was being unduly pessimistic about her chances of finding someone to fix her pipes or her water tank or whatever needed attention; perhaps she'd struck lucky with Yellow Pages, and had rushed over to Notting Hill. She might even be able to move back into her flat before the week was out, restoring Loretta to her much missed solitude. Feeling a little guilty at entertaining such selfish thoughts, Loretta sipped her tea and decided to leave the office in time to do some shopping on the way home. She flipped idly through the latest copy of *Fem Sap*, a feminist academic journal of whose editorial collective she was a member, pleased to discover a long article about the writing of George Sand, a novelist whose work she had recently read for the first time. It bore a promising title, *Le style est la femme même*, and Loretta made a mental note to read it that evening. Then she closed the journal, stuffed it into her shoulder-bag, and went back to work.

This time, things did not go so well. She could not recall where she had found the quotation in the text, a pithy comparison of Edith Wharton's work with that of Henry James by Eileen Chester, an American academic; Chester had not written a book on Edith Wharton, but she was an active contributor to quarterly journals and to volumes of American literary criticism. Loretta began taking books down from her shelves, gradually creating chaos in a room which was usually notable for its order, but the origin of the quote remained elusive. It must be in one of the journals, but which one? It was tempting to remove the passage altogether, she thought, looking back at the text on the screen, but it made a neat bridge between two ideas which dominated the middle section of chapter eleven.

"Shit," she said, dropping her head into her cupped hand and staring fixedly at the screen. She had always known she

21

was taking a risk in leaving the notes until the end of the book, a practice scorned as unprofessional by most of her colleagues in the English department, but Loretta prided herself on her memory, at least where academic matters were concerned. Now, it appeared, it had let her down. She rapped the desk in front of her several times with her knuckles, taking her frustration out on the nearest inanimate object. Then she sighed, pressed a key to instruct the computer to store the work she had completed that day, and removed the disc. She collected Edith Wharton's novels together and put them in a neat pile on her desk, locked the computer disc in her top drawer, and let herself out of the department at ten minutes to five.

Loretta walked briskly towards Oxford street, five minutes from her office, hoping her favourite Italian deli in Soho would still be open. She was suddenly ravenous; she amused herself by devising a menu of pasta shells with sun-dried tomatoes, followed by *melanzana alla parmigiana* if she could find a couple of aubergines. And she would buy one of the wonderful puddings the shop imported from Italy—*tiramisú*, perhaps, or a *tartufo*. This charming fantasy was rudely interrupted as Loretta rounded a corner into Oxford Street and found herself swept along by a tide of shoppers anxious to make the most of the January sales; they had started prematurely the day before, Loretta remembered, as she struggled through to the kerbside. She lost her balance for a second, propelled off the pavement by a couple carrying a colour television in a large cardboard box, and skipped back to avoid a taxi which had jumped the lights just as she lost her footing. It flew past, hooting furiously and spraying Loretta's calves with dirty water from the road, and she looked down in dismay at the dirty splashes it had deposited on her black stockings. She shook her head, waited for the lights to change and crossed the street without mishap, striking off into Soho as soon as she got to the other side.

When she reached the little Italian shop, it turned out that it was closed for the whole week. Loretta looked at her watch:

22

quarter past five, and the shops around her were getting ready to shut. She set off at a fast pace for another deli a couple of streets away, arriving just as the proprietor was locking the shop door. He relented on seeing her look of disappointment, and Loretta was able to buy everything on her shopping list with the exception of a pudding. The owner even produced two very battered aubergines from the back of the shop; they would be all right, he assured her, letting her have them half price, as long as she used them that evening. Thanking him profusely, Loretta left the shop and made her way to the nearest bus stop. She waited twenty-five minutes for a bus, and then had to stand all the way to Islington, crammed in between two elderly women who conducted a lively conversation across her chest about the numerous health problems of a mutual friend. Loretta breathed a sigh of relief when the bus reached Upper Street, jumping off at the first stop and gladly walking the rest of the way home.

Ten minutes later she turned the key in the front door of her flat. The aroma of roasting meat impressed itself upon her as soon as she pushed open the door, and at that very moment Sandra appeared from the kitchen. She was wearing an unattractive PVC apron Loretta had been given for Christmas by an elderly aunt, and held a grubby tea towel in one hand.

"Surprise!" she called out. "Dinner is served!"

"But—" Loretta thought of all the trouble she'd gone to in order to get the ingredients for her Italian supper—the aubergines certainly wouldn't last until tomorrow night. Then, watching Sandra's smile fade, she made an effort to simulate pleasure. "Why, Sandra, this is—how kind of you. I had no idea—"

"You didn't leave me your number," Sandra said accusingly. "I had no idea how to get hold of you. I thought the least I could do was make you some supper. Obviously I shouldn't have bothered." She turned abruptly and went back into the kitchen, leaving Loretta standing in the hall with her shopping. There were sounds of pots and pans being banged about, and a cupboard door slammed noisily. Loretta sighed,

23

put down the plastic carrier bag, and took off her coat. Then she pushed open the kitchen door.

"I'm sorry, Sandra, I didn't mean to upset you," she said, addressing her back. "I did try ringing, but you weren't here . . ."

"I had to go and get the food—I can't stay in all the time, you know."

Sandra's voice was muffled, and to Loretta's horror she sounded on the verge of tears. Loretta took a step forward, putting out a hand to touch the woman's arm. "Honestly, Sandra, I didn't mean—What is it?"

Sandra shook it off without looking at her. She removed her glasses, dabbed at her eyes, and put them on again. Then she turned to face Loretta, her face flushed. "I'm sorry, I've had a terrible day," she said in a low voice. Loretta waited for her to explain, but she didn't.

"No luck with the flat?" she asked after a moment, thinking it hardly accounted for Sandra's tearful state.

Sandra shook her head. "I was on the phone most of the morning—I kept getting answering-machines, and the only man who was willing to come out worked for one of these big firms. They charge forty-odd pounds just for turning up this week, and to tell you the truth I'm a bit short of money . . ." Sandra said this last bit with her head down, as though she found it an intensely embarrassing admission.

Loretta stared at her, wondering if she should offer to pay for the plumber herself. It would be worth forty pounds, she thought, then realized she had no idea what the eventual bill might be. And it would amount to buying Sandra out of the flat, she realized, suddenly ashamed of her lack of charity. Surely she could put up with a few more days' inconvenience?

"I'm sorry," she said. "It sounds as though you were right this morning—never mind, you know you can stay here . . . Dinner smells delicious. Is there anything I can do? I'll just put this stuff in the fridge . . ." She went into the hall and picked up her shopping, smiling nervously as she

24

returned to the kitchen. She was relieved to see that Sandra's high colour was fading.

"I was just about to make the gravy," Sandra said in a more normal voice, picking up a measuring jug and giving its contents a stir. "It won't take long."

Loretta began putting things in the fridge, pushing away the now familiar feeling of being a visitor in her own flat. She had got to the last item, a large piece of *pecorino* cheese, when she spotted a half-full tin of cat food on the bottom shelf.

"Oh!" she exclaimed, taking it out. "Where's Bertie? Didn't he want to be fed?"

"I don't think I've seen him all day," Sandra said off-handedly. "Where do you keep that carving knife you used for the pheasant?"

"In the second drawer down. You mean—God, Sandra, you haven't let him out?" She stood staring at the other woman, horrified by the thought that the cat might have escaped into the street.

"Of course I haven't let him out. I expect he's gone to sleep somewhere, that's all. *I* don't know."

Loretta thrust the can back into the fridge, slammed the door, and rushed into the hall calling the cat's name. She peered round the drawing-room, quickly averting her eyes from the untidy heap of bedding and clothes which Sandra had left in one corner, and rushed upstairs. There was no sign of the cat in her bedroom, and it was with a feeling of rising panic that she flung open the bathroom door. She was immediately aware of a faint miaow, and was looking anxiously round the room when she realized that the noise was coming from the airing-cupboard. She pulled open the door and was conforted by an angry cat who leapt down from the shelf above the hot water tank and walked in circles on the floor, letting out a series of disgruntled wails.

"You poor old thing," Loretta said, bending down to stroke him. "Come downstairs and I'll feed you."

The cat preceded her down the stairs, disappearing into the kitchen before Loretta had reached the bottom step.

"He was shut in the airing-cupboard," she told Sandra crossly, her sympathy of a moment before evaporating.

"I'm not surprised," Sandra said, looking up from carving a joint of beef. "You know, Loretta, this flat is hardly a suitable environment for a cat. He's under my feet all the time."

Loretta opened her mouth, but decided against saying anything. She was perfectly aware that the flat was not an ideal home for an animal, but she had taken in Bertie when nobody else wanted him, and the two of them had developed a warm and comfortable relationship. She moved to the fridge, took out the opened tin of cat food, and emptied it into Bertie's dish.

"Where shall I sit?" she asked, washing her hands.

"There," Sandra said, indicating one of the two places she had set. "I hope you like your meat rare."

The beef was not so much rare as raw, and Loretta ate as little as possible, picking half-heartedly at the rock-hard roast potatoes and overcooked green beans which accompanied it. Sandra appeared not to notice the meal's shortcomings, carving herself two more slices of beef when her plate was empty. To Loretta's relief she didn't seem to be offended by her refusal of seconds, and Loretta was sufficiently cheered to venture a suggestion.

"You haven't—you don't think it's worth going back to the flat to see what sort of state it's in?" she asked. Sandra wouldn't be able to move back until the place had been cleaned up, and that was presumably something she could do before the water system was mended. "I could come with you," she added nobly, "we might be able to do something with the carpets—get them to a cleaner or hang them up . . . I mean, they're going to smell otherwise . . ."

"I'm not worried about the *carpets*," said Sandra, looking at her oddly. "It's a furnished flat, they belong to the land-lord. I tried him again today, before you ask, and there's still no answer." Her colour was beginning to rise again. "God, you really are anxious to get rid of me, aren't you? I thought

26

you said you had a book to finish—it doesn't sound to me as if you you've got time—"

"I was only trying to help," Loretta protested, feeling obscurely that Sandra had wrong-footed her again. "I mean, it's up to you what you do . . . I know I'm not the best hostess, I've lived on my own for too long . . ." She tailed off, wondering why she was apologizing for her offer of assistance. "I think I'll make some tea," she said shortly. "Will you have some?"

Sandra sat back in her chair. "I do appreciate what you're doing, Loretta," she said unexpectedly. "If I'd had anyone else to turn to, I really wouldn't have troubled you—"

"Oh well . . ." Loretta got up, unable to cope with Sandra's abrupt changes of mood. Had she always been as volatile as this? She seemed to have developed an aversion to any mention of the problem of her flat, but she'd have to face the mess sooner or later. Loretta stood by the table, wanting to point this out, but afraid of Sandra's reaction; she was tired, hungry in spite of the meal, and she didn't think she could face another scene.

"Would you rather have coffee?" she asked abruptly.

"I'll get it. No, I'd like to. I'll make us both a nice cup of tea." Sandra was also on her feet. "You go into the drawing-room, and I'll bring it through in a moment."

Loretta paused, then obediently left the kitchen. She dropped on to the sofa in the drawing-room and leaned back, eyes closed. She was feeling utterly miserable, and she tried to work out how much longer she would have to put up with Sandra. It was Tuesday today, and Thursday was New Year's Eve. Friday was a bank holiday, then there was the weekend. Things wouldn't be back to normal until Monday—almost a week. Loretta wondered whether she could stand it. Perhaps *she* should go away—but it was ridiculous, was she going to allow Sandra to drive her out of her own flat? There was her book to think of . . . Loretta opened her eyes, sat up, and looked around for her shoulder-bag. It occurred to her that she'd left it in the hall and she went to get it, returning with the issue of *Fem Sap* she'd started reading that morning. A couple of minutes later she tossed it to one side with an exclamation of disgust, just as Sandra entered the room with a tray.

"What's the matter?" Sandra put the tray down on a small table, balancing it precariously close to the edge while she moved the answering-machine a few inches.

"Nothing—I was just reading a very silly article in this," Loretta said, indicating the journal. "It's supposed to be about the style of George Sand, but it turns out to be about her *clothes*, not what she wrote. I can't imagine how it got in . . ." Now she had something else to worry about; the journal's standards had been slipping since a damaging split in the editorial collective a couple of years before. Loretta thought she would have to make some phone calls before the next meeting, and tried to remember when it was.

"My God!" Sandra exclaimed suddenly. "It's in French!" She had picked up the discarded copy of *Fem Sap* and was regarding it in astonishment.

"Some of it is," Loretta agreed. "It's an international journal—we accept contributions in three languages."

"Hmmph. No use to me—my French doesn't extend beyond reading menus." Sandra tossed the journal back on to the sofa and went over to a chair by one of the windows. "Well, Loretta," she said, picking up the tea strainer and starting to pour the tea. "You're quite the intellectual on the quiet, aren't you?"

Ten minutes ago, in the kitchen, Sandra's tone had become conciliatory; now it was combative again. Loretta looked at her watch and saw it was only half past eight: the evening stretched unbearably ahead of her, and she made a decision.

"Crikey, is that the time? I had no idea—don't bother with tea for me, I'm going to be late!" She jumped to her feet, smiled brightly at Sandra, and moved towards the door. Sandra was staring at her as if she had gone mad.

"Sorry—film I want to see at the Screen on the Green," she said breathlessly, anxious to get out of the flat before Sandra could offer to accompany her. "Thanks for dinner—delicious! Don't wait up. Bye!"

28

She was out of the front door and running down the stairs, coat and bag clutched in one hand, before Sandra had had time to utter a single word.

3

AT HALF PAST TEN ON THURSDAY MORNING
Loretta typed the last footnote into her computer and sat back
to gaze at the screen with a quiet sense of satisfaction. She
had even managed to recall the source of the quotation which
had eluded her on Tuesday, tracking it down in a long article
from the *New York Review of Books*. Her one remaining task
was the title; Loretta opened a drawer and took out a sheet
of paper, feeling that this was a problem for old technology.
Ten minutes later she stared at all the disjointed phrases and
crossings-out which littered the page and realized she was no
further on. She screwed it up into a ball, tossed it into the
waste-paper basket, and started again. This time she wrote
the only real candidate so far—''Edith Wharton: A Literary
Life''—at the top and looked glumly at it. It was accurate
enough, there was no doubt about that, but it didn't exactly
. . . sparkle. Loretta had no illusions about having written a
bestseller, but surely she could come up with something that
wasn't quite so dull? She wanted people to read the book,
after all.

She got up and began pacing up and down the room, one
hand supporting her chin. She had postponed thinking about
the title, assuming that when the time came a phrase from
one of the novels or from a letter would stand out, something
short and memorable which might catch the imagination of
the general reader as well as the specialist. A thought oc-

curred to her, and she returned to the computer, removing the disc which contained the final chapters of the book and replacing it with another on which she had stored the introduction. Moving the cursor through the text she found what she was looking for, assessments of Edith Wharton by Edmund Wilson and Virginia Woolf. Wilson had described her as a "passionate social prophet"; Woolf said she wrote about "men and women who confront their fate." Loretta shook her head, disappointed. Her memory had played her false; neither phrase was pithy or memorable enough to turn into a title.

"Shit," she said, swapping the discs back again. She was wondering whether to have a break—a visit to the sales was a tempting distraction after two days' solid work—when the phone rang.

"Hello?" Loretta said into the receiver, surprised. She was the only person in the silent English department, and she was not expecting any calls.

"So you really are at work—quite the busy bee, eh?"

"Sandra?" Loretta's heart sank. She had left her work number scribbled on a piece of paper the day before in response to a request from Sandra, but she was far from happy to hear her voice. After the scene on Tuesday evening she had done her best to avoid her; hadn't even inquired whether Sandra had acted on her suggestion of cleaning up the Notting Hill flat.

She realized that Sandra was asking about the progress of her book, a subject in which she had previously shown no interest. Puzzled and wary, Loretta explained that the text was complete, but the title was giving her trouble.

"But that must be the easiest bit," Sandra told her. "All you need is two or three words, and you've already written— what, fifty thousand?"

"Ninety-eight thousand," Loretta said proudly, having run a word count on the computer that morning. "Not including notes and the bibliography, of course. And there's still the index, but I think I'm going to pay someone to do that."

"Blimey," said Sandra, "who's going to read all that?

Ninety-eight thousand words! Sorry, I shouldn't have said that, I'm sure . . . Why don't you use one of her titles? That's what she's famous for, isn't it? I read a couple of them years ago and all I remember is the titles, I couldn't tell you the plot. Not the title exactly, but something—you know what I mean.''

"Yes, I think . . ." Loretta paused, looking at the spines of the Edith Wharton novels sitting on her desk: *The Mother's Recompense, The House of Mirth, The Custom of the Country, The Age of Innocence, The Fruit of the Tree* . . . She had the beginnings of an idea.

"So—what are your plans for this evening?"

"Sorry?" Loretta has missed the question completely, her mind fully occupied by the business of her title.

"This evening—New Year's Eve. I just wondered if you'd got anything planned . . ."

"Oh yes, I'm going to a party," Loretta said absently. If she took the Virginia Woolf quote and turned it around . . . It took her a moment to realize that Sandra had gone uncharacteristically silent.

"Sandra? Are you still there?"

She heard a sigh. "Yes. Don't worry—I remember now, you said Robert was coming . . . I was going to suggest taking you out to dinner, but—it doesn't matter." She sounded forlorn.

"Oh Sandra, I'm so sorry." Loretta suffered an attack of guilt, suddenly conscious that Sandra had now spent the best part of a week alone in the flat. And it was generous of her to offer to buy dinner when she'd admitted to being short of money . . .

"We're meeting a couple of friends at a restaurant and going on to a party," she explained. "Robert arranged it ages ago—I'm terribly sorry."

"Forget I mentioned it, really." Sandra tried to sound casual but Loretta could tell she was disappointed. It occurred to her to invite Sandra to the party, but she restrained herself on account of Robert's probable reaction.

"Oh dear," she said lamely, "I didn't think—I tell you

32

what, why don't we go out to lunch tomorrow? Somewhere's bound to be open. We could go for a walk afterwards . . ." Robert wouldn't be enthusiastic about this plan either, Loretta thought; she wasn't keen herself, but she felt better for making the offer. He might well decide not to come, which would be the most satisfactory solution.

"Yes—lunch sounds great." Sandra sounded a bit more cheerful. "I must go—I'm keeping you from your work."

"It doesn't mat—"

There was a click, and the line went dead. Loretta pressed the rest and got a dialling tone, but hesitated and put the receiver back. There was no point in speaking to Sandra again; the arrangement with Robert had been made long before her unexpected phone call on Christmas Eve. Loretta thought for a moment, staring into space, then returned with renewed energy to the question of the right form of words for her title.

She arrived home that evening clutching a thick parcel which contained the typescript of her book. It had churned out of the department's two laser printers in the course of the day while Loretta hurriedly marked a pile of essays which she was due to hand back at the beginning of the spring term. She had also slipped out to the sales and the product of that trip, a little black dress from Liberty's, was wrapped in tissue paper in a purple carrier bag which she put down on the hall floor as the stair light went out behind her.

"Sandra, it's me," she called out, suddenly aware of the silence in the flat. At the sound of her voice the grey cat padded downstairs, a light shape in the darkness, letting out the low miaows which signalled both hunger and pleasure. Loretta turned on the hall light, bent to stroke him, then straightened up and peered into the kitchen. Unwashed dishes from Sandra's breakfast stood haphazardly on the table, and a half-chewed crust of bread lay on the floor, presumably abandoned there by the cat.

"Wait a minute," she told him, leaving the kitchen for the drawing-room. She switched on the light and was dismayed by what she saw; the sofa-bed had not been folded up, and a jumble of bedding and clothes, including Sandra's lilac kimono, lay on top of it.

"Oh God." Loretta groaned, staring at the mess. She turned, went out of the room, and started up the stairs.

"Sandra?" The light was on in the bathroom but the door swung open to Loretta's touch, revealing a used bath towel on the floor but no other evidence of Sandra's presence. Loretta grunted, stepped backwards and put her head round the door into her bedroom. One glance was enough to tell her that it was as she had left it; at least Sandra had spared this room her attentions. Loretta went back downstairs, fed the cat, then set about tidying up. It had occurred to her to leave everything just as it was until Sandra returned to the flat—she had not left a note, and would probably reappear shortly—but Loretta could not bear to see the place in such a state. Grumbling silently to herself, she washed up the plate from which Sandra had eaten bacon, egg and tomatoes, the frying-pan, a dish which appeared to have had the egg broken into it, sundry knives and forks, a mug with thick coffee sludge at the bottom, and a crumb-strewn tea-plate. Then she wiped the table with a damp cloth, switched on the kettle for a cup of tea, and headed for the drawing-room.

There she folded up Sandra's kimono, along with a newly ironed blouse and skirt which seemed to have been tried on and then thrown to one side. Reluctant to open either of the bags standing in a corner of the room, she made a neat pile of the clothes and bedding, restored the sofa-bed to its upright position, and left them on top. Then she returned to the kitchen, made herself a cup of Earl Grey tea, chatted to the cat while she drank it, and went upstairs to run a bath.

"Not *more* black." Robert, who had just kissed her, stepped back to examine Loretta's new dress.

"But I *like* black," Loretta said lightly, trying not to think about Sandra's remarks a couple of days before. She was particularly pleased with this dress, knee-length black wool with black beading round the neck, which she wouldn't have been able to afford had it not been half price in the sale.

"All right, I was only teasing," Robert said, putting his arms round her again. "You look very—sophisticated."

"Thank you." Loretta relaxed, and returned his kiss. She felt a tingling sensation in the pit of her stomach, and was glad Sandra hadn't come back. She was about to slip her tongue into Robert's mouth when, oblivious of her mood, he released her.

"No Sandra?" he asked, putting his head round the door of the drawing-room. "Do I take it she's—oh, I see she hasn't."

"She's out," Loretta said, smoothing down her dress to hide her disappointment. "I don't know where she is. Can I get you a drink?"

"Depends who's driving."

"Oh, we can get taxis, surely?"

"We *might* have trouble getting back," Robert pointed out. "It is New Year's Eve."

"But we won't be in a hurry." The later they got back the better, Loretta thought; Sandra had waited up for them on Christmas Eve, and Loretta had felt oddly embarrassed when the time came to say goodnight and go upstairs with Robert.

"No-o. But—well, if you don't mind taking the risk . . ."

"I'd rather do that than drive."

"So be it. Let's skip the drink, anyway. We can have one at the restaurant."

Loretta shrugged, reaching for her coat, and picked up her bag. Robert strolled out on to the landing, turned on the stair light, and waited while Loretta shooed the cat back inside the flat. Then he led the way down, pausing at the street door to ask Loretta if she wanted to bet on how long they'd have to wait for a cab.

"Certainly not." She sighed, wondering why Robert was in a bad mood, and opened the street door. Stepping out on to the pavement, she hoped he would not be like this all evening. Then she lunged forward, waving frantically at a taxi which was speeding down Liverpool Road towards her.

It screeched to a halt several yards beyond her, and Loretta hurried to the window to tell the driver where they were going. She heard Robert come up behind her, turned to him and pulled open the back door of the cab.

"After you, sir," she called out, gesturing inside. Robert hesitated, gave her a quizzical look, and preceded her into the taxi. As it moved off Loretta felt her spirits rise. Her book was finished, a new year was beginning, and she was aware of a sudden surge of affection for Robert. She leaned towards him, gave him a peck on the cheek, and looked away to conceal a smile as he turned to her in surprise.

They arrived back at Loretta's flat at two-thirty in the morning of New Year's Day, drunk and in high spirits. Loretta tiptoed up the stairs to her front door with exaggerated care, frequently turning, finger on lips, to remind Robert that they mustn't wake Sandra. The effect was spoiled when she noisily dropped her keys; she cast an agonized glance at the top of Robert's head as he picked them up for her, sure that Sandra wouldn't have slept through the clatter.

"Let me," Robert enunciated clearly, ignoring Loretta's outstretched hand. To her delight, he succeeded in fitting the keys in the lock only at the third attempt.

"See! *You're* drunk too—"

"Shhh," Robert hissed, flapping one hand behind his back as Loretta followed him into the flat. "Remember what you said—oh." He stopped abruptly in the hall, and Loretta bumped into him from behind. "She's . . . not here."

"Not here?" Loretta repeated the words as if unable to grasp their meaning, then pushed past him. "Oh. I see." She swayed towards the open door of the drawing-room, where the light from the hall was sufficient to reveal that the sofa was as she had left it, Sandra's clothes and the spare bedding in a neat pile at one end.

"Stra-ange." Loretta turned, staring at Robert as though he might be able to provide the answer to this mystery, then moved towards the stairs. "Sandra!"

"Shhh!" Robert said for the second time.

Loretta, by now halfway up the stairs, peered down at him. "Don't be silly," she scolded, unnaturally loud. "She's not here. Sandra!" She turned and looked upwards into the darkness.

"If she's not here," Robert said with wounded dignity, "why're you calling her?"

Loretta ignored him and continued her slow progress up the stairs, holding the rail tightly with her right hand. There was a miaow from behind, and she looked back to see Bertie rubbing himself joyfully against Robert's calves. She resumed her journey, pausing on the landing before checking the bathroom and bedroom. Both were as she had left them.

"Not here," she said, coming slowly down the stairs, a preoccupied look on her face.

Robert shrugged his shoulders. "Gone to a party," he said confidently.

Loretta shook her head. "No. No one to go with. Wanted to come with us. She was at loosh—a loose end." She swallowed, aware of a strange, dizzy sensation in her head, and a dryness in her throat. "Drunk too much." She swayed unhappily towards Robert.

"Never mind." He leaned forward, putting one hand clumsily round the back of her head and attempting to stroke her hair. "Come to bed." He tried to kiss her. Loretta pushed him away.

"What—" She summed up her remaining strength. "What we going to do about Sandra?"

"What about her?" Robert pulled Loretta towards him, getting a firmer grip this time. "Let's go . . . bed." The words came out slurred, and they both swayed a little.

"But—"

"*She's* all right. She's having . . . a wonderful time." He kissed Loretta again, simultaneously moving her towards the stairs.

She resisted half-heartedly, torn between the sensations produced by his hand on her left breast and an uneasy sense that there was something she ought to do. She gave in, allowing herself to be propelled upstairs and into the bedroom.

"Let's . . . on the bed. Out!"

Skilfully for one who had drunk so much, Robert manoeuvred the cat on to the landing and slammed the bedroom door. He pushed Loretta in the direction of the bed, and she was aware of a sharp pain in her shoulder as they collided with the rail of the brass bed. Then they had rounded the tricky corner and Robert was pressing her down on to the quilt. One of his hands was at her knees, rolling up her tight black dress, and she sat up to help him, pushing him away just long enough to drag it over her head and toss it to the floor. Then she lay back, pulling Robert with her, naked to the waist and oblivious of everything but her desire.

They spent the morning in bed, Loretta waking just after eleven with a splitting headache while Robert was still asleep; she made her way painfully downstairs in search of orange juice, vitamin C, and a couple of paracetamol tablets. Bertie protested noisily on discovering that he was expected to survive on mackerel-flavoured dry biscuits, but Loretta felt too nauseated to face opening his usual can of Whiskas. She returned to bed and went almost immediately back to sleep, waking up a couple of hours later to find herself alone. After a few minutes Robert appeared; he had a surly look on his face, carried a cup of black coffee in one hand, and was stark naked.

"Robert! What about Sandra?"

"She's not back. Sorry, you were still asleep when I got up." He put down the cup, climbed into bed and lay back against the pillows, a hand to his head.

"Not back?" The events of the night before were hazily coming back to Loretta. "Then where—"

"*I* don't know."

"Wait a minute, what's the time? *Quarter past one?* But I'm supposed to be having lunch with her!" Loretta looked down at Robert, who was lying with his eyes closed.

"I expect she's forgotten. Lie down, Loretta, let's go back to sleep."

"But—I think I'll have a bath. Don't forget your coffee."

Loretta got out of bed and stood uncertainly beside it, not knowing what to make of Sandra's continuing absence.

"Mmm?" Robert suddenly opened his eyes.

"I said don't forget your coffee."

"No, I—" The rest of what he said was inaudible as he rolled over and went back to sleep.

Loretta frowned, hooked her dressing-gown off the back of the door, and went to the bathroom.

When Sandra still hadn't returned the next morning, Robert suggested she had managed to track down friends whose company she found more congenial than theirs.

"I don't know why you're making such a fuss, Loretta," he told her shortly. He rarely consumed enough alcohol to give him a hangover, and this one seemed to be lasting a very long time—or its effect on his temper was. "You admit you can't stand her—you should be grateful she's not here."

"I just don't understand it," Loretta persisted, anxiety getting the better of her. "Her missing lunch yesterday, I mean. I had the impression she was a bit lonely, I thought she was keen. And she hasn't left a note—"

"For heaven's sake, Loretta, you're not her keeper. She'll come back in her own good time."

Robert was buttoning his overcoat, getting ready to go back to Oxfordshire. Loretta knew it was a mistake to labour the point of Sandra's non-appearance, but needed reassurance.

"I hope you're right," she said without conviction.

"Of course I'm right!" Robert leaned forward and touched her cheek. "Now—stop worrying! Promise?"

"Mmm," Laura said noncommittally.

Robert shook his head. "You—ah, while I think of it, what about the concert on Friday?"

"I'll have to ring you," Loretta said distractedly, running a hand through her hair. "I haven't got a new diary and I don't know whether I'm supposed to be going out to dinner on Friday evening or Saturday. Is that all right?"

Robert sighed. "It'll have to be, won't it? Let me know as soon as you can—I don't want to waste the other ticket."

"I will." She allowed him to kiss her cheek and watched as he started down the stairs. "Bye," she called as he reached the bend.

He was right, of course, she told herself, going back into the flat and shutting the front door. What Sandra did was up to her—though it did seem odd that she should go off without a word. Perhaps she'd been in touch with her husband? Presumably he'd be back from his skiing holiday by now. Loretta wondered if she'd ever had his telephone number, and doubted it. Nevertheless she went into the drawing-room and opened a pine corner cupboard, rummaging among old notebooks and out-of-date lecture notes until she came across what she was looking for, a stack of *Spare Rib* diaries held together with an elastic band. She was just opening her 1980 diary when the phone rang, so she put it down and hurried across the room, half expecting to hear Sandra's voice when she picked it up. Instead there was a loud humming noise and the sound of distant, barely audible voices.

"Hello? Hello? Is anybody there?" She pressed the receiver close to her ear, trying to make out what the voices were saying, not even sure they were speaking English. She was about to put the phone down in exasperation when another, marginally less faint voice came on the line and spoke her name.

"Yes, yes, this is she. Who's that?"

"Happy new year!"

"John—is that you?"

"Course it's me. I was just . . ." His voice trailed off and she did not hear the rest of the sentence.

"Sorry, I can't hear," she shouted. "Where are you?"

"Nicosia. How are you?"

"Very well. I thought you were somebody else."

"Charming! I spend a fortune ringing from Cyprus and . . ." Tracey's voice faded again, then came back loud and clear. "New boyfriend on the scene, is there?"

"You haven't rung from Cyprus to ask me that?" Loretta

picked up the phone and settled into a chair, ready for a lengthy conversation. Tracey's telephone bills were paid by his employer, the *Sunday Herald*, and he had never shown any inclination to economize on their behalf. "How's things? What did you do for Christmas?"

"It was terrific." The improvement in the line was maintained, with Tracey's voice as clear as if he were in the next room. "I went swimming on Christmas Day, and this little taverna put on Christmas dinner for the English corrs— roasted a whole lamb. The Reuters bloke put me on to it— it's a sort of tradition in these parts. Not a turkey in sight. Brilliant."

"We—I didn't have turkey, either." Loretta was about to cover her mistake by telling Tracey about Sandra when he interrupted her.

"Actually, Loretta, there's something I want to talk to you about. I've been thinking—you know, New Year and all that— makes you think about . . . life and things. Neither of us is getting any younger, and it's been a while . . ."

"Go on," Loretta said, her suspicions aroused by these incoherent philosophical ramblings.

"Well, I was just wondering—don't take this wrong. I was just wondering how you'd feel about us getting divorced."

"Divorced?" Loretta repeated the word in astonishment.

"You sound amazed. But it makes sense when you . . ." Tracey faded away in a storm of crackles and hisses.

"I can't hear you," Loretta shouted, taking the phone from her ear and giving it a violent shake. "Hello? Are you there?" John's voice muttered inaudibly in the background. "You'll have to speak up, I can't—oh, that's better."

"Can you hear me?"

"Yes, I can now. But I missed everything you said after the bit about divorce."

"Well, like I said, neither of us is getting any younger, and we haven't lived together for years, so I just thought— why not make it official?"

"Yes, I suppose . . ."

41

"What's the matter, Loretta? You don't sound very pleased."

"It's just rather sudden, that's all . . . we've never really discussed it before."

"Yes, we did—when we first separated."

"I know, but it seemed a lot of bother, and we couldn't do it straightaway."

"We can now, though," Tracey pointed out. "Good God, Loretta, I didn't expect you to react like this. Anyone would think you want me back after all this time."

"No thanks!" she said hurriedly, without thinking. "I mean—sorry, that didn't sound very nice."

"Don't worry, the feeling's mutual," Tracey said with asperity. "Look, Loretta, it's just a formality. All you've got to do is fill in a few forms and send them to me—"

"All *I've* got to do?"

"Well, it's easier for you—you're in London and I'm not."

"But I haven't the faintest idea how to go about it."

"Go and look it up."

"Where do you suggest I start? The town hall?"

"Why not? That's where we got married, isn't it?"

"Yes, but—"

"Come on, Loretta, you're not stupid. I'm sure I can leave it all in your capable hands. And I'm quite willing to go halves, whatever it costs."

"That's very generous."

"Loretta!"

She sighed. "All right, I'll make inquiries and let you know. But it may take some time. Term begins soon, and you know how busy . . . There's no hurry, is there?"

"No—no."

"You don't sound sure."

"No, of course not, you're quite right . . . Oh, while I think about it—don't forget to put your real name down on the form," Tracey added maliciously. "We do want it to be legal."

"John—" Loretta was sensitive about the fact that she'd changed her name from Laura to Loretta when she went to

42

university, and Tracey knew it. There was a brief silence, then Tracey apparently decided he'd gone too far.

"So—how are you, anyway?" he asked lamely.

"I'm—very well," Loretta paused. An unfamiliar element of formality seemed to be entering their relationship, and she wasn't sure how to deal with it. She heard Tracey's voice, but it had become faint again. "Sorry, I can't hear you—"

"I'll ring you another time," Tracey bellowed, "line's breaking up. Bye, Loretta. Happy new year!"

She replaced the receiver and put the phone back on the table. Then she sat back in her chair, unsettled by the conversation. Tracey was quite right, they hadn't lived together for years, and there was no reason why they shouldn't formalize the situation. But *I* left *him* she thought indignantly, plucking at a loose thread in the arm of the chair, a consequence of Bertie's habit of sharpening his claws on the furniture.

Suddenly Loretta laughed out loud, reluctantly admitting what was wrong: she had been piqued by the fact that Tracey had suggested the divorce. The absurdity of her reaction amused and embarrassed her, and she got to her feet shaking her head at this demonstration of human frailty on her part. She stood in the middle of the room, trying to remember what she had been doing when Tracey rang until the sight of the open cupboard door reminded her. She returned to the 1980 diary and flipped through its pages to the section which contained telephone numbers. She found an entry under Neil, but it was a London number, the one for Sandra's old flat in Blackheath. Loretta put the diary back, debating with herself as to whether she should check the others. Sandra might turn up at any moment, and she would not thank Loretta for contacting her husband behind her back—on the other hand, since she'd gone to the trouble of getting them out . . .

Loretta had a quick look in her 1981 diary. The Blackheath number was there under Neil, and it appeared again in 1982 and 1983. Then it disappeared. Loretta breathed a sigh of relief, winding the elastic band round the diaries and putting

43

them back in the cupboard. There was nothing she could do, and she might as well put the problem of Sandra out of her mind and think about more pressing matters. How did you go about getting divorced? She toyed with the idea of ringing up one or other of her divorced friends and quizzing them on the subject, but the prospect made her feel foolish. It occurred to her that Tracey's suggestion of looking it up wasn't such a bad one, and the obvious place to try was Islington Central Library in Holloway Road. She wondered if it would be open on 2 January; she stretched, thinking she felt like a walk. It would do her good after the alcohol-induced lethargy of the last couple of days. She turned on her answering-machine, went into the hall and took down her coat.

4

LORETTA AWOKE ON MONDAY MORNING IN the confident expectation that her absent guest would turn up at some point during the day. She had had no word from her since the morning of New Year's Eve, but the longer Sandra was away the more likely it seemed that she had been offended by Loretta's grudging hospitality and had taken herself off for a long weekend somewhere. Today was different: shops and businesses would be back to normal for the first time since Christmas, and the question of sorting out the waterworks at the Notting Hill flat must be assuming some urgency. It was already 4 January, and while Sandra had been vague about the starting-date of her new job, Loretta had the impression that it was imminent.

Cheered by the thought that the small mystery of Sandra's whereabouts was certain to be cleared up soon, Loretta parcelled up the typescript of her book, which she had read through in the course of the weekend. There were still one or two passages which weren't entirely to her liking, but she was delighted with her title, an adaptation of the quote from Virginia Woolf—*A Woman and her Fate: A Life of Edith Wharton*. As she stapled and sellotaped the bulky parcel and wrote the address of Vixen Press in large felt-tip letters on the front, she speculated that Sandra might already be at her flat, letting in a plumber. Loretta hummed under her breath as she weighed the parcel in her hands, savouring the joy of authorship.

When she went out on her errands to the post office and the County Court—she had discovered from the library that this was where she would acquire the forms needed for her divorce from John Tracey—she was careful to switch on her answering-machine, but was rewarded on her return only by a long message from her mother and one from Robert reminding her about the concert on Friday. Loretta clasped a hand to her forehead, realizing she had forgotten to check whether or not she was free, and spent half an hour getting hold of the friend who had invited her to dinner at the weekend. It turned out that the dinner party was on Friday, the same evening, and she had an uncomfortable phone conversation with Robert, who pressed her to drive up to his house in Oxfordshire on Saturday night instead. Loretta agreed reluctantly, not looking forward to the journey on a dark winter's evening, and went upstairs to her tiny utility room to put on some washing.

Then, in a rather less cheerful frame of mind than she had started the day, she sat down at the kitchen table to study the forms relating to the divorce. They did nothing to improve her temper; having written Laura Anne Lawson in the box which asked for her full name, she was then required to supply her maiden name. Loretta glared at the form, wondering what to write; it was about time, she thought, that the people who designed such documents recognized that an increasing number of women no longer followed the convention of giving up their surnames on marriage. She wondered if she should attach a covering letter to this effect, then decided against it and simply wrote "None" in the space provided. As she read on, pen poised, it occurred to her that some literal-minded official might misread the entry, and she smiled briefly at the thought of receiving correspondence addressed to Dr. L. A. None. She went on filling in the form, then discovered that she was required to produce her marriage certificate, a document she had neither seen nor given a moment's thought to for several years. She wasted a considerable amount of time looking for it, turning up old letters, Christmas cards, even Bertie's vaccination record, but not the certificate. Eventually she sat back on her heels on the bedroom floor, surrounded by cardboard boxes, and concluded that it must be among John Tracey's papers, not hers. She should have thought of this solution before, for Tracey was far more sentimental than she; she would have to ask him about it when she wrote to explain the divorce procedure, and to get his signature on the forms.

She looked at her watch, saw that it was a few minutes before three, and frowned as she realized there was still no word from Sandra. It was frustrating, not having the Notting Hill address and phone number, and Loretta began to feel uneasy again. Uneasy and not a little angry; what on earth was Sandra playing at, disappearing for days like this? She really was most inconsiderate—Loretta shook her head crossly. Pushing the cardboard boxes back into the bottom of the wardrobe, she went downstairs and stood looking at the phone in the drawing-room. She bit her lower lip, telling herself there must be some way of tracking down her lodger, and an idea came to her. Sally Wilkins, Sandra's closest friend in the women's group, had kept in touch with Loretta; she glanced at the mantelpiece, where Sally's Christmas card was standing next to one from her parents. Perhaps she had heard something? It was even possible that Sandra had despaired of Loretta and had gone to stay with Sally. On the other hand, Sally's flat was very small, hardly big enough for herself, her lover Peter and their baby . . . Nevertheless it was worth a try. Loretta went to get her address book, looked up Sally's number and dialled it.

"Sally? Hi, it's Loretta. How are you?"

They exchanged news, Sally telling Loretta about the progress of her year-old daughter, Felicity, and the difficulties of combining motherhood with even a part-time job. Loretta told Sally about her Edith Wharton book, then explained why she had phoned.

"I was wondering if you'd heard from Sandra Neil lately?"

"Sandra Neil? Gosh, not for ages—it must be a couple of

47

years. No, wait a minute, less than that—it was just after I was pregnant with Felicity. She rang out of the blue and I didn't have time to talk, I was on my way to the ante-natal clinic . . . She sounded a bit depressed, but I was pregnant and—well, I should have phoned her back but you know how it is. We'd sort of lost touch a bit anyway . . . Why d'you ask?''

"Oh, only that she's been staying with me—"

"*Staying* with you? Heavens, Loretta, I thought you two didn't get on. How on earth—"

"I didn't have much choice. She rang on Christmas Eve and said her pipes had burst. I'm surprised she didn't ring you . . ."

"Maybe she did—Peter and I were away over Christmas. Is she still with you?"

"Well, that's the thing—I haven't seen her since last week. I came home on Thursday, that was New Year's Eve, and she'd gone. There was no note or anything, but she's left all her clothes behind . . . I'm getting a bit worried—I hoped you might have heard from her.''

"Not a thing. Have you tried her husband?"

"I thought of that but I don't know his number. You don't happen to have it, do you?"

"I might. Can you hold on?"

"Of course.''

A moment later Sally was back. "Found it. Have you got a pen?'' She dictated a Winchester telephone number. "I shouldn't worry," she added reassuringly. "I'm sure she can take care of herself. Her life was always a bit complicated, what with her being up here and the kids away at school . . . How is she, by the way? Still working for Westminster?''

"No, she's given up social work, it turns out. She's starting a new job in a health club.''

"A *health* club? Sandra?''

"Oh dear, that's what I thought. But I—she obviously didn't want to talk about it but I got the feeling she was fed up with social work.''

"That doesn't surprise me in the least. I always had the impression it was tougher than she expected—that's the trou-

48

ble with women who've not worked before. When did she leave Westminster?''

"That I don't know. It must be quite some time ago—she said she'd been working away from London.''

"Don't tell me she went back to Tom!" Loretta heard a throaty chuckle. "I always thought . . . That was Sandra's problem in a nutshell—when something went wrong she always had Tom to fall back on. What I never understood is what he got out of it.''

"But Sally, I thought you liked her. You always used to see a lot of her outside the group.''

"I know, I'm sorry. I just got a bit cynical—she only seemed to get in touch when something was wrong . . . When she'd had a row with Tom over the kids, or there was a problem with one of her clients. That's all we had in common, really, the job. I'm probably doing her an injustice, it's just I always thought she'd go back in the end. It's all speculation— as I say, I lost contact with her a while ago.''

"I wonder—she was very vague about where she went after Westminster. I assumed she'd moved because she got a new job somewhere. It didn't occur to me that she'd gone back to him. It didn't *sound* as if they were on good terms, but . . . Well, thanks for the number.''

"Honestly, Loretta, I shouldn't worry too much. You'll probably find she's gone off to see Tom and the kids and it hasn't occurred to her that you'd be worried . . . Nice to hear from you.''

"And you.''

"By the way—there's another number here you could try— it's a place they've got down on the coast, he keeps a boat there. I went for a weekend once with Sandra, years ago now. It was lovely, in the New Forest, right on the water. Tom likes sailing, apparently, though I don't think she's keen.''

"I'd better write it down—there's no harm in trying. I'm probably wasting my time, but you never know . . . Thanks, Sally.''

Loretta took down the number, which had a code she didn't recognize, and said goodbye. After she'd put the phone down she sat staring at the piece of paper, reluctant to dial either number. She remembered how vehemently Sandra had reacted to Loretta's question about her husband on Christmas Eve: "We are *separated*, you know." It occurred to Loretta that perhaps Sally was right, that Sandra had indeed returned to her husband but had now left him again. If that were the case, Tom Neil would hardly welcome a phone call from someone who wanted to quiz him about his wife's movements. Loretta stared glumly at the paper, her extreme reluctance to involve herself in Sandra's affairs doing battle with her mounting anxiety over her non-appearance. Anxiety won, and she picked up the receiver.

She dialled the Winchester number and listened, in both relief and frustration, to the forlorn sound of a phone ringing in an empty house. After a while she dialled again, checking that she hadn't got a wrong number first time round. There was still no reply. She tried the second number, the house on the coast, with the same negative result. Loretta looked at her watch, thought that Tom Neil might not have come home from work, and resolved to try later.

By the time she left the house at half past six, for a yoga class which she hoped would help her relax, she had dialled each number half a dozen times without getting an answer. That didn't mean anything, of course, but she was very conscious of the fact that it was now four days since she'd heard from Sandra. She walked round the corner towards Upper Street, toying with the idea of going to the police, and decided to wait until the next morning before taking so drastic a step.

It was after ten when she got back to the flat, having allowed herself to be persuaded by two women from her yoga class to join them for a sauna and a vegetarian Indian meal. There was still no sign of Sandra, nor any message from her on the answering-machine, and Loretta promised herself she would ring Tom Neil first thing in the morning.

The phone was picked up on the third ring and a tired male voice recited the Winchester number Loretta had got from Sally.

50

"Mr. Neil?" She was far from encouraged by his tone.

"Speaking."

"I'm a friend of Sandra's—" she began, wondering how to phrase her request.

"Oh." She heard a long sigh. "You're ringing about the funeral?"

For a second Loretta's mind went blank. "The funeral?" she repeated, exactly echoing his inflection. Suddenly she remembered that Tom Neil had taken the children on a skiing holiday, and an awful possibility struck her with the force of a blow. Oh God, that would explain Sandra's hasty departure from the flat, why there was no note . . .

"The children—"

"They're as well as can be expected," Tom told her, misconstruing her concern. "Felix has taken it better than Lizzie, I'm just hoping after today . . ."

"Oh—so it's not—" Loretta felt a wave of relief. She groped for words, anxious to find out which of Sandra's relatives had died but not wanting to ask outright. She decided that the simplest way of finding out was to speak to Sandra herself. "Is she there? Can I speak to her?"

"Speak to her? Speak to who?"

"To Sandra. She is there, isn't she?"

"Oh *Christ*." There was a stunned silence at the other end of the line. "You haven't heard—I'm sorry, I assumed you knew. Sandra's—it's Sandra's funeral."

Loretta gripped the phone tightly, unable to speak.

"I didn't—it was in the paper, and lots of her friends have—I'm sorry. It must be a terrible shock."

"Yes, I—I can't—you must be—oh!" Tears streamed down Loretta's face.

"I'm sorry to have told you so—so abruptly. That's one of the things you discover at a time like this, there's no way of— I've had a lot of it in the last few days."

"But I don't—was she *ill*?" Loretta was incredulous.

"Oh no, nothing like—it was an accident, a car accident."

"Did she—when?"

51

"We don't know—some time on New Year's Eve. There wasn't—no one else was involved."

"I—I see."

"The funeral's this morning—she's being cremated. There's a service at eleven, if you'd like to come . . ."

Loretta glanced at her watch. Its face swam before her, indistinct through the tears, and she wiped her eyes impatiently with the back of her hand.

"I can't—it's too late—"

"That's all right—I understand. I'm afraid I ought to—people are starting to arrive . . ."

"Oh yes, I mustn't . . . Thanks for telling me, and I hope . . ." She tailed off.

"I *am* sorry—I hoped people would see it in the paper. You've had a shock."

"Yes. I—thank you. Goodbye."

Loretta put the phone down blindly, leaned forward with her elbows on her knees, and gave way to the sobs rising in her throat. Her head was full of images—Sandra on Christmas Eve, in the hall taking off her damp raincoat; on Christmas Day, wearing a silly paper hat; in the kitchen, eating breakfast in her lilac kimono. Sandra dead—Loretta couldn't believe it.

She sat up, wiping her eyes on a tattered paper handkerchief she had found in the pocket of her skirt. New Year's Eve: it had happened on the very day Sandra left the flat. She had been dead all this time, and Loretta had carried on with her own life, stupidly unaware; she had even found out too late to get to the funeral . . . She looked at her watch again, checking that there really was no chance—it was twenty-five to ten, far too late to get to a funeral in Hampshire at eleven. Loretta gave a heavy, shuddering sigh, and dabbed at her eyes again. She tried to remember what she'd said to Tom Neil, so shocked by her discovery that she couldn't even recall whether she'd said the conventional things—that she was sorry, and if there was anything she could do . . . She wasn't even sure whether she'd told him her name, in fact

52

she probably hadn't. And what had he told her, apart from the fact that Sandra had died in a car accident? Loretta realized she hadn't asked where it had happened, whether Sandra had died instantly or—that bit didn't bear thinking about.

She bit her lip, realizing she had forgotten to tell Tom Neil that his wife had been staying with her, and that Sandra's belongings were still in the flat. She would have to ring him again, though she flinched from doing it today. He had the ordeal of the funeral to get through; whatever the state of his relationship with Sandra, the news of her death must have come as a devastating blow—and what about the children? Felix and Lizzie, those were their names; how were they coping? The whole thing was awful, unbelievable. Loretta's numbed mind drifted away from practical considerations to the still astonishing fact that Sandra had walked out of this very room some time last Thursday—perhaps only a few minutes after Loretta had turned down her invitation to dinner—and was dead within a matter of hours. Loretta remembered her own return home from work, her annoyance at finding the mess Sandra had left in the flat, and was overwhelmed by a fresh wave of grief and guilt.

5

"I STILL CAN'T BELIEVE IT. SHE WAS DEAD ALL that time and I didn't know—I hardly made any effort—" Loretta broke off, afraid she was going to cry again. She cradled the phone under her chin while she felt in her pockets for her errant handkerchief.

"I do think you're being a bit hard on yourself, Loretta," Robert told her. "Obviously it's a shock, and it's going to take a while to recover, but there was no reason for you to think anything like this had happened. If you assumed the worst every time you didn't hear from someone for a few days you'd be in a constant state of hysteria."

"Yes, but I even missed the funeral," Loretta pointed out. "If I'd rung Sally last week, when she first disappeared, I could at least have gone to the funeral."

"I can see that, but it hasn't made any difference to Sandra, has it? Look, don't you think guilt has a lot to do with this? Not that you've anything to be guilty about—you gave her a bed in spite of the fact that you didn't like her. Now, Loretta, you know you didn't get on—"

"All right, but it doesn't help, does it?" Loretta was beginning to regret ringing Robert. She had needed to tell someone the terrible news and her first choice had been Sally, who was out. She was no longer sure why she had fixed on Robert next, but the conversation certainly wasn't making her feel better.

"Anyway," she said, anxious to get off the phone. "I mustn't keep you—were you working?"

"Yes, as it happens. On another of those piano pieces— the ones I played last time you were here. But it doesn't matter—it's you I'm concerned about."

"Oh, don't worry about me. I'll—I've got various things I can get on with," Loretta said vaguely. "I'll be all right."

"Are you sure?"

"Yes—I'll see you on Saturday."

"Oh, we'll speak before then. I'll give you a ring to see how you are. Try not to reproach yourself, Loretta."

"Yes—bye now."

"Bye."

Loretta sat back in her chair, staring at a point on the floor. She remained in this position for perhaps two minutes, punishing herself by dwelling on the stratagems she'd adopted to avoid spending time with Sandra in the flat. Whatever Robert said, her behaviour had not been kind. She longed to speak to Sally, and eventually she picked up the phone and tried her number again. There was still no reply and she wondered if Tuesday was one of the days Sally worked. Frustrated, she put down the phone and started moving restlessly round the room, coming to a halt in front of a card which showed the Virgin Mary standing outside an NHS maternity hospital with a "Closed for Christmas" sign on the door. Her face brightened as she picked it up, but fell again as she saw what was written inside. The sender was Bridget Bennett, another former member of the women's group, and the message gave the date of Bridget's return to England from Connecticut, where she had gone to stay with her cousin and his wife. For a brief moment she had entertained the hope that Bridget would be back this week—*she* would understand her feelings, Loretta was sure—but the note inside the card said "back on the 14th," more than a week away.

Loretta returned the Christmas card to the mantelpiece, feeling very isolated. Even John Tracey was out of the country—and in his case there was the divorce to think of. It was not yet clear what difference it would make to their relation-

55

ship, but Loretta couldn't believe that things would go on as they had before. She blinked several times, suddenly aware that her eyes were sore and puffy, and went into the kitchen where she bathed them messily with kitchen paper soaked in cold water. Then she went to the fridge, remembering that she hadn't had anything to eat since the night before. She reached inside and took out a bowl of cold rice salad left over from the weekend, wrinkling her nose at its aroma—an unappetizing combination of stale cheese, stringy meat, and bits of green pepper which had begun to curl at the edges. She couldn't imagine why she had kept it, and it was the work of a moment to slide the solid white mess into the bin. The rest of the stuff in the fridge was hardly more appealing, and Loretta decided a trip to the Sainsbury's superstore at the bottom of Liverpool Road would be good for her mentally and physically.

The weather had turned bitterly cold again after a mild weekend and Loretta was very glad when she got home with her shopping. She had left the central heating on and it was warm and cosy in the flat. She started emptying her carrier bags on to the table, and was putting a pack of kitchen towels in the cupboard under the sink when she realized she was on the verge of more tears. It wasn't really surprising, she thought, straightening up and wiping her eyes; she had managed not to think about Sandra while she was pushing her trolley up and down the crowded aisles in the supermarket, but it was more difficult now she was back in the flat and vulnerable to its associations. She hurried through the rest of the unpacking, leaving out a carton of ready-made soup which she poured into a pan on the cooker as soon as everything else had been put away. Then she cut a couple of slices of wholemeal bread from a fresh loaf and laid a place at one end of the table.

She had just finished eating and was stroking the cat in a dispirited manner when the phone rang. Loretta got to her feet, letting Bertie slide gently to the floor, and wondered if it was Robert. She went to the phone reluctantly and answered it with an unenthusiastic "hello."

"Loretta? You sound awful. Have you got a cold?" It was Sally.

"No—I'm all right." Unprepared, Loretta didn't know how to tell Sally about Sandra. She hesitated, and Sally continued in a cheerful voice.

"Well, I can't talk for long—I'm ringing to see whether Sandra's turned up. I was thinking about it last night, and I'd quite like to speak to her—I feel a bit guilty about losing touch. I know what I said, but I do have a soft spot for her . . ."

This speech made things worse, and Loretta found herself replying in a rush.

"I did try to get hold of you earlier—I don't know what to . . . Listen, Sally, it's bad news, this is going to be a shock—I rang Tom—and she's dead. It's awful—there was a car crash. Isn't it dreadful?"

"Dead? Oh, Loretta . . ."

Sally didn't say any more but Loretta heard snuffling noises at the other end of the line.

"I'm sorry," she said miserably. "You must be terribly shocked—I am, I've been bursting into tears all day."

"She—you said a car crash?"

"Yes. That's all I know. It's stupid—I didn't think to ask anything else."

"Well, that's—you spoke to Tom? How was he? Hold on while I blow my nose."

"All right, I suppose. It's hard to tell, I've never met him."

"Have you told the others?"

"The others?"

"Yes—the group."

"Gosh, I didn't think . . . I was going to ring Bridget, but she's in the States till next week . . ."

"I was just thinking, I'd like to go to the funeral and I'm sure Sue—"

"Oh—it's too late. The funeral was today—eleven o'clock. I'm sorry, if only I'd got hold of him earlier . . ."

"It's all right, Loretta, you weren't to know. I wonder—d'you think we should have a meeting? As we've missed the funeral, I mean? It might be better . . . Funerals are such an awful way to remember people."

"A sort of memorial meeting, is that what you mean?"

"Well, nothing formal—just a chance to talk about—what's happened."

"But would we—" Loretta was unsure. It was one thing for the members of the group to meet again at a funeral, an event whose purpose and structure were clear. The success of Sally's suggestion would depend on their ability to recreate the old intimacy of group meetings, and without it there might be embarrassed silences into which people would feel constrained to fling mawkish remembrances of Sandra. She tried to remember when the group had last met. Was it 1981 or 1982?

"Would we—you sound doubtful?"

"No, I—I'm just wondering if it would work. After such a long time."

"I know what you mean. But I can't help feeling we should do *something*. The group was an important part of my life—all our lives. We can't just ignore—"

"Of course not," Loretta said uncomfortably, sensing an unspoken accusation that her attitude was unfeeling. "No, if you think—How do you want to go about it? As I say, Bridget's away till next week, and in any case she isn't often in London . . ."

"It may not be possible to get everyone—we may have to make do with you, me, Sue and June. If you're willing, that is? God—in that case, leave the arrangements to me. Where d'you think—shall we meet at my flat? Oh"—Loretta heard a faint wail in the background—"there's Felicity, she's woken up. Sorry, Loretta, I'll have to go."

After she'd put down the phone it occurred to Loretta that Sally was, like herself, troubled by guilt. Sally had been critical of Sandra the previous afternoon, but had apparently regretted her remarks even before she knew about the fatal car crash. Her attempt to get the women's group together was

58

probably a way of assuaging that guilt, which didn't make Loretta feel any better about the meeting. What would they talk about? It was years since she'd seen June Price or Sue Corbett, and the brutal fact of Sandra's death would dominate the meeting . . . Loretta told herself she was too tired to think about the subject any longer. The idea was Sally's, and it was up to her to do the worrying. Loretta glanced at her watch, went into the drawing-room and turned on the *Six O'Clock News*.

On Saturday night Loretta stepped reluctantly out on to the pavement, pulling the street door shut behind her. A gust of freezing rain stung her eyes and she turned up the wide collar of her coat to protect her face, hurrying round the corner to her car. The weather was wild, had been all day, and her only consolation was that she didn't have far to go. Sally had contacted Sue Corbett and June Price, and this was the only evening in the next couple of weeks when all three of them could make it. Loretta wasn't free, in theory, having promised to spend the night with Robert in Oxfordshire, but the complications which arose when she mentioned this fact to Sally were so great that she had given in and cancelled the trip. Robert reacted coolly to the change of plan, so much so that Loretta took an instant and unplanned decision to conceal the reason from him. It seemed easier to take refuge in a small lie about having to go down to her mother's than to explain about the meeting, especially as she still had doubts about the wisdom of it. The phone conversations with Sally and Robert had left her feeling resentful of their demands on her, and with a slight impression from a remark of Sally's that she was not alone in her lack of enthusiasm for the reunion.

Now it was too late to do anything about it. Loretta turned the key in the ignition, waiting for a gap in the traffic in the side street where she had parked the car. She pulled out, peering hard through the filmy windscreen at the wet road in front of her and the reflected light of the street lamps. The rain suddenly got heavier, bouncing off the road and drumming on the roof of the car, and she was glad Sally lived nearby. It was not the evening for map-reading her way through unfamiliar suburbs of London. Loretta turned left into Upper Street, heading for Highbury Corner, and at the roundabout took another left into Holloway Road. The traffic was light and she made rapid progress, eventually slowing the car and moving into the centre of the road just before Jones Brothers. She turned into Sally's street, passing the cinema on the corner which had long been converted into a billiard hall, though Loretta dimly remembered having once seen a film there—the Coronet, that was what the place had been called. The short road was full of double-parked cars and she had to negotiate a zig-zag course to the end, turning into another street before spotting a gap large enough for her Panda. She squeezed it into a narrow space between a brand new sports car and a beaten-up purple Capri, struggling to put up her umbrella as she got out of the car. Then she set off in the direction of Loraine Road, buffeted by a wind which threatened to turn her umbrella inside out at any moment. A couple of minutes later she bounded up the steps of the house in which Sally and Peter had the upper-ground floor flat; their bell was the middle one of three.

"Loretta!" Sally leaned forward and up to plant a kiss on Loretta's cheek. She was small and thin, her short black hair framing a heart-shaped face which gave her the look of an inquisitive pixie.

"Come in." She had lowered her voice to not much more than a whisper, and she glanced over her shoulder into her flat as if she wanted to say something without being overheard. All that came out, though, was: "They're in here."

Loretta, puzzled, followed Sally into the flat. Something was wrong, that much was clear, but there had hardly been time . . . She glanced covertly at her watch and saw she was only a few minutes late.

"Don't worry about being quiet," Sally said in her normal voice, pushing open the door of the front room. "Peter's taken Felicity to his mother's for the night."

Loretta stepped into the room over a toy fire engine which

was lying on the threshold. Gently, she moved it away with her foot so she could close the door. When she turned round she was surprised to find not two but three women looking expectantly at her. Two of them said hello, while the third, a complete stranger, offered an uncertain grin. She was young and pretty, in short skirt and patterned tights, and she sat close to June Price on Sally's old Habitat sofa. Nobody said anything for a moment and Loretta looked to Sally for guidance.

"This is a friend of June's," Sally announced, opening her eyes wide. "Carol—sorry, I'm terrible at surnames."

"Carol Macklin," June supplied. "D'you want to sit here, Loretta?"

She gestured to the space beside her, on her left, but it was a polite rather than a welcoming gesture. Loretta had a sense that, accidentally or otherwise, June and Carol had set up an exclusion zone at the heart of the room. She wondered who Carol was, and why June had brought her.

"No, it's all right, I'll—" She looked quickly across the room and moved towards a battered armchair. "Is this free?"

"Yes, help yourself. Tea, Loretta? You don't drink coffee, do you?" Sally waited by the kitchen door.

"Tea would be wonderful!" Loretta said fervently, sitting down. She realized at once that her enthusiasm was out of all proportion; she had been offered a drink, not a three-course meal. It must be the atmosphere in the room, she thought, feeling stiff and unable to relax. She concealed her discomfort by reaching for the loose cushion behind her, trying it in several positions as though it was the only source of her unease.

"That's better," she said at last, flexing her shoulder muscles and looking across at June. "Well, how are *you*? Still in the same job?" The last time they had met June was working as an administrator in a law centre, an endlessly frustrating position with long hours and inadequate resources.

"Yes, but I only do three days a week now. There's no money—the council's rate-capped, of course. But it does

61

mean more time for other things—I'm doing a part-time MA, so it's worked out quite well . . .''

June shot a glance at Carol, who had turned away to examine the contents of a revolving bookcase next to the sofa. Loretta waited for June to continue the conversation, observing that her hair was shorter and lighter, and her customary jeans had been replaced by a skirt and hand-knitted jumper. When June remained silent she gave a slight shrug and turned to the remaining member of the group.

"How about you, Sue?" she asked brightly. "You're looking well."

"Oh—yes." Sue closed the magazine she'd been flipping through and gave Loretta a startled look. Loretta had the very strong impression that she, too, would much rather be elsewhere. "I'm sorry about Sandra," Sue said abruptly, pushing her longish hair behind her ears.

Loretta acknowledged this remark with a slight nod, reluctant to talk about the accident until Sally came back from the kitchen. She had no clear idea about the form the meeting was supposed to take, and she wondered what was keeping Sally.

"Where are you working these days?" she asked, to keep the conversation going. "Same school?"

"Yes—I'm just about standing it. We got a new head last year, and he's not very . . . Well, I'm looking elsewhere," she said shortly. Sue taught physics in a comprehensive school in Hackney.

"I thought I had some Earl Grey," said Sally, coming back into the room and handing Loretta a mug. "Careful, it's hot. I couldn't find it, so I'm afraid it's Indian." She drew up a Lloyd Loom chair, recently painted white, from a corner of the room and sat down. "Oh, thanks." She leaned forward and took a handful of photographs from June. "I'll show you these later, Loretta," she said, putting them back in an envelope. "They're just of Fliss."

Silence fell, and Loretta noticed out of the corner of her eye that Sue had picked up her magazine again. She studied a framed poster over the fireplace, a well-known Hockney print of a swimming-pool, and tried to recall whether meetings of the group had always started as awkwardly as this. Perhaps at the very beginning, she thought, straining to remember, but not later on; once they'd got to know each other, there was always someone who wanted to pass on a piece of news—Sue announcing that she'd finally told her violent boyfriend to move out, Sally talking about her ex-husband's attempts to persuade her into a reconciliation, Sandra confiding that living alone in London was more difficult than she'd anticipated.

"Um—I suppose it's up to me to start," Sally said suddenly, sitting up straight with the photographs in her lap. "This meeting was my idea, I thought of it as soon as Loretta told me—"

"Actually—" They all looked at June, surprised by the interruption. "Actually, before you get going, there's something I'd like to say."

Loretta glanced at Sally and back to June, noticing that next to her on the sofa Carol was examining one of her shoes in minute detail. There was something about the women's proximity, their intense awareness of each other even when their attention was apparently elsewhere, that gave Loretta a sudden inkling of what June was going to say. The knowledge was so unexpected, so great a diversion from the stated purpose of the meeting, that she immediately sensed trouble ahead. She was pleased for June, of course, but how would they get back to the subject of Sandra?

"I didn't *want* to come tonight," June was saying, a little defiantly. "When Sally rang me I said—I told her there wasn't much point. It's dreadful hearing someone's died but—well, it hasn't got anything to do with me now . . . I sort of feel—to be honest, I don't think I should ever have been in the group."

"Why not?" Sally looked puzzled, and Loretta realized she was still in the dark.

"OK." June took a deep breath. "Remember when the group started? I was still living with Geoff—I must've driven you all mad. One week I was going to leave him and the next

63

I'd changed my mind—I was scared. I remember saying that, but not why—'' She bit her lip and went on. ''I had these feelings, I'd had them for ages, and I thought if I left Geoff . . . You didn't make it any easier, you were all so bloody *het*.'' She stopped and looked at Carol for support.

''Oh, June! Why didn't you say?'' Sally had at last understood the situation, and she looked astonished. ''That was the whole point of the group, being able to say—''

''That's what I'm *telling* you,'' June interrupted. ''I *couldn't* say anything. It didn't seem—I suppose when I saw the ad in *Spare Rib* and it said a group for separated women I sort of hoped—but I soon got the message. All the rest of you were interested in was *men*. That's not exactly what I mean, I'm not putting this well—I know we talked about different sorts of relationships, but always with men. You know, whether it was different if you weren't married, or you didn't actually live with them . . . I don't think the group helped me at all, looking back, I just felt the odd one out all the time.''

''So did Sandra,'' Loretta said without thinking.

''Sandra?'' June looked astonished. ''But she—she dominated the group. There were times, only once or twice I admit, when I was going to say—wait a minute, why are we always talking about heterosexuality, and then I looked at her and I just couldn't—''

''Why not?'' Sally demanded.

''Because she—'' June opened her hands in front of her as though her point was too obvious to be worth making.

''You mean—you think she was anti-gay?'' Sally's tone gave the impression that she was ready to argue.

June gave a short laugh. ''Not so much that as—I don't normally use words like heterosexist, but she behaved as though gay people never existed. Especially after she had an affair with that man, the one she met at the health farm.'' She raised her eyes to the ceiling to convey what she thought about health farms. ''It was all—oh, he's so good in bed, I just never knew it could be like this—''

''She *is* dead,'' Sally said coldly, glaring across the room.

64

"It was you who wanted me to come here," June shot back. "I'm just explaining . . ."

"You have to allow for her background," Sally protested. "She'd never lived in London before, she'd spent all her life in Hampshire being a wife and mother—you have to admire her for having the courage to break away from that. Where she came from, there probably weren't many gay people—"

"You're saying there aren't any lesbians in Hampshire? Or any gay men?"

"Of course not! But I doubt if it's so open—you've just told us how difficult you found it to come out in *London*. All I'm saying is, I'm sorry you feel like this about Sandra and I think you're being a bit unfair. It was very hard for her, leaving Tom and the kids—"

"She hadn't really left him."

June crossed one leg over the other and described circles in the air with her right foot. Loretta, feeling in some obscure way that the argument was her fault for innocently mentioning that Sandra had felt left out, was reminded of an angry cat twitching its tail. She noticed that Sue had wisely gone back to her magazine and sighed, wishing she had one.

"What do you mean?" Sally was waiting for June to elaborate.

"Well, she was still sleeping with him."

"Was she?" Sally sounded surprised.

"Oh yes. I met her once at the Special Clinic, she'd got some infection from the bloke at the health farm—ironic, isn't it? And she was worried to death about giving it to Tom."

"Do we have to have this discussion?" Sue asked sharply, shutting her magazine and tossing it on to the floor. "I'd really rather *not* sit here while you two argue about Sandra's sex life."

"*I* didn't bring it up," Sally protested.

"It's the last thing I want to talk about," June insisted.

There was a strained silence and Loretta looked at the sunlight on the water in the Hockney painting. Even though it was only a print it glinted with captured light, and she shivered, suddenly aware that the room wasn't very warm.

"I'm sorry," June said helplessly, after a moment. "This is exactly why I didn't want to come."

"It's my fault," Sally said, gripping the arms of her chair. "It was my idea."

"June—remember the time," said a voice Loretta didn't recognize. She swivelled round from the Hockney to see that Carol was speaking for the first time. "We said we'd try and be there for the beginning . . ."

"Oh." June looked torn. "Some friends of ours are playing at a club in Stoke Newington . . . We said we'd get there by half nine. I'm sorry."

"Well—" Sally seemed to be about to say something, then changed her mind.

"I'm glad to have seen you all," June continued, rather formally now. "Our coats . . ."

"Your coats—oh shit!" Sally had jumped to her feet, scattering photographs of her baby all over the floor. She went down on her knees and began picking them up.

"I'll do it," Loretta knelt beside her, glad of something to do. "You get the coats."

Sally got heavily to her feet and disappeared through a door which she shut behind her. She was gone for a couple of minutes, and Loretta was looking for a safe place to put the envelope containing the photos when she came back into the room.

"June." Sally handed her a black coat. "Carol."

The two women stood up.

"Well—thanks for the tea." June moved towards the door, Carol in her wake.

"Don't—I hope you enjoy your concert." Sally trailed behind them.

Loretta called "Goodbye" and a moment later heard the sound of the front door being opened. Sally came back into the room and threw herself down on the sofa.

"God," she said, propping her right elbow on the back of it. "I had no idea."

66

"What of?" asked Sue. "That June was gay or that that was going to happen?"

"Either. Did you, Loretta? I know you weren't keen on the meeting."

"Only because we hadn't met for so long—" Loretta began.

Sally interrupted her. "I feel terrible about the whole thing. The group, I mean, not just what she said about Sandra. It never occurred to me that she . . ."

"That was her point, I think," Sue said succinctly. "Feeling awful doesn't help. What're we going to do now?"

"Now?" Loretta looked at her watch. "Go home, I suppose."

"Oh no," moaned Sally. "You can't leave me here in this state. Can't we—does anyone fancy a pizza? That place on Islington Green? Anything to take my mind off it."

"I suppose I could eat something," Loretta said slowly.

"I don't mind," Sue said, getting up. "I'll get the coats." She disappeared into the room Sally had gone into earlier.

"I'm sorry, Loretta," said Sally, not looking at her. She was carrying the Lloyd Loom chair back to its corner.

"Oh, forget it—it might've worked. Maybe if Bridge had been here . . ."

"Maybe. I was going to ask you—I thought it would come up naturally, but as it hasn't . . . Did you get hold of Tom? You were going to ask him about the accident, where it happened and so on."

"No, I didn't." Loretta shook her head. "I've tried him several times and he's always out. I wondered if he'd gone away for a few days. I'll have to speak to him some time, I've still got Sandra's clothes and things . . ."

"Will you let me know? It doesn't make any difference, really, I'd just like to know—"

"Yes, I'll give you a ring." Loretta remembered the photographs and went over to the table where she'd put the envelope, anxious to get off the unhappy subject of Sandra. There were about a dozen pictures, most of them showing

Felicity, or Felicity and Sally. "Gosh, she's big for her age. She's got a nice smile."

"She's very advanced—it's not just me that thinks so, it's the clinic as well."

There was the sound of a lavatory flushing—Loretta remembered Sally's bathroom was off the bedroom—and Sue came back with her own and Loretta's coats in her arms.

"Weighs a ton," she said disapprovingly, handing Loretta her fake fur.

"It's very warm," Loretta pointed out. "Ready?"

"Yes," said Sally, eagerly leading the way. "Just slam the door—I've got the keys."

Loretta brought up the rear, making sure the door to the flat was firmly shut. "Is it still raining?" she called out, retrieving her damp umbrella in the hall.

"Pouring. Whose car shall we go in?"

"Let's take mine." Loretta joined Sue and Sally on the steps, a gust of wind snatching at her umbrella and turning it inside out.

"Oh hell," she said, trying to right it. "I've broken one of the spokes. We'll just have to run for it."

The three women hurried down the steps into the wild night, pausing on the pavement to link arms against the wind. Then, proceeding like some ungainly, night-fearing animal, they struggled up the street to where Loretta had left her car.

6

LORETTA WAITED UNTIL THE FOLLOWING afternoon before trying Tom Neil's number again. She did so reluctantly, and only because of the practical problem of Sandra's luggage. Until the previous evening she had managed to push her own guilty feelings about Sandra to the back of her mind, but the events at Sally's flat had revived them. It did not help that June's remarks, however justified, had demonstrated the partial truth of Sandra's claim that the women's group had been hostile towards her. Loretta thought that the sooner she came to some arrangement with Tom Neil the better, then she could forget the whole business.

She was so used to getting no reply from the Winchester number that she was unprepared when the phone was picked up. A female voice requested her to hang on; she heard a clatter as the receiver was put down, and a whine in the background which sounded like a vacuum cleaner. It stopped abruptly, and the phone was lifted again.

"Hello?" The voice, that of a youngish woman, was suspicious, and Loretta wondered whether she'd got a wrong number.

"I'd like—is that Tom Neil's house?"

"Are you the police?"

"The police? Good God, no! I'm a friend of Sandra's—of Mrs. Neil."

"Oh. Well, Mr. Neil's not here." If Loretta had expected

69

to dissolve the woman's hostility by identifying herself as a friend of the family, she was disappointed. She tried again.

"When *will* he be there?"

"Tuesday—after the inquest."

"The inquest? You mean—on Sandra?" It had never occurred to Loretta that Sandra's death would be the subject of an inquest, and she was momentarily astonished. Ignorance vied with curiosity: was this a matter of routine, or were the police unhappy about—about what? After all, Sandra had died in a car crash. How could there be anything sinister about that?

"Yes—waste of time and money, isn't it?" The woman at the other end of the line had read her own interpretation into Loretta's expression of surprise and was now rather friendlier.

"I—I had no idea. Do the police . . . ?" She hesitated, wanting to ask questions, but hampered by not knowing who she was talking to. The conversation was so at odds with what she had expected when she dialled Tom Neil's number that she was temporarily unable to gather her wits.

"The *police*," the woman snorted. "They were round here again yesterday, soon as he got back—he only came to pick up his letters. Three times they've been now, four if you count the ones that come to tell him . . . you know. Not that it's any of *my* business, *I* wasn't here—I don't normally come weekends, only tomorrow's a bit awkward . . . It was Mrs. Fraser two doors down saw them. She was out of her house this morning, soon as I arrived, fishing. I told her—*I* don't know what it's all about. All I know is the inquest's on Tuesday morning, half past ten, and Mr. Neil's coming back here after."

"Half past ten," Loretta repeated, still turning the information over in her mind.

"That's right—you want to leave a message? There's—hang on—there's an envelope here I can put it on the back of."

"No, don't worry. You've been very helpful."

70

"No trouble. I've got to go, my husband's coming to pick me up at three and I've got the upstairs to hoover. Bye."

The line went dead. Loretta put the receiver back in its cradle and leaned back in her chair, a frown creasing her forehead. What was she to make of what she had just learned? It had already occurred to her that the inquest meant nothing; she had occasionally seen newspaper reports of inquests on road accident victims, not that she made a habit of searching out such stuff. Only the most spectacular cases, multiple pile-ups on motorways and the like, got into the *Guardian*, but for every one that made the nationals dozens must go unreported, or appear only in the pages of local newspapers. By itself, the inquest wasn't significant.

She was more perplexed by Tom Neil's visits from the police. They had been round three times, the cleaner had said, in addition to bringing the news of Sandra's death. Obviously Neil would have been interviewed, that was only to be expected—in all likelihood it would have happened when he went to identify Sandra's body or shortly after. A small shiver ran through Loretta at the picture she had conjured up, and she moved her thoughts on swiftly. Why had the police needed to see him on three more occasions? A car crash was an unpleasant but relatively straightforward way to die; there could be grounds for suspicion only if the police had found evidence of mechanical interference with Sandra's car, with the brakes or . . . Loretta's knowledge of such things was hazy. In any case, the notion that anyone had tampered with Sandra's car was outlandish, not worthy of serious consideration—except that she had been a social worker, and there were cases of social workers being attacked, even murdered, by psychotic clients. Perhaps the police had discovered something amiss, and were keeping Tom Neil informed . . . Loretta seized the phone and dialled the Winchester number again.

"Hello—I called a minute ago. I forgot to ask, where's the inquest being held?"

"Lymington."

"Lymington?" Loretta repeated the name blankly, unable

for a moment to think where it was. She realized she had expected the woman to say Winchester—illogically, since she had not yet inquired where the accident took place. Then she remembered the other phone number Sally had given her and the Neil's house on the coast.

"Is that where—isn't that where their other house is?"

"Well, just outside." The woman sounded eager to get off the line.

"And that's—is that where the crash happened?"

"Yes. If you don't mind . . . my husband's waiting outside."

"Oh, right. Sorry. Thanks very much."

Loretta put the phone down a second time and got up from her chair, moving to a window. Outside in the street a red London bus thundered past and she glanced down into the sparsely populated upper deck. She caught a glimpse of two teenage boys who appeared to be wrestling each other in one of the front seats, and a black woman in a hat at the back, well out of their way. The weather was unchanged, wet and blowy, and she wasn't surprised that so few people had ventured out.

Another odd circumstance struck her—the fact that the inquest was taking place *after* Sandra's funeral. She thought about it for a moment, then decided it wasn't so strange after all; weren't inquests sometimes opened and adjourned so that the body could be released to relatives? She was probably making far too much of the little the cleaner had told her. On the other hand, what was behind those visits from the police? The thought nagged at her, and didn't fit easily with a simple road accident. Then another question began to bubble in her mind: why had Sandra rushed off to the house near Lymington? She hadn't mentioned any such intention when she rang Loretta at her office on New Year's Eve; on the contrary, she had suggested dinner in London that very evening, and if Loretta had accepted . . . She pushed away this thought, concentrating on the fact that everything pointed to a very sudden change of plan on Sandra's part. It was an awfully long way to drive on a dismal winter afternoon,

72

especially when the alternative was a warm London flat—unless Sandra had arranged to meet someone there? It seemed an odd choice for a rendezvous. Sally hadn't said much about the house except that it was right on the water, and that Tom Neil kept a boat there. Loretta thought it fair to assume it was bleak and unwelcoming on a bitterly cold December night.

She turned away from the window, aware that there was a simple way of getting answers to all these questions. Her gaze travelled round the peaceful room, taking in the cat stretched sleekly in front of the log fire, the book lying open on the sofa. It was an appealing domestic scene, and she felt a surge of resistance to the idea which had taken shape in her head during her first conversation with Tom Neil's cleaner. She certainly didn't *want* to go to the inquest, the trip would be tiring and she had so many other things to do—term started on Thursday . . .

At the same time, she had already made the decision. She knew her motives were far from altruistic, though a less honest person might have claimed to be doing it for Sandra's sake. Loretta accepted that going to Hampshire was a way of allaying guilt, of being able to feel she was doing something after the fiasco of the women's group. She was still standing with her back to one of the windows, and her glance fell on Sandra's luggage in the far corner of the drawing-room. She cheered up, thinking that this was another reason for attending the inquest: she could take the bags with her and hand them over to Tom Neil. Relieved to be thinking of practical matters, she turned her mind to the journey. How long would it take to drive to Lymington? She had never been there but she had been to Southampton a couple of times, to conferences at the university, and it was in the same general direction. The M_3 went most of the way, so it shouldn't take more than—what? An hour and three-quarters? Better allow a little more, to be on the safe side—a couple of hours should be enough. Loretta noticed that the fire was burning low and went over to add some logs, taking care not to disturb Bertie as she did so. Then she went to the kitchen in search of a carrier bag for the neat pile of clothes still sitting where she had left it on top of Sandra's suitcase.

When Loretta's alarm went off at seven-thirty on Tuesday morning, the trip to Hampshire seemed momentarily less attractive. She stirred, leaned across to turn off the insistent beep-beep of the clock-radio, and inadvertently rolled Bertie off the bed on to the floor. He picked himself up, dazed with sleep, and leapt back on to the quilt.

"Sorry, Bertie," she said, pulling up her legs from under the duvet and swinging them over him. "I've got to get up."

She padded barefoot into the bathroom, shivering because the central heating hadn't yet come on. It was still dark outside, and she groaned as she turned on both bath taps. She went downstairs to put on the kettle, stretching, yawning, and longing for another half hour in bed as she waited for it to boil. She discovered mould on the last few slices of bread in the breadbin, and her resolution wavered. Pushing away the temptation to forget the whole thing, she rummaged in a cupboard and found an elderly packet of porridge oats. At least porridge didn't go off, she thought, mixing the oat flakes to an unattractive sludge with water and turning on the cooker. Then she remembered that she'd left the bath taps running, and had to abandon the porridge for a moment while she ran upstairs to prevent an overflow.

"Damn," she said mildly, putting her hand in the deep, tepid water. There was far too much cold, and the hot water had now run out. She pulled out the plug, letting the bath drain to the last couple of inches before putting it back. Then she opened the airing-cupboard and switched on the immersion heater, half-heartedly hoping there'd be enough hot water by the time she finished breakfast.

The result of these delays was that Loretta left her flat late, pulling the front door shut behind her just after half past eight. She struggled down the stairs with Sandra's suitcase in one hand and her large holdall in the other, opening the street door just as the postman reached for the letter-box.

"Oh—thanks." She put down the luggage and glanced

quickly through the envelopes, automatically sorting out those addressed to her downstairs neighbour, Shahin, which she placed on top of the meter cupboard. She was left with three: a credit card bill which she put unopened in her shoulder-bag, an airmail letter from Cyprus addressed in John Tracey's hand, and a white envelope franked "Vixen Press." Her heart beat more quickly at the sight of the latter; she had not expected to hear from Vixen so soon—it was only eight days since she posted the typescript—and she was suddenly afraid that the envelope contained a rejection slip. She tore it open, anxiety tightening her chest as she smoothed out the single sheet of paper inside. Then, as she read, her cheeks began to glow. Her editor, Susie Lathlean, wrote that this was a preliminary note to say the typescript was "fabulous"; she had taken it home last week when she was struck down with the flu and found it "riveting, a tremendous read." The letter ended with the information that Susie had given it to another Vixen editor to read, but she was sure there wouldn't be any major problems. Vixen would be delighted to publish the book, and did Loretta have any ideas about illustrations? Loretta was still basking in the praise heaped on the biography when she got to a handwritten PS at the bottom of the letter: "Are you very attached to the title?" Susie had scrawled. "My instinct is for something simpler."

Loretta tutted her disappointment, suddenly ready to defend *A Woman and her Fate: A Life of Edith Wharton* to the end. She read the letter through again, this time with a slightly jaundiced eye, asking herself if the praise wasn't a bit overdone—a rather hasty judgement. There must be *something* Susie didn't like, apart from the title. She was already marshalling her arguments when she remembered why she was standing on the doorstep and looked at her watch. Quarter to nine; if she didn't set off now she was going to be terribly late. She stuffed the letter from Vixen into her bag, followed it with the unread airmail envelope from Tracey, and hoisted Sandra's luggage for the short walk to her car.

* * *

Loretta's progress across London was slow, and included an unexpected halt in standing traffic on the Westway as a result of roadworks. There was no further hold-up in Shepherd's Bush, and even though the motorway was relatively empty going west, the final stretch on A-roads through Lyndhurst and the New Forest took longer than she'd anticipated. Loretta arrived in Lymington a little after eleven, eager to find the coroner's court and in no mood to linger over the beauties or otherwise of the town. She headed into the centre along a prosperous shopping street dominated by a rather ugly parish church on her left, and stopped a passer-by to ask for directions. The woman couldn't help her, nor could the next person she consulted, an elderly man with a small, fierce terrier.

"Have you tried the police station?" he asked, struggling to prevent his dog attacking Loretta's car. "They—sit, Charlie!—might know."

His directions to this building turned out to be excellent—if you were on foot. Loretta promptly got lost in a one-way system, and it was twenty past eleven when she drew up outside a wide, two-storey building with the words "Hampshire Constabulary" over its porticoed double doors. She parked her car and hurried inside, where she was surprised to find the reception area empty. A laconic desk sergeant appeared after she had rung the bell on the counter several times; he stared for a full thirty seconds at her red fake fur coat, then informed her offhandedly that inquests took place in a room at the side of the police station. Loretta thanked him and went back outside, following his directions to the public entrance. She was half convinced that the case was already over, but when she pushed open the unmarked swing door she found a lobby populated by three people, all of whom stared at her with interest through a haze of stale cigarette smoke.

"Is it—is the inquest still going on?" she asked, addressing the question to the uniformed policeman who appeared to be single-handedly responsible for the pollution.

"You a witness?" He lowered his copy of the *Daily Express*. "No."

"Go on in then." He jerked his head towards the double doors in front of her. "You'll have to be quiet—he started ages ago."

Loretta had never been in court before, and she did her best to open the right-hand door silently. It swung inwards with a dismaying creak, and she had a momentary impression that everyone inside had turned to stare at her. Then they went back to the business in hand, leaving her stranded at the back of the court. She had no idea where to sit, and the small, bare room with tables along three walls was not what she had expected; there was no dais, and she was able to identify the coroner only because he was sitting opposite her, under a picture of the Queen. A policeman sat on his left, staring fixedly at a stack of manila files tied with pink ribbon. A few chairs had been placed haphazardly in the well of the court, only two of them occupied, and Loretta glanced around for a less conspicuous spot. She found it in the shape of a small table on her right, at the back of the room, and tiptoed across to join a middle-aged man who was sitting behind it. He gave her a surprised look, then went back to sketching a harbour scene on a yellow pad on his knees. It occurred to Loretta that she should have brought a notebook.

She transferred her attention to the coroner, a portly, balding man in a dark suit and gold-rimmed spectacles which had slipped down his nose. His sharp little eyes peered over them at a witness, a tall, spare man with wavy, iron-grey hair who appeared ill at ease in the portable witness stand in the far corner of the room. It took Loretta a moment to get the hang of what was happening, and when she did she was surprised by the snail-like pace of events. Each of the witness's replies was laboriously written down by the coroner, leaving long silences in between. After observing this numbing procedure for a couple of minutes, Loretta had gleaned that the tall man was a pathologist and that he was halfway through his evidence. He was describing Sandra's injuries in some detail, but in medical jargon so obscure it might have been another language. Loretta found his explanations hard to follow, but thought this was just as well; the dry, medical language

77

blunted the horror of his subject. His delivery was rapid, and he had just moved on to another point when the coroner intervened.

"Mr. Brown—I have mentioned this before," he said testily. "We don't all have the benefit of a medical education—is this a matter of substance, or merely a medical curiosity? We've already spent a considerable amount of time on your evidence and there is another witness to follow."

"It does raise an interesting question," the pathologist said eagerly. "If I could just explain—very broadly, vital reaction appears to have set in at the site of this laceration and—"

"Vital reaction?"

"The massing of leucocytes—"

"White blood cells, Mr. Brown!"

"Sir?" Brown seemed bewildered by the further interruption. "The massing of—of white blood cells at the site of a wound in a living body is observable in the form of inflammation at its edges. Such repair work is visible, naturally, only in living tissue." He had speeded up, and was giving nervous sideways glances at the coroner. "Different types of leu—white cells appear in sequence, over a period of forty-eight hours—"

"Doctor, we are not interested in a period of forty-eight hours in this case," the coroner snapped. "We've already established that a period of, at the very most, two hours elapsed before the unfortunate lady expired from the massive injuries you have described. The relevance of this—" The coroner shrugged crossly.

It took Loretta a few seconds to grasp the import of his speech, and then a fullness came into her throat. She stared at the table in front of her, clinging to its ordinariness as an antidote to the ghastly picture which had come into her head. Sandra had survived the crash, had lived for up to two hours afterwards—Loretta pushed the image away. She had not immediately understood the pathologist's reference to some sort of reaction in living tissue, but now it was clear. She blinked back tears, trying to calm herself by lifting her head and

78

concentrating on the two actors in the drama—on the dull rhythm of question-and-answer. The argument was still going on, however.

"—seems a somewhat arcane point." The coroner glanced at his watch. "If you could be brief—"

"Vital reaction after injury is generally observable within two hours, although it has been recorded in as short a period as thirty minutes," the pathologist gabbled. "In this case, there were few traces of leucocyte infiltration at the edges of the lacerations, with the exception of the one below the left eye. Inflammation *was* microscopically visible there to a rather greater degree—"

"Just one moment. You've told us that the margin within which this reaction occurs is a wide one—between half an hour and two hours. Am I correct?"

"Yes, but—"

"Then I do not see—"

Both men paused.

"I was simply pointing out the fact that the reaction was visible at this site and not at others," the pathologist said unhappily.

"Not at all at the others?"

"I wouldn't put it as categorically as that—"

"So the reaction *was* visible elsewhere?"

"Not to a marked degree."

"In any degree at all?"

"Yes."

"Thank you." The coroner took out a handkerchief and mopped his brow. "I think we'll move on. If you would be so kind as to bear with me for one moment . . ."

He pushed his glasses up his nose with a practised movement and bent his head. The court was so quiet that Loretta could hear the scratching of his pen. She sat with furrowed brow, her hands clasping her knees, not daring to relax. The important thing was not to think about the crash— the minutes, hours even, Sandra had spent lying in the wreckage . . . She fidgeted in her seat, crossing and uncrossing her ankles, wishing that the journey from London had taken even longer—long enough for her to have missed the pathologist's evidence. She looked at her watch and saw it was ten minutes to twelve.

"Mr. Brown—"

The pathologist swivelled his head, an uncomprehending expression on his face. Loretta thought he had sensed the coroner's hostility, but was genuinely puzzled by it.

"Mr. Brown, if we may turn to another area—the question of the level of alcohol in Mrs. Neil's blood. I trust you have the figures?"

It was like pressing a switch; the pathologist began reeling off numbers, starting with Sandra's blood-alcohol level at the time of the post mortem. He followed it with a long and complicated lecture—during which the coroner grew increasingly restive—on its relation to the level at the time of death. Loretta found it no easier to follow than the rest of his evidence and gave up the attempt, allowing the words to flow over her. Eventually he came to a halt, like a clockwork toy winding down, and the coroner rapped out a question.

"In other words, the amount of alcohol in the deceased's blood was insufficient to explain her loss of control?"

"I wouldn't like—" The pathologist looked alarmed.

"Let me put it another way. She was not inebriated—her blood-alcohol level was not above the limit prescribed in law for drivers?"

"I—no."

"If you would be so good as to run through those figures again?"

Brown complied. The coroner recorded them, then fired another question at the pathologist.

"And you found no medical condition which might explain Mrs. Neil's accident?"

"I—I did not." Short answers obviously unsettled him.

"Thank you, Mr. Brown. The court is grateful for your help." The coroner gave a curt nod of dismissal.

The pathologist hesitated. "If I may be excused," he said, "the hospital—"

"Of course. We must count ourselves lucky that the hospital is close by, and hope your attendance here has not taken up too much of its valuable time.''

The sarcasm was obvious, but the pathologist seemed to miss it. He gave a nervous smile and stepped down, hurrying with long strides to the back of the room; the door creaked as he went out. The coroner leaned to one side and conferred in a low voice with the uniformed policeman, and Loretta saw both men consult their watches. Then the coroner shook his head vigorously, apparently disagreeing with something the policeman had said. Loretta remembered that he had mentioned another witness, and wondered who it was.

''Who are you with?''

She jumped, taken by surprise by the man sitting next to her. She stared at him for a moment, not knowing what he meant.

''I'm not with anyone,'' she whispered back, puzzled. ''I'm on my own.''

''Aha, freelance,'' he said knowingly. ''Don't see many of your sort in this part of the world. Who's interested then? Doesn't look much in it to me.''

Loretta took in the man's notebook and crumpled raincoat. ''Oh—I see,'' she said, suddenly realizing he was a reporter. ''I must be in the wrong place—I thought this was for the public.'' He was probably from the local paper, she thought, wondering why she hadn't noticed before. She had arrived late, of course, and rather flustered . . .

''What you doing on the press bench, then?'' He was regarding her suspiciously.

''I just said—I didn't realize. Where'm I supposed to be?''

''Oh, very good—I suppose you've never been in court before, either. Pull the other one. Come on, what's the angle? You'll need my help, you missed most of it. Not that there's much to tell.''

''Look, I'm really not—''

Loretta heard a loud cough and looked up to see the coroner frowning at her. She shrank into her coat and looked down at her hands, feeling like a naughty schoolgirl.

''Sergeant Harris—next witness, please.''

The sergeant rose ponderously to his feet and passed the press bench on his way to the back of the court. He disappeared through the double doors for a moment, with the usual squeak, and returned with a short, smartly dressed man in his wake. Loretta watched as the newcomer stepped confidently into the witness box.

"I must remind you that you are still on oath—"

The man gave a brisk nod, and Loretta was impressed by a sense of energy and confidence. It occurred to her that he was another expert witness—something to do with Sandra's car, perhaps. She remembered her speculations of the previous afternoon and sat up straight, wondering if she was about to learn the reason for the police interest in the case. There had been nothing in what she had heard so far to explain it.

The coroner, who had been consulting his notes, raised his head.

"You told the court last week that your full name is Thomas Edward Thornton Neil . . ."

Loretta stifled a gasp. This was Sandra's husband? She was not sure what she had expected, but this man was older, too self-assured—his appearance gave no hint that he had a personal interest in the case.

"You gave your address as Paternoster Square, Winchester. You also said that you own a small house about three miles from Lymington, with a water frontage. A location known as Hardimans Deep—Shore House, I believe it is called?"

"That is correct." Neil's voice was loud and firm—that of an altogether larger man, Loretta thought, oddly.

"You are forty-five years of age, and your occupation—you are a wine shipper?"

"Correct."

Neil's tone reminded Loretta of something—she couldn't place it for a moment. Then it came to her: he sounded like a contestant in an up-market quiz show, eager to get the preliminaries out of the way and start on the real questions. She was astonished by his self-control, the absence of any hint of grief; then she reminded herself that he and Sandra had separated years ago. It was not as if theirs had been a close relationship.

"You also told the court—" the coroner paused, searching for the right words. "Last week you also told us that two police officers called at your home, your home in Winchester, on the afternoon of January the first this year—New Year's Day—with the news that your wife had been involved in a road traffic accident. A fatal road traffic accident."

"Yes." Neil nodded emphatically.

"You subsequently drove to the mortuary in Lymington where you identified the body of your wife, Mrs.—" the coroner checked his notes "—Mrs. Alexandra Patricia Neil, who was thirty-seven years of age at the time of her death?"

"I did."

The coroner fiddled with his spectacles. "Ah, Mr. Neil, if this is distressing for you—"

Neil interrupted him. "It's quite all right—I understand."

The coroner looked affronted. Loretta thought it was his standard speech to bereaved relatives, and he was used to finishing it. "I was about to say that if at any time you would like to adjourn for a few moments, or you would like to sit down—you must feel free to mention it." He frowned at Neil, who appeared not to notice.

"Thank you, I'm grateful."

The coroner hesitated, then resumed questioning.

"I believe you returned to England only the day before your wife's accident?"

"I understood there was some doubt as to the time of the crash—whether it was on New Year's Eve or in the early hours . . . I returned to England on the thirty-first of December. We—my children and I—arrived home from the airport around lunchtime."

"I see. I am right in thinking that your wife did not accompany you on this holiday?"

"That is correct."

"Can you—could you tell me when you last saw your wife, prior to her accident?"

"It was at the beginning of December." The answer was given without hesitation; Neil did not seem to be embarrassed about his separation from Sandra. "Perhaps I could explain—my wife worked in London, and had done so for some years . . ."

His voice tailed off; there was a distinct loss of assurance, but that wasn't the only reason Loretta looked at him in surprise.

"Sandra had a very—" he hesitated "—a very exacting job at a rehabilitation unit in West London, and her case-load was particularly heavy at that time of year. She usually returned home—to the family home, that is—as often as possible. The period before Christmas was very busy, and she was unable to get away . . . Sandra was very conscientious."

A deep frown creased Loretta's forehead. Her memory wasn't sharp about everything Sandra had told her over Christmas, but she clearly recalled their telephone conversation on Christmas Eve. "I've been working away from London," Sandra had said, giving it as the reason she'd lost touch with her friends in the city.

"—went to Switzerland without her," she heard the coroner saying, and realized she had not been paying attention. "I'm sorry to pry into your private affairs in this manner . . ."

"There's no need—" Neil gestured with one hand, and took a deep breath. "It is—was—our usual practice to take the children skiing at Christmas . . . Sandra was in fact an accomplished skier. This year I left it rather late to book—it was impossible to get flights which fitted in with her work schedule. Obviously the children were very disappointed . . . after some discussion on the phone we decided I should take them alone. That is a decision I—obviously I regret it."

The coroner looked puzzled.

"Why is that, Mr. Neil?"

"Because—because of subsequent events," Neil said, conveying the impression that the answer was self-evident.

"You mean—the fact that your wife did not see her children over Christmas? Of course, with hindsight—"

"No, not that. I—I think it may have exacerbated a state of anxiety—of overwork . . . ." He pursed his lips.

"Mr. Neil, are you suggesting—was your wife . . . *depressed* in the period leading up to Christmas?"

Neil looked down at his hands, which were resting on the brass rail of the witness box. "I—"

"Mr. Neil, I don't want to press you—"

Neil lifted his head. Loretta was shocked by the change in his face, by his abrupt transition from confidence to a visible struggle to maintain control. He tugged at the knot of his tie, as though he was finding it hard to breathe, and the first time he opened his mouth no sound came out.

"Sandra was—some years ago Sandra decided she wanted to train as a social worker. The children were growing up, and she felt she needed . . . I was hostile to the idea at first, but then I saw how much it meant . . . My wife was—energetic, and she wanted to do something that would make her feel—useful. She left school with A levels, but she didn't work after we got married . . . She got a place at a college in London, but it was always her intention—we agreed she would look for a job nearer home as soon as she was qualified—when she'd got some experience.

"That never—she had been looking for a job in Hampshire for some time, but nothing suitable seemed to . . . Her job in London was—well, I thought it made too many demands on her. She became more and more exhausted . . . The business of Christmas was the last straw, I thought she needed a holiday and the children needed her . . . There was a row—I urged her to give the job up. She refused, and there was a—coolness between us. I think my decision to go ahead with the holiday was—ill-judged."

He stopped, staring at the jug of water on the table in front of the coroner. "Could I—some water?"

"Sergeant Harris."

The policeman got up, filled a glass and took it over to the witness box. Neil finished it in three long gulps and handed it back.

"Thank you."

The coroner cleared his throat. "Mr. Neil, may I get this clear? What you have described is a—a rather unusual domestic arrangement, but you are not suggesting that you and your wife . . . that your marriage had broken down?"

"Certainly not!"

Neil's tone was heated. Loretta bit her lip and, without realizing what she as doing, began to twist the ends of her hair around the fingers of her right hand.

"But you *are* saying that your—um—domestic arrangements, that is to say, your wife's absence from the marital home as a consequence of her job, had caused a certain . . . *froideur* in the approach to Christmas?"

"I—yes." Neil was contemplating his hands again.

"And you are further suggesting that your wife's state of mind as a result of this—this disagreement—may have had a bearing on . . . subsequent events?" The coroner's tone was ice-cold.

Neil shook his head, opening his hands and closing them as if he didn't know what to say. "I—it crossed my mind."

"Was your wife—had she been treated for depression?"

"Not as far as I know."

"And we have heard from Detective Constable—from the police that nothing was found at Shore House to indicate why your wife was there—certainly no note—"

"No, but—"

"But?"

"But it seems odd," Neil finished lamely. "She was—she knew we'd be back on the thirty-first, I thought she'd be keen to see the kids . . . When she didn't get in touch I tried ringing her in London, I tried all day, but she wasn't there. And she didn't—what she was doing at Shore House? She didn't even like the place much, she thought it was too isolated—I keep a small boat there, a dinghy, but she was always reluctant . . . And the police say—apparently there was nothing wrong with her car—"

"With respect, Mr. Neil, this is all speculation." The coroner looked stern. He observed Neil over his glasses for a moment, then began adding to his notes.

Loretta dug her hands deep into the pockets of her coat, unconsciously shredding an old bus ticket. She had no idea what to make of Neil's evidence, of the almost unrecognizable portrait he had drawn of his marriage and his bizarre suggestion that Sandra—*Sandra*, of all people—might have crashed her car deliberately. Loretta could no more imagine Sandra killing herself than—than *Fergie*. She had been upset over Christmas, it was true, but there was a steely selfishness about her, a degree of self-regard which was at once the reason for Loretta's dislike of her and a powerful argument against the notion that she was a candidate for suicide. Everything about Tom Neil's story was at odds with Sandra's version of events, but it wasn't just her ignorance of court procedure that held Loretta back. His anguish seemed genuine; she had been very struck by his emotional collapse as soon as he started talking about his wife. Loretta was conscious of feeling sorry for him, something she found hard to square with the fact that he appeared to be telling lies. She jerked out of her reverie, anxious not to miss anything.

"—distressing for you, especially in view of the circumstances," she head the coroner say. He hesitated, giving the impression that he was reluctant to refer directly to the Neils' unconventional matrimonial set-up. "But you seem to be suggesting that your wife's death may have been—intentional. I have to ask whether you have any evidence for this, other than an inference drawn from her supposed state of mind in a period—at a time when you yourself admit to having had little contact with her?"

"I—no."

"It is the case, would you not agree, that the deliberate crashing of a car is a most unusual and uncertain method of committing suicide?"

"I suppose so. Yes."

"Mr. Neil—if I may offer a word of advice. In my experience it is not uncommon for the bereaved to search for explanations of the deaths of their loved ones which—which do not meet the facts of the case. Particularly when an element—however unjustified—an element of guilt may be involved.'' The coroner fiddled with his papers. "Now, if I may press on—" He examined his notes for a moment, then began to speak in altogether firmer tones. "The police officer in charge of the case has told us that your wife was not wearing a coat at the time of the accident, and it appears that her departure from the house was somewhat hasty. Is this a matter on which you can throw any light?''

"No, sir.'' Neil's tone was chastened.

"Your wife was—she was a competent driver?''

"She had no convictions, if that's what you mean.''

"And she was familiar with the approach to Shore House?''

"Yes. We've been going to the place regularly for ten or eleven years. She wasn't fond of it, but she knew the road.''

The coroner made a further note, then took off his glasses. "Mr. Neil, there is one further matter on which you may be able to throw light. During their examination of the house, the police discovered a broken window in the downstairs bathroom. Were you aware that this damage had taken place?''

"I don't think—no. I was at the house in September, shutting it up for the winter. I thought I made sure before I left that everything was secure.''

"It has been suggested that the broken window is the result of a break-in, or an attempt at burglary. Is anything missing from the house?''

"No.'' Neil's voice had audibly regained its strength. "The police asked me to check . . . there are one or two valuable pictures, and a video recorder. Nothing's been taken.''

"Thank you, Mr. Neil. You may step down.''

The coroner checked his watch. "Court will adjourn for ten minutes,'' he announced unexpectedly.

"Court rise!''

Taken by surprise, Loretta was still getting clumsily to her feet as the coroner pushed back his chair, gave a perfunctory bow in her general direction, and disappeared through a door in the side of the room.

7

"GO ON—YOU CAN TELL ME. WHO'RE YOU doing it for?''

It was the reporter again, and Loretta felt a surge of irritation as she sat down. She was preoccupied with the problem of Tom Neil's evidence, and she wanted time to think. Before she could say anything, however, he was off in the same vein.

"Bet it's one of the nationals—" He shook his head, apparently determined to disbelieve her earlier denials. "You know something I don't, that it? What's it all about, then, the husband making out she did herself in?''

"I haven't the faintest idea," Loretta said flatly, and with complete honesty. "Look, I'm nothing to do with the press.''

She noticed Tom Neil heading for the doors at the back of the room and jumped to her feet, intending to follow. Then she realized she had no idea what to say. The question she wanted to ask—why Neil had apparently lied to the coroner— was neither tactful nor likely to get results. She could mention Sandra's bags, and hope things would develop from there; if, on the other hand, he simply thanked her and took them off her hands, what then? She decided to take the coward's way out and wait until the end of the inquest. It seemed safe to assume that Neil wouldn't leave the building before then. She leaned back in her chair, comforted by this logic, and saw that the reporter was watching her with narrowed eyes.

"How many times do I have to tell you, I sat in the wrong place," she said, wondering if she should move. Not that she was doing any harm where she was, but he was getting on her nerves. "If I'm a journalist, where's my notebook?"

Her neighbour grinned unpleasantly, showing nicotine-stained teeth. "Think I was born yesterday? Got a tape recorder in there, haven't you?" He pointed at Loretta's shoulder-bag, which was standing open on a chair on her other side. "It's illegal, you know, but I don't suppose you worry too much about that. Do I get a whiff of a love triangle? Got a girlfriend, has he?"

"I'm *not* from the papers!" Loretta lost her temper. "Sandra was a friend of mine—"

"Yeah, and my name's Nigel Mansell. All right, have it your own way. I would've helped you out, but . . ."

He picked up his notepad, tore a clean sheet of paper from the middle, and began composing his story. Sensing that Loretta was watching him, he hunched protectively over the table to prevent her getting a glimpse of what he was writing. She shook her head, turned to her other side, and ostentatiously fastened the catch of her shoulder-bag.

Her mind went back to Tom Neil, and she felt tired and dispirited, a reluctant participant in events she didn't understand. Then, quite suddenly, she remembered a remark June had made on Saturday evening to the effect that Sandra had gone on sleeping with her husband long after leaving Winchester. Loretta brightened, thinking that Neil's evidence wasn't necessarily untruthful—it could be an alternative version of reality. Perhaps he really believed his wife had gone to London only to train as a social worker; perhaps she had let him believe it. Sandra's view of the world was markedly solipsistic, and it would not be out of character if she had chosen to keep her options open.

This explanation ironed out some of the discrepancies, though not all of them. There was still the question of *where* Sandra had been working, and Neil's motive for suggesting

90

that she had committed suicide. Loretta put up her hands and pushed her hair back from her face, letting her head fall backwards until it touched the wall behind. When she returned to a sitting position she saw a man watching her from the well of the court, the place she now realized was intended for the public. He met her gaze unabashed, and his right eye closed in a brief wink. Loretta stared at him in surprise, and went on looking after he had turned back to the magazine on his knee. He was in his mid-twenties, thick-set, and with dark curly hair; good-looking in a very masculine sort of way. Loretta wondered who he was, but had no time to speculate, for at that moment the police sergeant appeared through the side door, followed closely by the coroner.

"Court rise!"

There was a general shuffling of feet and Loretta noticed Tom Neil slip in and take a seat near the handsome young man. At least she had been right in assuming he would stay to the end. She turned to look at the coroner, listening attentively as he began what she guessed was his summing-up.

"I have been inquiring into the death of Mrs. Alexandra Patricia Neil," he said gravely, "a married woman with two children. It is a case with an unusual feature, which relates to the deceased's date of death. The fatal road traffic accident in which she died occurred without witnesses; no other vehicle was involved; and Mrs. Neil survived the crash for an indeterminate period of time before life became extinct. Hence it has been more than usually difficult to establish either the time of the accident or the time of death with any degree of accuracy; Mr. Brown, the pathologist, places the collision very roughly between ten forty-five p.m. on the night of December the thirty-first last year and twelve-thirty a.m. on January the first. The significance of these dates will immediately be apparent; although the margin of error appears small, it is sufficient to leave unanswered the question of whether Mrs. Neil's death occurred in 1987 or 1988.

"Mrs. Neil's car, a Ford Sierra registered two years ago and which she bought last February, left the road and collided with a tree. The accident happened on the road from

Shore House, a residence owned jointly by herself and her husband. A post-mortem was performed, and revealed the cause of death to be multiple injuries. Mrs. Neil had earlier consumed some alcohol, but was below the limit laid down for those about to take control of a vehicle.

"It appears that Mrs. Neil, who spent Christmas alone in London because of her work commitments, did not inform anyone of her intention to visit Shore House. With the help of Mr. Sanders, who was staying at the house next door and heard her car, I have been able to establish that she arrived at Hardimans Deep on the evening of her death at just after eight p.m. Unfortunately for this inquiry, Mr. Sanders went out at approximately eight-thirty on the evening in question, noticing as he did so that Mrs. Neil's car was parked by his gate, there being no direct vehicular access to Shore House. Mr. Sanders attended a New Year's Eve celebration in Romsey, and did not return home until just before ten-sixteen the next morning, a time fixed by the 999 call he made on discovering his neighbour's body in the wreckage of her car.

"It appears that Mrs. Neil left the house in some haste, or that she was contemplating only a short journey, since she was not wearing a coat. Additionally, Mr. Sanders later found his gate had been left open. We can only conjecture as to her destination, police inquiries at neighbouring houses—if they can be described as such in this somewhat scattered locality—having failed to unearth anyone who admits to having contacted her in the course of the evening. Nevertheless, I have to bear in mind the date and the possibility that Mrs. Neil, like her neighbour Mr. Sanders, had received a last-minute invitation to a New Year's Eve party. Let us bear in mind that Mr. Brown's estimate of the time of the accident— between ten forty-five p.m. and twelve-thirty a.m.—favours the period before midnight rather than after, suggesting that she may have been in a hurry to reach her destination in time for the customary celebrations. This may also account for the rather excessive speed at which Mrs. Neil's car appears to have been traveling when it left the road.

"The police have, quite rightly, raised a puzzling feature

of the case. That is the broken window in the downstairs bathroom. I believe I am correct in saying that the police have considered the possibility that Mrs. Neil disturbed an intruder in Shore House, and crashed her car in an attempt to escape. Against this I must weigh the facts that no unidentified fingerprints were discovered in the house, and that the fragments of glass had been swept up and placed in a waste bin in the kitchen. Most significant of all, Mr. Neil tells us that nothing had been taken, and I conclude that the most likely explanation is that Mrs. Neil discovered the damage, which may well have been caused during the celebrated storm last October or by children playing on the nearby public beach, on her arrival at Shore House and dealt with it to the best of her ability.''

The coroner stopped and poured himself a glass of water, sipping from it delicately. Loretta was surprised by the fluency of his delivery, and wondered if the purpose of the brief adjournment had been to give him time to rehearse.

''This situation I am called upon to consider,'' he continued, pushing the half-empty glass away, ''is one in which a young woman gets into her car probably before midnight on New Year's Eve, drives at speed along a thickly wooded stretch of road, and unhappily crashes into a tree. Her husband has told me that Mrs. Neil was depressed—in effect, of his suspicion that her action was deliberate. He has produced no evidence for this claim, and indeed had not seen his wife for almost a month prior to her tragic accident—a somewhat unusual state of affairs which, you might think, in itself goes some way to explain the burden of guilt which he appears to have taken upon himself.

''If, however, we rule out suicide as the cause of Mrs. Neil's unlucky accident, as I propose to do, what other explanations remain to be considered? The police inform me that her car was in excellent mechanical condition, and Mr. Brown was able to find no medical condition which might have caused a fit or blackout. The accident happened on a moonlit night when visibility was good, and the ground was dry with little frost.

"Let us consider the location of the accident a little more closely. Shore House, though a private residence, stands on the edge of the New Forest. It is reached by a long road, one might even call it a track, which crosses fields and then traverses a somewhat dense tract of woodland. The accident occurred just after Mrs. Neil's car entered this belt of trees and although it was, as I have said, a clear night, this fact is virtually irrelevant at this point in her progress. Indeed, the abrupt passage from bright moonlight to darkness may go some way towards explaining Mrs. Neil's loss of control. I have also to take into account the fact that, while not actually inebriated, her judgement may have been marginally impaired by her earlier intake of alcohol." He paused for a second and took a surreptitious glance at his watch.

"The police have, as I noted earlier, raised the question of whether Mrs. Neil's death was precipitated by the action of another person. The question I have to consider is whether the possibility of outside agency is strong enough to prompt an open verdict. I am reluctant to consider such a verdict, especially in a case where there is no evidence of foul play and in which the relatives of the dead woman may seize upon it as a signal that some degree of self-blame is in order. I have in mind the fact that no evidence has been produced to show that another person was in Shore House that night, nor is there anything to suggest that Mrs. Neil was not alone in her car when the accident happened. There is certainly no suggestion—and this is surely the salient point—that her injuries were sustained anywhere or at any time other than in the vehicle and in the course of the collision. This is a tragic case, in which a healthy young woman has been robbed of her life, two children have been left motherless, and Mr. Neil has lost the companionship of his wife. I may say that it is a salutary reminder to us all that the motor vehicle is a far from unmixed blessing. Having given due consideration to all the matters raised by the case, it is my intention to record a verdict of accidental death."

He stopped and looked sternly ahead of him, his eyes com-

94

ing to rest on the figure of Tom Neil, who was leaning forward, hands clasped together.

"Mr. Neil—" Neil raised his head. "I should like to put on the record the court's sympathies in this matter. Thank you."

"Court rise!"

Sergeant Harris's voice boomed across the room, once again catching Loretta unprepared. She had not expected the inquest to end so abruptly, and she was still in her seat when the reporter pushed past, muttering something she could not make out.

"Wait—" She put out a hand but he was already opening the door at the back of the court. Out of the corner of her eye she saw Tom Neil get up and she turned towards him, observing the slightly dazed expression on his face. As she watched he squared his shoulders, straightened the knot of his tie, and moved ponderously towards the exit. Loretta snatched up her shoulder-bag to follow him, but the movement dislodged its magnetic catch and her belongings slid in an untidy heap to the floor.

"Oh shit!" she exclaimed, forgetting where she was, and went down on her knees to retrieve everything. Neil must have come by car, she thought, stuffing her purse, her makeup bag, and that morning's post back inside—perhaps she could catch up with him in the car park. She seized the paperback crime novel she had brought with her and her cheque book, stretching under the table in an attempt to reach her brand new diary. Too late: a pair of shiny black loafers came into view, and a man's hand scooped it out of reach.

"Allow me."

The voice was friendly and teasing. Loretta manoeuvred awkwardly in the confined space and got to her feet, clutching the strap of her shoulder-bag in her right hand.

"*Women Painters Diary 1988.*" It was the good-looking man who had winked at her from the well of the court. "You interested in art?"

"I—yes. Thank you." Loretta took the diary from his outstretched hand and began sliding out from behind the press

95

table, anxious to catch up with Tom Neil. The man moved with her.

"Who are you with, then?" He smiled, making light of the fact that he was now barring her way. Loretta felt a paralyzing sense of *déjà vu*, and glared at him.

"I only meant—makes a nice change from Len Miller," he said disarmingly. "Same old face, day in, day out. He's almost part of the furniture."

"I'm not a journalist," Loretta said shortly. "Now if I could get past—" She took a step forward, wondering what sort of pervert would hang around inquests trying to pick up women.

"Not a relative, are you?" He had moved back a pace but was still between her and the door.

"No. A friend. Look—"

"Of Mrs. Neil? Or Mr. Neil?" His tone was quite different—sharp, inquisitive.

"Of Mrs.—of Sandra. What is this?"

"Did you know her well?"

"Yes, but—"

"Got time for a coffee?"

"A coffee?" Loretta was getting desperate. Tom Neil would surely be gone by now; was she going to have to follow him to Winchester?

"Just a little chat, nothing official."

"Offi-" Loretta stared at him. She turned her head sideways and read the title of the magazine he had been reading earlier: *Police Review*. He was also holding a file, a manila one tied with pink ribbon like those she had seen on the table in front of the uniformed sergeant. "You're a policeman?"

"Yep. This is my case."

"Oh . . ." She thought rapidly. She had probably missed Tom Neil, and it couldn't do any harm. She didn't have to tell him anything if she didn't want to—

"All right."

"There's the canteen—or there's a caff about ten minutes' walk from here. That too far for you?"

96

"No," she said quickly, preferring it to the police canteen.

"OK. Let's go."

He stood back at long last and allowed Loretta to precede him to the door. She reached for the handle but he was there first, holding it open and motioning her in front of him.

"After you."

It was said in a natural tone, not as if he was making a point of his chivalry. Loretta hesitated, decided not to argue, and walked past him into the smoky lobby.

"Great place, this," said the policeman, biting into a sausage sandwich with tomato ketchup oozing thickly from the edges. "You don't know what you're missing."

Loretta said nothing, unwilling to admit she had been tempted to join him. She watched him eat, her mouth watering as the sandwich disappeared before her eyes. The cup of black tea she had ordered was strong and bitter, hardly a substitute for locally made herb sausages . . . She didn't know why she had been so abstemious. Reaching for the bowl of white sugar standing in the middle of the Formica table, next to a jar of English mustard and an encrusted bottle of brown sauce, she added a few grains to her tea in the hope of making it more drinkable. She appraised her companion covertly as she stirred it, taking in the square-cut baggy suit, the fashionably narrow tie partially obscured by the paper napkin he had tucked over it. He was not her idea of a policeman, resembling neither the old *Dixon of Dock Green* stereotype nor the over-eager, officious breed she had occasionally encountered in London. If it hadn't been for his very slight Hampshire accent she would have assumed he was foreign, from somewhere in the Mediterranean; it would account for his olive skin and deep brown eyes, the dark curls forming a widow's peak over his wide forehead. He really was very good-looking, not in a way that attracted Loretta, but the young waitress in jeans and apron who took their order had lingered at the table, joking with him and blushing. Sausage sandwiches weren't even on the menu, which featured dishes with archly rustic or nautical names—"The Forester's Feast" and "The Bosun's Beef Casserole" had stuck in Loretta's mind. It was clear that the policeman was a favoured customer.

"You can still have one, you know. Julie won't mind."

"Sorry?"

He grinned across the table, removing the napkin and wiping his fingers on it. "You should see the look on your face. Anyone'd think you hadn't eaten for weeks."

"Oh—" She shrugged it off, embarrassed.

"Suit yourself. We haven't been introduced," he added, pushing his empty plate to one side and drawing the manila folder towards him.

"Lawson. Loretta Lawson."

"Loretta? Doesn't sound very English. Not Italian, are you?"

"Italian? Not as far as I know."

"Thought you didn't look it. It was the name made me wonder—you don't meet many Lorettas. How'd you get it?"

"I changed it. From Laura."

"Oh?" He was interested. "Sometimes think I should've changed mine, soon as I got into this game. They can't spell it, not even on my pay slips—they always leave the H out. Derek Ghilardi—that's G-H-I-L-A-R-D-I. Detective Constable. Pleased to meet you." He stretched his stubby right hand across the table and gripped Loretta's firmly. "My dad's from Sicily, that's why I asked about your name. He was a cook on a ship—he's got a restaurant in Southampton now." He released her hand abruptly, resting his own on the manila folder in an absent sort of way. "You local?"

"Me? No, I live in London."

"Thought so, dressed like that." He grinned and gestured towards her coat, which was draped over the empty chair next to her. "Which bit?"

"North London—Islington."

"Isn't that near the Arsenal?"

"Quite."

"Thought so. Been there when I was a kid—used to follow

98

the Saints. The Saints—Southampton," he added, seeing her blank look. "I don't any more—had enough of it when I was in uniform, Saturday afternoons on the terraces. One of the reasons I was glad to get into CID, though I'm not so keen on Lymington . . . What you do there? In London?"

"I'm a lecturer. At London University. I teach English."

"I should've gone to university. Too keen to earn some money, that was my trouble. My sister's there now—Leeds. She's doing French. Funny, isn't it—you'd think she'd want to do Italian. She gave me a book for Christmas—*Nausea*, it's called. By Jean-Paul Sartre. You read it?"

"No." Loretta shook her head, annoyed with herself for being surprised. Why shouldn't he have read Sartre? She excused herself by thinking that whatever she'd expected on her way to the café, this definitely wasn't it.

"Anyway—about your friend."

Loretta waited.

"What d'you make of the inquest?"

"What did I make of it? I suppose it was pretty straight-forward . . ." She was cautious, reluctant to say much until she knew more about what the detective wanted from her.

"What about the medical evidence? You missed the beginning—were you in time for Brown, the pathologist?"

"He'd already started when I arrived, but I think I heard most of it."

"So you were there when he was talking about vital reaction?"

"About—oh yes." The corners of Loretta's mouth turned down. "I gathered—he seemed to be saying she didn't die straight away."

Ghilardi sighed and shook his head. "You didn't get it either." He leaned back, folding his arms. "I'm not surprised—not the way Brown explained it. I had a word with him this morning—told him to keep it simple. It's not as if he doesn't know what Robinson's like—Robinson's the coroner, by the way. Well, you saw what happened."

Loretta looked at him blankly.

"Hopeless state of affairs," Ghilardi went on, uncrossing

his arms and fingering the pink ribbon of the folder irritably. "They'll have to do something about it eventually—Robinson can't stand Brown, thinks he's trying to put one over him. He isn't, actually—Brown's not like that. He's very good at his job—after all, he was the one who picked up on this vital reaction business. He can't put it across, that's all—he behaves in court same as he does in the hospital, as if he's got an audience of brain surgeons. Robinson loses his temper every time—takes too long, you see. All he cares about is getting to his country club for lunch—he belongs to one of those places that looks like a private nursing home except they let the inmates out between meals. Did you notice he kept looking at his watch? He was desperate to be finished by one."

"Why does he bother, if he feels like that?" Loretta asked.

Ghilardi shrugged. "Makes him feel important, I suppose. He's just a jumped up country solicitor—Buggins's turn."

"But—you're saying he missed something? Something to do with the medical evidence?"

"Oh—yes. This business of vital reaction—funny, isn't it? One minute you haven't heard a word before, and suddenly it comes up all the time . . . The point is, your friend had a cut on her face under her left eye—just about here." He indicated a point just above his cheekbone, his fingers dragging down the delicate skin. He paused. "This upsetting you?"

Loretta shook her head vigorously, trying to remain detached.

"This cut—Brown gave us a ring after the PM and said he didn't like the look of it. Hummed and ha-ed, of course, wouldn't commit himself—but the point is he thinks it's older than the rest. That it happened *before the crash*. You with me?"

Loretta's eyes opened wide. "Before—"

"Yep. Brown thinks someone punched her in the face before she went anywhere near the car."

"But—good God."

"Odd, isn't it?" The detective seemed very calm.

"It's more than odd—surely it means the verdict's wrong?"

"More than likely. Stuck with it now, though, aren't I?"

"Can't you . . ."

"What? Go to the High Court? That's what you have to do if you want to overturn a verdict. There's nowhere near enough evidence—far as we're concerned, it's finished. I had a chat with my boss last night, he said it all depended on Brown doing his stuff. From his point of view, the boss that is, the way it's turned out's no bad thing. We've got a nasty murder on our hands—you've probably read about it, kid who was helping with the Christmas post. *And* a building society job on Christmas Eve, not to mention a couple of con-men going round old folks' houses nicking their savings. Why go looking for trouble? It's not as if it affects the clear-up rate— at the moment there's no crime to clear up."

"I—but that's terrible."

Ghilardi shrugged and finished his coffee. "That's life."

"But you—you must have a theory."

"Not so much a theory—just a lot of facts that don't add up. One, she was probably attacked before she got in the car. Two, she went out without a coat on a freezing cold night. *And* without her handbag. D'you ever go anywhere without your handbag? Especially on your own in a car at night? What if you break down? You wouldn't have any money . . . Three, someone broke the window in the downstairs bathroom."

"Who d'you think—"

"That's what I wanted to ask you about. You don't happen to know—sorry if I'm treading on toes—you don't happen to know if she had a boyfriend? Someone down here the husband wouldn't know about?"

Loretta thought. "She didn't mention it, but that doesn't mean—she was a bit secretive about things like that." She was remembering Sandra's remark about living like a nun, her obvious determination not to talk about that aspect of her life. "I'm sorry—I don't think I can help you. Though it did cross my mind that she might have been meeting someone. It was so odd, the way she rushed off without saying a word."

"Rushed off?" The detective looked puzzled.

101

"Oh—I haven't explained. She stayed with me over Christmas—the pipes had burst at her flat—"

"This the place in Notting Hill?"

"Yes."

"Neil gave us the address. Go on."

"I got home on New Year's Eve and she wasn't there. The place was in a mess, her things were everywhere and the lights were on—I was very surprised, she hadn't mentioned going anywhere. She rang me at work that morning, you see, and wanted to know what I was doing in the evening. Unfortunately I was already fixed up . . ."

"What time did she ring?"

"Oh—ten-thirty, eleven maybe. Before lunchtime."

"And you got the impression she was going to be in London that evening?"

"Oh yes, definitely. That was why I was so surprised when she wasn't there . . . Is it important?"

Ghilardi sighed. "Probably not."

"You were going to say something."

"Oh, it's just speculation. It could mean several things—that she arranged to meet someone at the last minute—a married man, maybe . . . The important thing is that presumably no one knew she was coming—apart from this man, if he exists—which makes it quite possible that she did disturb somebody. That business of the broken window—I don't like it. Whoever swept it up was very careful—wore gloves and all that—not even a decent gloveprint."

"Surely that doesn't prove anything? Maybe it was Sandra, and she didn't want to cut her hands."

"Maybe. On the other hand, it could be that someone was planning to walk off with the pictures. Did you know he collects modern art? Amazingly stupid place to keep them."

"Wouldn't they have seen the lights?"

"Not necessarily. The lounge is on the front of the house, the sea side. And the curtains are very thick—I've checked. Even if they came by sea—well, if they came by sea that would explain why they didn't notice her car, wouldn't it?"

"Crikey," said Loretta. The thought that burglars might

have assaulted the house from the water hadn't occurred to her. She imagined the scene for a moment and shuddered. "It's every woman's nightmare—being alone in a house and hearing intruders."

"Sure. Though we don't know that's what happened—that's why I asked about a boyfriend. You ever been to Hardimans Deep?"

"No. I only ever saw Sandra in London."

"It's as quiet as the moon—like the moon with trees. There are these two houses, right on the Solent. You can't see them from the road, it's about a mile away and they're hidden by trees. Anything could've happened."

Loretta pulled a face. "It's certainly not impossible, Sandra having a lover, I just can't think of anyone who would know . . ." She hesitated, wondering if she should mention the discrepancies in the version of events Tom Neil had given at the inquest; recalling his anguished face, she was reluctant to draw suspicion on to him if it didn't already exist. On the other hand, Ghilardi had been frank with her . . . she decided to make light of it. "One thing—there's probably nothing in it, but I wouldn't take what Tom Neil said in court as gospel—"

"I'd already worked that out," Ghilardi interrupted her. "I'd very much like to know what he's up to—you say you saw her at Christmas. Did *you* think she was depressed?"

Loretta frowned. "Well—she wasn't very happy, but then she wouldn't be—it's not much fun, sleeping on somebody's sofa, especially not at Christmas. I mean, you always have the feeling everybody else's enjoying themselves, and if you're not . . . That's one of the things I hate about Christmas . . . When he said—well, I was flabbergasted."

"You weren't the only one. We've spoken to him several times this week, one way or another, and he never said a thing—today was the first time he even hinted she might be depressed."

"Maybe he feels guilty," Loretta said, unable to forget Neil's near-collapse in the witness box. "You know, like the coroner said."

"Funny he only mentioned it now, though, after he'd got the message we weren't happy with the case."

"Did you tell him about—the reaction, I've forgotten it's name?"

Ghilardi shook his head. "No. Sometimes you get more out of witnesses by not being specific—just letting them get the feeling something's not right. What were you going to say, by the way? When you said we shouldn't treat his evidence as gospel."

"Oh—" Loretta felt suddenly awkward, like a child called on to tell tales about other pupils. "Just that—all that stuff about his marriage. As far as I know they split up years ago, and not just because of Sandra's job. She only went back to see the children—at least, that's what she told me. Though she may have told Tom something different, of course."

"I hope you don't mind me saying—she doesn't seem to have been a very nice person."

Loretta shrugged, not wanting to go into her own feelings about Sandra.

"I thought straight away it was a funny set-up," Ghilardi went on when she didn't say anything. "Him down here and her up in London—it's not what you'd call a marriage, is it?"

"I don't know—I suppose not." She was discomforted by this appeal for her opinion.

"You married?"

Loretta remembered John Tracey's unopened letter, waiting her shoulder-bag. "I was. Not any more."

"Me neither. Not that I'm against it, don't get me wrong. It's difficult, though, in this job."

"Yes, yes, I can imagine." Loretta bit her lip, and decided it was time to turn the subject back to Sandra. "There is something else. This morning he said—Tom Neil, I mean— he said Sandra had a job in London. I can't imagine why he should lie about it, but as far as I know she didn't—she definitely told me she'd only just come back. She said she'd got a new job in a health club, and she wasn't due to start till the new year—that seemed odd in itself, but you'd only see why if you knew Sandra." She paused and added: "I've no idea

104

what it means—it seems such an odd thing to lie about. Oh, another thing. Didn't he say she couldn't go skiing because of work—that she couldn't get away? She told *me* she didn't *want* to go because she'd hurt her leg last time—something like that." Loretta frowned, hoping her memory was reliable.

Ghilardi took a deep breath and expelled it, his chest deflating visibly. "Let's have a look . . . ." he said thoughtfully, untying the ribbon circling the manila folder. He removed a sheaf of documents, pausing to slide a set of large colour prints back inside. There seemed to be dozens of typewritten sheets, and after flipping through them he drew out four which had been stapled together.

"Here we are—Tom Neil's first statement. 'My wife worked as a social worker at a rehabilitation unit in West London . . . Work commitments prevented her from getting away in time to come on the family holiday in Switzerland . . .' " He went on reading in silence, then returned all the sheets to the folder and closed it. "Interesting. I'll put in a request to the Met, see if they can clear up the work angle. Don't get excited," he added, noticing Loretta's eager expression. "It's like beaming a message to another planet, trying to get anything out of the Met. Especially on a low priority case like this. Funny, though—if he is lying, I can't see any point . . . Sure she was telling you the truth?"

Loretta held out her hands, palm up. "I assumed so—I can't see why she should lie about it, either. The whole thing's—bizarre."

"Unless—I do just wonder what she was doing there. At Hardimans Deep, that is. It's a bloody peculiar place to choose on a cold winter's night."

"She wasn't the only one, though, was she? Didn't the coroner say the man who owns the other house—I've forgotten his name. Wasn't he the one who found her?"

"Sanders." Ghilardi grinned. "The interesting Mr. Sanders. Who knows, maybe she was up to something with him."

"You mean—an affair?" The possibility hadn't occurred to Loretta.

"Doubt it. I'd be surprised if Mr. Sanders was interested in women—in that way, that is. It's the professional connection I was thinking about. He's an importer. Wholesale. Cheap jewellery, brass—wouldn't give it house room, myself. It's where he gets it from that's interesting—Pakistan and North Africa."

"So—" Loretta couldn't see what he was getting at.

Ghilardi laughed. "It's all right, I'm only joking. I don't really think Mr. Sanders is the Mr. Big of the Lymington drug scene. Anyway, he's got an alibi."

"Has Tom Neil?" Loretta demanded, surprising herself.

"Not as such. The kids stayed the night with friends, apparently—didn't come home till the next morning. He says he gave them lifts to their parties, got home about half past eight. He was tired, they'd only got back from Switzerland that morning, so he made himself something to eat and went to bed around ten-thirty. There's no evidence, either way. I can't arrest him for that."

"No, of course," Loretta said quickly. She lowered her eyes, ashamed of sounding suspicious of Tom Neil. "Those photos—the ones in there." She pointed at the folder. "Are they—"

Ghilardi's hand hovered over it. "I don't mind showing you, but they aren't very pleasant."

Loretta took a deep breath. "I'd still like to see them," she told him, though she wasn't sure why.

Ghilardi opened the folder again and slid out a number of garishly coloured ten-by-eights. He looked through them quickly, selected one and passed it across the table.

The photograph had been taken at a little distance from a maroon Ford Sierra, showing its off-side front wheel in the air and the bonnet crumpled against the gnarled trunk of a tree. Loretta could see where the car had slewed off the track, leaving a trail of destruction through the undergrowth before the actual collision. A figure was visible in the driver's seat, its head slumped back against the head-rest. Loretta shivered and returned the picture to Ghilardi.

He had another one ready. Loretta saw that it had been taken through the window of the driver's door. Sandra's right eye was open, staring upwards at an odd angle because of

106

the way her head had been thrown back. Her skin was deathly white, and there was a large, livid bruise on her right cheek.

"Have you—I'd like to see the cut the pathologist was talking about," she said bravely, giving the photograph back.

Ghilardi flipped through them again. "That's it," he said in a neutral voice, putting a print down on the table and pointing to a laceration below Sandra's left eye.

Loretta stared at the inch-long wound, trying to ignore the other cuts and the streaks of blood on Sandra's face. She had a horrible feeling that the open, sightless eyes were watching something, and she pushed the picture away.

"Amazing—that he could tell so much from that," she said in a strangled voice.

Ghilardi put the photographs away. "You're not all right, are you?" he demanded. "Julie!"

The waitress came eagerly, then backed off as she saw Loretta's face. "Is she—"

"She'll be all right. Can you bring us another cup of tea? Black, is that right?"

Loretta nodded.

"A black tea and a black coffee. Hang on, Julie." His hand rested lightly on the waitress's arm. "You should have something to eat, Loretta."

She shook her head, surprised by his use of her name. She managed a weak smile, and the waitress disappeared behind the counter.

"I told you they were grim," Ghilardi said accusingly, clasping his hands together on top of the folder as if to keep the horror at bay.

"It's all right—I wanted to see . . . ." Her misery was suddenly replaced by anger. "You won't leave it like this, will you? You *can't*." She fixed her eyes on his, desperate to get his promise that he wouldn't drop the case.

"My hands are tied," he began. "Look, are you willing to make a statement? That would help."

"I haven't told you much. Of course."

"It's a start. And I'll see what I can get from the Met—though, as I say—Thanks."

Their drinks had arrived and Loretta stirred a heaped spoonful of sugar into hers. She disliked very sweet tea, but she was feeling slightly faint: hypoglycaemia, she told herself, trying to forget the photographs.

"Better?" Ghilardi watched as she sipped from the cup.

Loretta nodded.

"Can you come back to the nick with me? I might as well take your statement now."

"My car's there, anyway. I'll just drink this."

"Take your time. You've had a shock."

"I suppose you get used to it. Bodies, I mean."

Ghilardi pulled a face. "It's the worst part of the job. Children are—that's what really gets me." He lifted his cup and drank some of his coffee. "Julie—can we have the bill over here?"

The waitress tore a sheet of paper from the pad she kept in the pocket of her apron. Loretta tried to read it as she put it on the table in front of Ghilardi but he waved her away.

"It's not going to break the bank. Best sandwiches in town," he said, smiling up at Julie as he took three pound coins out of a small leather purse and handed them to her. "Keep the change. When she's collected enough she's going to take me for a night on the town, aren't you?" he asked the waitress teasingly. She blushed and went to answer a summons from an elderly couple on the far side of the room.

"Ready?" he asked Loretta.

She finished her tea and got up. Ghilardi was already pulling on the heavy overcoat he had brought with him from the police station, and he did up the buttons while she put on her fake fur.

"Great coat," he remarked, leading the way to the door. He opened it and stood back for her.

Loretta felt a welcome blast of cold air on her face and realized how warm it had been inside the café. She turned up the collar of her coat and stepped gladly out into the street.

8

"SORRY IT TOOK SO LONG," SAID GHILARDI, coming back into the bleak interview room where Loretta had been reading for at least three-quarters of an hour. She had begun to think he had forgotten her.

"If you could just sign here, and here."

He placed two typewritten sheets on the table. Loretta put down her book, a detective story by Nicholas Blake, and cast her eyes rapidly over the pages.

"Seems all right," she said, taking Ghilardi's pen and signing her name at the bottom of the first sheet. "And here?"

She returned the pen. "What happens now?"

Ghilardi picked up the novel and read the blurb on the back cover without comment. "Depends what we get from the Met," he said, not looking at her. He seemed subdued, and Loretta wondered if it was the effect of being back in the police station.

"You off to London now?" He had opened the book and was studying it closely. "This any good?"

Loretta hesitated, then decided to answer his first question. "Well, I was wondering—I thought I might go and have a look at Hardimans Deep." The idea had come to her during Ghilardi's lengthy absence; it was probably her only opportunity, since she had no plans for a second visit to Lymington.

Ghilardi looked surprised and glanced at his watch. "You'd better get a move on—it'll be dark soon. D'you know how to get there?"

"No." Loretta shook her head.

"Oh, yes, you said. Tell you what, I'll draw you a map." He sat down on the other side of the small table and started making a sketch on a blank statement form. "It's only about three miles," he remarked, pausing to think with his pen in mid-air, "but it's not the easiest place to get to."

Loretta watched in silence for a moment. Then a thought occurred to her: "Gosh, what if Tom Neil's there? It might be a bit awkward—"

"You could always ring first," Ghilardi suggested, not looking up. "You got the number?"

"Yes. Could I—" She looked round the room for a phone but couldn't see one. Of course, they wouldn't put them in interview rooms; she remembered that suspects were allowed only one telephone call, and sometimes not even that. "Don't worry, I'll do it from a call box. Oh—thanks." She took the map from Ghilardi.

"I won't try to explain it," he said, getting up and straightening the jacket of his suit. "I think it's pretty self-explanatory." He moved towards the door.

"I'm sure . . . Well, thanks for the tea." Loretta felt as if she'd been drinking it all day, but at least it had given her something to do while Ghilardi was getting her statement typed. "What shall I do with—" She gestured to the empty cup and saucer.

"Oh, leave it." Ghilardi sounded preoccupied. He grasped the door handle, then turned back to Loretta. "You will be careful, won't you?" he said abruptly. "The boss may think this case is finished, but—"

"What? You mean you've spoken to him already?" Loretta stared at the detective in dismay. So *that* was the reason for the lack of animation she'd noticed since he returned five minutes ago.

"Only in the corridor. Bit tactless of me, really," he admitted. "I'll try again after you've gone—he may change his mind when he sees this.'' He held up the typed sheets. ''Anyway, that's my worry . . . Look, I'm quite serious about you being careful. God knows what happened that night, but I don't like to think of another woman there on her own in the dark—you'd better give me that map back.''

Loretta placed her hand protectively on the catch of her shoulder-bag. ''I'll be all right. I can't just—somebody's got to do something, and if you're not allowed to . . .''

''It'll be all right,'' he insisted. ''I caught him at a bad moment, that's all. There's been a development on that murder, the one I was telling you about. Her bag's been handed in and he wants more house-to-house inquiries . . . Come on, you won't find anything, there's just a couple of houses— we've been over the place with a fine-tooth comb.''

Loretta stood her ground. ''I'm over twenty-one you know,'' she said coolly, keeping her hand on the flap of her bag. She was slightly irritated by Ghilardi's manner, but realized it was better not to show it. Silently, though, she couldn't help reflecting that she was seven or eight years older than the detective, which made his protectiveness absurdly misplaced. It was a consequence of having so few women in the police force, she supposed—their absence fostered these ridiculous notions of chivalry . . .

''I suppose I can't actually *stop* you.'' Ghilardi's voice interrupted her reverie, and she looked at him in surprise. There was a genuine note of anxiety in his tone, and his forehead had creased into a worried frown.

''Heavens, anyone would think I was Little Red Riding Hood setting off to meet the big bad wolf,'' she joked, trying to quell an answering sensation of nervousness. ''All I'm going to do is—is look.''

''OK, but . . .'' Ghilardi tailed off, still frowning. ''Promise me you won't get out of the car?''

''What on earth—oh, all right.'' She could do what she liked when she got there, Loretta thought, crossing her fingers in her coat pocket. She moved towards the door, expecting Ghilardi to open it now that the matter was settled, but he remained in the same position.

"One more thing." He was looking slightly embarrassed. "If you do—if you notice anything—you will get in touch?"

"Of course," Loretta said impatiently, beginning to feel she'd never get out of Lymington police station. "Shall we . . ." She gestured towards the door.

"Oh, right." He jerked it open and Loretta hurried into the anonymous, cream-painted corridor.

She heard Ghilardi close and lock the door, then he caught up with her and, to her astonishment, placed his hand under her left elbow. Loretta moved instinctively away, and at that moment a door opened at the end of the corridor. A burly man with thinning sandy hair came towards them, slowing as he took in Loretta's presence.

"Watcha, Del," he said with a sly grin, looking from the detective to Loretta and back again.

"Steve." Ghilardi gave him a cool nod and ushered Loretta past.

She reached the heavy door to the reception area first, pulling it open and anchoring it with her foot. When she turned to take her leave of Ghilardi, she saw over his shoulder that the big man was still hovering in the corridor, an expression on his face she didn't much care for.

"Thanks very much, Dr. Lawson," Ghilardi said loudly, putting up his hand to take the weight of the door from her. "You've been very helpful." He placed his shoulder in front of the door and held out his right hand.

"Goodbye," she said, taking it briefly, and was surprised to see him incline his head very slightly backwards and raise his eyes to the ceiling. It suddenly occurred to her that he might not get on with his colleagues in CID; if he wasn't her idea of a policeman, it seemed equally likely that he wasn't theirs, either. She gave him a smile of genuine warmth, stepped backwards in the direction of the main door, then turned and went out of the police station.

Inside her car, Loretta unfolded Ghilardi's map and pored over it. After a while she gave up trying to make out the route in the rapidly gathering shadows and turned on the interior light. A moment's study was enough to confirm that Ghilardi's directions were rather complicated, and Loretta thought it a fair bet that she'd get lost. Only the first bit sounded easy—she was to follow signs for the Isle of Wight ferry. She turned off the light, started the engine, and drove out of the police station car park.

Before long she came to a roundabout she recognized from her journey round the town that morning, and was relieved to see a sign for the ferry. A moment later she spotted a telephone kiosk and remembered her intention of ringing Shore House to make sure Tom Neil hadn't stopped off there on his way home. She parked the car in a side street, walked back to the phone and dialled the number nervously. If Neil answered, what was she to say? It seemed cowardly just to put the phone down, but on the other hand—

The ringing tone went on and on, and Loretta was thankful that the problem hadn't arisen. She left the phone box and went back to her car, glancing at Ghilardi's directions again before continuing her journey. Soon she was driving across a causeway, the first indication she'd had all day that Lymington was remotely near the sea. Dozens of masts rose in prickly formation on one side of the car, while the wind ruffled dark water, gun-metal grey, on the other. The absence of other human beings from an area which in summer would be bustling with life was unsettling, and Loretta was glad when she reached the far side.

She turned right, following Ghilardi's instructions, and drove past the small ferry terminal. Within a couple of minutes she had left the town behind and was in a country lane flanked by high hedges. She mentally ticked off one of Ghilardi's landmarks on her left, the illuminated sign of the Fairlawn Hotel, and thought she must be about halfway by now. The hedges soon gave way to unfenced moorland, and Loretta hurriedly switched on her headlights. The road here was rutted and patched, badly in need of resurfacing, and she found it impossible to circumvent every single pot-hole. It was uncomfortable driving, and she was hardly aware of the uneven scrubland to either side. There were few houses and

113

no signs of wildlife, not even the occasional New Forest pony. Loretta wondered where they went in winter.

She slowed as she came to a fork in the road, realizing it was too dark to read the old-fashioned signpost which glimmered in the dusk without getting out of the car. Instead she signalled right from memory, pausing before the turn to make a perfunctory check for other traffic, and set off down a narrow lane. It was fortunate that she was driving slowly, for almost immediately she spotted another, narrower lane going off to the right and brought the car to a halt to check her map. There was no sign on it of this second fork, and Loretta hesitated, wondering if Ghilardi had deliberately left it off or had simply forgotten its existence. She decided that the former explanation was the more likely and continued her cautious journey, peering through the windscreen for the gateway which marked the beginning of the drive to Shore House. After about half a mile she noticed a change in the light ahead, a silvery glow which made her think of the sea, and was filled with doubt about the route she had taken. She kept going, more and more convinced she was on the wrong road but unable to turn round, and eventually came to a gateway beyond which she could make out an expanse of mud sloping down to water.

Loretta stared for a moment at this lonely scene, then sighed and got out of the car. There was a noticeboard planted in the mud beyond one of the gateposts and she went to read it, discovering that the land on which she was standing was a wildfowl sanctuary, and that fearful penalties existed for anyone who disturbed its inhabitants. Walking a few paces forward, she was impressed by the lovely and desolate nature of the place, by a profound silence interrupted only by the murmuring of the sea and the plaintive cries of gulls. She could see land on the far side of the water, an uneven band of darkness between the lighter tones of the sea and the sky, but its dense mass betrayed few signs of human habitation.

Loretta shivered, suddenly remembering Ghilardi's joke about the Neils' neighbour, Mr. Sanders, and his business connections. It had seemed far-fetched at the time, but now

114

it struck her that this isolated stretch of coast was a perfect dropping-off point for something—not necessarily drugs. Sounds and pictures came unbidden into her head: velvety darkness, the soft plash of oars, men's muffled voices . . .

Loretta exhaled sharply, cross with herself, and thrust her hands deep into her pockets. It was all nonsense, the product of hunger and an over-active imagination. Apart from the inherent improbability of the scene she had just conjured up, there had been bright moonlight on New Year's Eve, not velvety darkness; she hadn't even got her facts right. She turned abruptly and headed back to the car, stamping on the ground in front of the gateway to see if it would take the weight of the Panda. It seemed firm enough, and in any case there was nowhere else to turn the car. She got in, switched on the engine and inched forward, aware of a flicker of anxiety as she left the pitted surface of the road. To her relief the car rolled smoothly forward, showing no tendency to sink into the mud; she swung it to the right, reversed, and drove back into the lane.

She was soon back at the second fork, the one which wasn't marked on her map. She turned left, and had driven perhaps a couple of hundred yards when she spotted a gateway on her right. A crooked, handwritten sign bore the words ''Shore House. Spinners Cottage. Private.'' She was in the right place. Loretta signalled and turned into the drive, which was little more than a mud track. It stretched ahead for quite a distance, running between fields, before disappearing into a low belt of trees. The engine whined and Loretta moved down a gear, hoping the suspension would be able to cope with the uneven ground. Her anxiety returned as she bumped towards the dark mass of the wood, wishing she had listened to Ghilardi; this was no place for a woman on her own. It occurred to her that she might feel better—or at least less conspicuous—without lights, and she flicked a switch on the dashboard and plunged the road ahead into darkness. The sensation of blindness was so alarming that she immediately turned them back on, regaining her composure just before the car entered the trees. She was on a narrow, twisting track

115

flanked by wooden posts which might or might not have a strand of wire stretched between them—it was simply too dark to see. Loretta drove carefully, craning her head forward; even so she almost missed a sharp bend to the left. There was a pale glow ahead which grew in size until she reached the last of the trees and came out on to a patch of moorland. Her headlights picked out a gate and she drew up in front of it, a collection of outbuildings on her left. A dark shape loomed against the sky on the other side of the car: Mr. Sanders's house, which Ghilardi had said was the nearer of the two dwellings. She could see no lights, no parked cars, and breathed a sigh of relief.

Loretta turned off the engine and sat quietly for a few seconds, letting her eyes get accustomed to the gloom. There were two paths leading away from the gate, one curving round to the front door of Spinners Cottage, the other stretching straight ahead to a second gate, then swerving right and disappearing round the low, pale bulk of Shore House. Loretta felt reluctant to get out of the car and wound down her window a couple of inches instead; she was immediately aware of a sound on her right, beyond the house, the gentle sucking of the sea against a pebbled shore. She wasn't far from the water, though she couldn't really distinguish it from the sky in the narrow patch of light between Spinners Cottage and the trees.

She turned her head and looked through the windscreen, on which a light drizzle had begun to fall, slightly obscuring her view. Spinners Cottage, in spite of its name, was larger than its neighbour—was, in fact, a rather substantial building. Shore House, on the other hand, was tiny and had been painted a pale colour which gave it an unreal, almost floating aspect in the darkness. She could make out a couple of rectangular shapes on the lower floor which were obviously windows, but no door. It must be on the far side of the house, out of sight, and Loretta opened the car door to go and have a look, telling herself firmly that she would come to no harm. She was half out of her seat when the cold, damp air stung her face, reinforcing her reluctance to leave the car. What was the point of exposing herself to the elements in this bleak and lonely place? There wasn't much to see—she didn't even have a torch—and any clues that had been missed by the police would have been washed away by the rain.

Loretta pulled the door shut, too late; the dampness had already invaded the car's interior. She shivered, clasping her hands together and blowing on them for warmth. The window on her side of the car was still slightly open and she hastily wound it up, trying to insulate herself from the bleak scene outside. She couldn't imagine why Sandra had chosen to come here, what had drawn her away from the cosy flat in Islington to this desolate location. A shudder went through her at this thought; until now she had successfully kept at bay the images planted in her brain by Ghilardi's photographs, but the blocking mechanism suddenly ceased to work. Loretta gripped the steering-wheel with both hands as she imagined Sandra running from Shore House, dragging open first one grate than another, hurling herself into her car . . . She turned to look over her shoulder as the film rolled on in her head, imagining the roar of an engine as Sandra set off too fast, the crump of the collision, the sound of breaking glass. Sandra's bloodstained face rose before her and Loretta shook her head as if to dislodge the photographic image. She took a deep breath and leaned back against the head-rest. Why was she doing this to herself? She had been mad to come here, she should have listened to Ghilardi—

Loretta reached for the car keys and started the engine. She had begun to feel light-headed; hunger had a lot to do with it, but she could not deny that the day had turned into something of an ordeal. She put the car into reverse and rolled back and to her left, taking care to miss the outbuildings. Once she was driving away from Hardimans Deep she felt better, though she took care not to look too closely at the twisted trees which surrounded the car like a petrified forest. She picked up speed as soon as she had negotiated the sharp turn she remembered from her approach, eager to escape from the wood. It was still cold in the car and she turned on the heater, moving up into second gear and then third. The

117

engine whined and complained; she dropped down a gear, reaching for the radio in the hope of soothing her nerves with the sound of human voices. She was relieved to hear the common sense tones of one of the presenters of *Kaleidoscope*, and reached the end of the drive in a calmer frame of mind.

As she was pulling out into the lane she saw headlights coming towards her. There wasn't room for the two cars to pass, and the unknown driver stopped and reversed to a gap in the hedge so that Loretta could get by. The person in the driving-seat was simply a dark figure, and Loretta had no idea of the car's make, but she had the distinct impression that he—if it was a he—turned to stare as she passed. She glanced in her rear-view mirror and saw the car turning down the track she had just left; she was seized by a momentary panic, a conviction that the car was going to stop and come after her, that the driver would demand to know what she had been up to at Hardimans Deep. The feeling was so strong that she increased her pressure on the accelerator and had to brake as she reached the junction which hadn't appeared on Ghilardi's map. Her heart was thumping and she turned up the radio before turning left, trying to interest herself in a discussion of an experimental production of *Antony and Cleopatra* with a Jamaican reggae singer in one of the leading roles. She found it hard to concentrate, preoccupied first by her unreasoning fear and then by the realization that she was behaving foolishly. The track to Shore House was far too narrow to allow anyone to make a three-point turn and come after her. Whoever had been driving the large car—she had noticed its size, if nothing else—would have had no choice but to keep going until he reached Hardimans Deep. In any case, what possible reason could he have for giving chase? Loretta turned down the over-efficient car heater and fixed her attention firmly on the review of the play. Did she agree with the female journalist who was claiming that the black Cleopatra emphasized the character's ambivalent status as both queen and outsider? In her present frame of mind, Loretta really had no idea.

* * *

An hour and a half later she was sitting at a plastic-topped table in the restaurant of a motorway service station, pushing away an empty plate. She felt better for the meal, even though the standard fry-up probably wasn't as good as the sandwiches she had watched Ghilardi consume at the café in Lymington. She sipped a glass of water, glad to be in a brightly lit room with lots of other people. Her back was stiff from driving, and her left arm ached a little; she sat up straight and brought both elbows backwards in an attempt to loosen her shoulders. She was over halfway to London but she didn't feel like resuming her journey yet; her gaze fell on her shoulder-bag, which was on the seat next to her, and she put out a hand and undid the catch. She felt inside and drew out the morning's post, taking the letter from Vixen Press from its envelope and re-reading it. A frown creased her brow: was she making a mistake in giving the book to a small feminist publishing house instead of one of the big academic presses like OUP? Susie Lathlean's letter was uncritical in its enthusiasm, and there was no mention of sending the typescript to other authorities on American literature to canvass their opinion. On the other hand, hadn't Loretta chosen Vixen precisely because it didn't play by the usual rules? Loretta knew very well what her chief academic rivals would make of the book, that they would be scandalized by her treatment of Wharton's sexuality and its relation to the novels. She should have more confidence in herself, she thought sternly; her argument was well-made, and the book's flaws were very minor ones. The only real problem was the title; deciding she didn't want to think about Vixen's objections for the moment, Loretta put the letter on the table and picked up the unopened airmail envelope from John Tracey. She slid her fingers under the flap and tore it open, smoothing out two pages of flimsy paper covered in Tracey's neat handwriting. She sipped her water and sat back to read, expecting the usual journalistic gossip and a query about how the arrangements for the divorce were progressing. Three-quarters of the way down the first page her mouth fell open, and she found herself re-reading the last paragraph in disbelief.

". . . not the sort of thing you can say over the phone," Tracey had written, getting to the point only after a great deal of prevarication. "And the trouble with you, Loretta, is that I never know how you're going to take things. But I thought it was only fair to come clean and let you know the reason I want a divorce, which is that I'm planning to get married again. This may come as a shock, and I suppose you'll disapprove, in fact I'm sure you will, but I do know what I'm doing. So does Soulla—I met her the week I came out here, and we've had plenty of time to get to know each other. She is in any case planning to come to London next year, as she's hoping to get a place to do an MA—she's just had a year off after getting her degree in Greece . . ." Loretta blinked at this confirmation that she had read the paragraph correctly the first time: Tracey must be around twice the age of his fiancée.

"Honestly," she said aloud, and looked up embarrassed when she realized someone was standing by her table.

"You finished?" A tall, thin boy with a white face and a paper cap on his dark hair was pointing to her greasy plate.

"Oh yes, take it," Loretta said, eager to return to Tracey's letter. "No—nothing else, thanks."

She began reading again, discovering that the unknown Soulla was twenty-three years old, had a degree in financial administration, and was currently working in her father's business, of which Tracey gave no details, in Nicosia.

"We would both like," Tracey continued, halfway down the second page, "a traditional Cypriot wedding, though of course it's impossible to set a date until things are sorted out at your end. Speaking of which, I'd be interested to know how all that's going. I've talked to Soulla about you, and she's very keen to meet you"—Loretta's eyes opened wide; she was not a little alarmed at the prospect—"and in fact we'd both like it very much if you could fly out for the wedding, whenever it may be. Meanwhile, drop me a line when you've got time and let me know how you are, and how long the divorce business is likely to take. Yours ever, John.''

Loretta sat for a while staring into space, Tracey's letter in her hand. There was no reason why he shouldn't get married again; unlike Loretta, he had had no doubts first time round, and didn't appear to share her view of marriage as a patriarchal institution. Now that the initial shock was wearing off, she really didn't think she minded. What was irritating—no, that wasn't quite the right word, it was more a sense of disappointment that she felt—was the fact that he'd chosen a woman half his age and one from what Loretta suspected was an unreconstructedly macho culture. Someone, in other words, who probably hadn't been touched by the feminism about which Tracey had made so many nervous jokes. And what on earth did a ''traditional Cypriot wedding'' involve?

As Loretta returned the letter to its envelope, it occurred to her that she might be doing Soulla an injustice. The woman had been to university in Greece, where there was a small but active feminist movement led by Margaret Chant Papandreou, the American wife of the prime minister. It was quite possible that Soulla shared some of Loretta's ideas; they might even get on rather well together when the meeting finally took place, a possibility which made Loretta smile. How would Tracey react to a sisterly alliance between his first and second wives?

She got up, paid her bill, and went out into the car park, conceding that the idea of Tracey's new fiancée took some getting used to. For one thing it raised all sorts of practical questions, such as where the couple intended to live. Tracey had hung on to his house in Brixton—it was currently rented out to a very pleasant gay couple, one of whom was an actor with a small part in a West End play—but perhaps he and Soulla would want to buy a place together. Loretta realized that Tracey hadn't mentioned his fiancée's surname, and wondered about Soulla's views on the subject; it had always galled him that Loretta refused to change hers.

She unlocked the car door, tossed her bag on to the passenger seat and slid behind the wheel. She felt exhausted in

121

spite of the hot meal she'd recently eaten, usually a sure-fire way of restoring her energy. Tracey's announcement, coming on top of all the other events of the day, had made her feel like the operator of an overloaded switchboard, struggling unsuccessfully to keep half a dozen lines uncrossed. She looked at her watch, remembering she'd intended to ring Robert when she got home, and wondered if she couldn't put it off until tomorrow. He might still be sulking about Saturday night, and she really didn't think she could cope . . . Loretta reached along the parcel shelf to where she kept her tapes, taking the first that came to hand and pushing it unseen into the cassette player. It turned out to be Joan Sutherland in the middle of the mad scene from *Lucia di Lammermoor*—a peculiarly appropriate choice, she thought, turning up the volume and starting the engine.

9

LORETTA PULLED OPEN A DRAWER OF THE London Library card index and ran her finger lightly along the top of its contents. She paused a third of the way in to check which bit of the alphabet she'd got to, then made a random plunge further inside. She was looking for a book by Baroness Orczy, a collection of detective stories under the title *Lady Molly of Scotland Yard*, and was delighted when she found a card bearing its details. She closed the drawer and set off for the lift to the upper floors where the Orczy novels were kept, stifling a yawn. She had slept badly after her trip to Lymington the previous day, and it was only the fact that the spring term began the next day that had prompted her to do some work. Towards the end of the previous year there had been a discussion among the more progressive members of the English department about the absence of popular fiction in the BA syllabus, and Loretta had been fired with enthusiasm for the idea of an optional series of tutorials on the detective novel. There was a serious point to her interest: women were so prominent in the field that she believed it would provide a starting-point for a debate on the question of whether there was an identifiably female form of fiction. Until Christmas the Edith Wharton book had prevented her from giving much thought to the structure of the course, but on Monday she had started drawing up a list of novels to fill in the gaps in her knowledge of the *genre*.

The lift doors opened and she stepped inside, still thinking about how to shape the course. It was important to go in with a strong proposal, for she was bound to meet stiff opposition from the traditionalists in the department. The lift moved upwards, came to a halt, and Loretta got out. She was turning towards the door into the fiction section when a stray and most unwelcome thought came to her: Sandra's luggage was still sitting behind the back seat of her car. She had completely forgotten it the previous evening when she parked round the corner from her flat, so battered by the day's events that she'd hurried straight home and run herself a hot bath. In fact, she hadn't given the bags another thought after leaving the inquest with Derek Ghilardi, even though they'd been one of the reasons for her trip to Lymington. What was she to do? If only she'd remembered while she was talking to the detective, she could have handed them over there and then; who knows, they might turn out to contain a clue—something that would provide him with the evidence he needed to reopen the investigation. Loretta felt a moment's excitement, as if she held the key which would unlock the secrets surrounding Sandra's death, and then common sense returned, and with it a sense of deflation. It was highly unlikely that Sandra's bags contained anything other than clothes and perhaps the odd book—Loretta remembered that Sandra had been reading some long historical tome over Christmas. She could ring Ghilardi, but would he be allowed to come all the way to London on a case that was officially closed? She wasn't even sure that the police worked like that, Ghilardi would probably have to contact Scotland Yard and ask them to come round to her flat—

"Oh, sorry." She moved hastily to one side, realizing she had been blocking the exit from the lift. A grey-haired woman with glasses glared at Loretta as she skirted round her, then disappeared through the door into the fiction section.

Loretta followed, still turning over the problem. She supposed she ought really to telephone Tom Neil and ask what he wanted done with the bags; strictly speaking, since he was Sandra's next of kin, they were his property. She bright-

124

ened slightly, thinking that she could suggest putting them on a train—Red Star, wasn't that what the British Rail parcels service was called? Tom Neil or Ghilardi, that was the choice . . . She walked gingerly along the narrow corridor between the rows of shelves, trying to avoid getting her high heels stuck in the decorative ironwork floor. She always meant to wear flat shoes for her visits to the library, and she almost always forgot. She reached the section she wanted, tugged a cord to put on the light between the high stacks of books, and turned left in search of Baroness Orczy. She was in luck; the books hadn't been borrowed by another reader, and she put her worries to one side for a moment as she examined its old-fashioned illustrations. Lady Molly was a willowy, glamorous figure, and Loretta was all the more surprised to find an uncompromisingly feminist statement on the first page:

> We of the Female Department are dreadfully snubbed by the men, though don't tell me that women have not ten times as much intuition as the blundering and sterner sex; my firm belief is that we shouldn't have half so many undetected crimes if some of the so-called mysteries were put to the test of feminine investigation.

Loretta laughed out loud, closed the book, and returned to the narrow walkway, pausing to switch off the light between the stacks. She had to wait a couple of minutes for the lift, which she passed by dipping further into the pages of the book. Downstairs she signed for it, collected her coat and went out into the weak winter sunshine in St. James's Square.

Ghilardi was out. Loretta tried his number as soon as she got home, around three o'clock and listened to the phone ring unanswered in the CID room. Eventually a woman picked it up and announced they were all out, Ghilardi included, and she had no idea when they'd be back. It wasn't her department, she said, she'd been passing and had answered the phone as a favour. She could take a message, but there was no guaranteeing that Ghilardi would be back today. Loretta raised her eyes to the ceiling, said she'd try again later, and put down the phone. It occurred to her that Ghilardi might be tied up on the murder inquiry he'd mentioned a couple of times the day before, the woman who'd been killed while delivering the Christmas post. In that case, perhaps she was wasting her time. If the whole of Lymington CID had been called out on the murder investigation, it seemed unlikely that Ghilardi would be allowed to waste time on an officially closed car accident. Loretta bit her lip, stood up, and went slowly to the hall where she had dumped her shoulder-bag. She took from it a piece of paper, returned to the phone and dialled Tom Neil's number.

"Hello?" It was a girl's voice. Loretta was taken aback for a moment, then guessed she was speaking to Sandra's daughter.

"Hello. Ah—is Mr. Neil there?"

"No. Daddy won't be back till this evening. About half past six."

Loretta hesitated. She was not having much luck.

"Can I take a message?" The girl sounded polite, well brought up.

"Yes, I—yes." She gave her name, spelling it slowly as the girl wrote it down, and her number.

"What shall I say it's about?"

"About? Um—your mother was a friend of mine, she left some luggage here—"

"What d'you mean?" The girl's voice was suddenly sharp.

"It's a bit difficult to explain—she was staying with me for a few days over Christmas." Loretta had not intended to get into a discussion, and she regretted the fact that she hadn't simply given her name and phone number.

"Why was she staying with you? Why wasn't she at her flat?"

"Well, because her flat was flooded. Look, I think perhaps I'd better wait and tell your father about it—"

"But I want to know—Daddy hasn't mentioned you. I've never even heard of you." She sounded accusing.

"I'm sorry. It happened after you'd gone away, there's no

126

mystery about it. Honestly.'' Loretta pulled a face as she told the lie.

There was a moment's silence, then the girl spoke in a small voice. ''All right, I'll tell Daddy.'' Loretta thought she was on the verge of tears.

''Thanks,'' she said feebly. She waited for a second, heard the phone go down at the other end, and replaced the receiver. She hadn't handled *that* very well, she thought guiltily, crossing the room to the sofa and picking up Baroness Orczy.

An hour later she put down the book, disillusioned. *Lady Molly* hadn't lived up to the promise of the first page, rapidly degenerating into a series of outlandish mysteries which the heroine solved through reliance on feminine intuition. Definitely a historical curiosity, Loretta thought, debating whether to include it in the course at all. She was still sitting on the sofa, her feet curled under her and her shoes kicked to one side on the floor, and she looked at her watch, wondering when Tom Neil would ring. Not for another couple of hours at least, she thought, still unhappy about her conversation with Sandra's daughter. Would he be angry with her for upsetting the girl? He must be finding it pretty hard going, adjusting to life as a widower with two teenage—Loretta realized she didn't know their ages, but assumed her guess was more or less correct—two teenage children.

She got to her feet, slipping on her shoes, and started for the kitchen. Had she done the right thing? Should she have waited until she got hold of Ghilardi, made absolutely sure he wasn't interested in the contents of the bags? She stopped by the door, turned, and went back to the phone; she had been intending to make a cup of tea, but it would wait. She dialled Lymington police station again, was put through to the CID room, and heard the phone ring unanswered. She had read that the police were understaffed, but this was ridiculous . . . She put the phone down and went back to the hall. The bags—more accurately a holdall and a suitcase, plus the few bits of clothing Loretta had stuffed into a carrier bag—were standing just inside the front door. She had deposited them there after collecting them from the Panda on her way home from the London Library; she wondered why she had bothered, since she would presumably have to take them by car to one of the London stations and put them on a train to Winchester. It occurred to her that she had secretly hoped for an excited instruction from Ghilardi: "Open them at once! This could be important!"

She grimaced, realizing how unlikely this was. On the other hand, would it really do any harm if she took a quick look inside—just to put her mind at rest? Before she could have second thoughts, Loretta seized the bags and heaved them into the drawing-room, lining them up by the sofa. She sat down, pulling the holdall towards her, and at that moment Bertie trotted into the room, woken from his nap upstairs by the sound of the bags being moved. He sniffed the holdall, put out a tentative paw and tried to insert it in the gap left by the imperfectly closed zip fastening.

"Bertie—" Loretta lifted him gently to one side and unzipped the bag. She pulled the sides apart and looked into the opening, seeing nothing but an untidy mass of clothes. She began taking them out, vainly attempting to smooth away the wrinkles in each skirt or sweater before placing it neatly on the sofa beside her. The task was interrupted by Bertie, who let out an interested yowl and jumped inside the bag, turning round so that his head stuck out from one end. Loretta laughed and lifted him out.

She went on removing clothes until she got to the bottom of the bag, where a pair of high-heeled purple suede shoes was lying squashed out of shape by the weight of sweaters, skirts and underwear which had been piled on top. Loretta put her hand inside the left one, trying to ease it back into shape, and noticed it was the work of an expensive Italian shoemaker. Why hadn't Sandra taken better care of them? She turned the shoe over and saw that the sole was hardly worn. She put it down and picked up the other, and as she felt inside her fingers encountered a wad of tissue paper. It was bright green and looked as if it had been put there to keep the shape of the shoe, but as Loretta removed it a tiny key fell out. She picked it up, and her eye fell on the lock of Sandra's suitcase. She inserted the key, noticing out of one eye that the cat was inside the holdall again, and it turned smoothly. She lowered the suitcase on to its side, pressed the catches with her thumbs and lifted the lid. A purple dress was folded neatly on top, and Loretta lifted it out, wondering if it had been bought to go with the shoes, or vice versa. It wasn't silk, as she had first thought, but a synthetic imitation, and as she held it up she saw it was cut so that it would drape rather oddly over the hips. It reminded her of the clothes worn by the women in those American television series she only ever saw at her mother's—*Dallas* or *Dynasty*. It certainly wasn't what she had expected of Sandra. Loretta pulled a face, thinking there was no accounting for taste, and began folding the dress. She added it to the pile on the sofa and turned back to the case, and her eyes opened wide in astonishment. There were several bundles of banknotes randomly distributed across the top layer of clothes, each of them secured with an elastic band.

"What the—" Loretta began, putting out her hand but not quite touching the money.

The cat leapt out of the empty holdall and sniffed at this new discovery, quickly losing interest in it. He turned his attention to chasing an ear-ring which had fallen on the floor. Loretta lifted one of the bundles, turning it over as though she didn't quite believe it was real. It was a wad of twenty-pound notes, so many of them that she had no sense of how much money she was holding. She removed the elastic band, dropped it to the floor, and began to count.

When she had finished she picked up the band and automatically twisted it round the notes. She might have miscounted by one or two, but the total was in the region of fifty-six. Making a rapid calculation in her head, she worked out that the bundle amounted to £1,120. There were three more, two of ten-pound notes and a thinner one of fives. Loretta got up, went into the hall, and came back with pen and paper. She picked up a bundle of ten-pound notes and started her second count.

Six or seven minutes later she stared at her notebook, checking her addition. The grand total was £2,440. Loretta was flabbergasted; she could hear Sandra's voice tearfully announcing that she was rather short of money as clearly as if the dead woman were standing next to her. Where had the cash come from, and what was it for? And why not keep it in a bank? Suddenly Loretta felt cross; she never kept large sums in the flat—not that she had them—and it irritated her to think that Sandra had behaved in a way that was an invitation to burglars. There had been a spate of break-ins in Liverpool Road in recent months, with some houses and flats suffering more than once. The last thing Loretta wanted was for word to get round that there was easy money to be had in her flat. This train of thought occupied her mind for a moment, until it was replaced by a more immediate dilemma. What was she going to do? The presence of the money in Sandra's suitcase was certainly an odd circumstance, but it didn't point in any particular direction. Maybe she had—Loretta shook her head, unable to think of any obvious reason for carrying so much cash.

She turned to the more immediate problem, thinking the best plan was to inform Ghilardi of her find but she might not be able to get hold of him before Tom Neil returned her call. Telling Neil about the cash might produce an interesting reaction, but could she bring herself to admit she'd been rifling through his wife's belongings? Another, and awful, thought occurred to her. How could she prove there hadn't been even *more* money, that she hadn't helped herself to some of it? Neil might take the line that someone who was unscrupulous enough to open the bags in the first place would not stop at searching them. She couldn't prove otherwise; the only person who could testify that she hadn't taken anything was Sandra herself, and that was no help at all.

Loretta looked down, saw the suitcase was still almost full, and decided she might as well see what else it contained. In for a penny, in for a pound—the phrase was rather appropriate in this instance, she thought. There were more clothes, including a couple of outfits in the same style as the purple dress. Loretta saw as she lifted them out that they had designer labels, not ones she recognized, and they didn't tell her much except to confirm that Sandra's taste had definitely changed for the worse. Perhaps it was the effect of her age, Loretta speculated, remembering Sandra's remark about being the wrong side of thirty-five.

She took out the last item of clothing, a badly creased cream satin shirt with shoulder pads, and saw a bundle of letters lying in the bottom of the suitcase. It was secured, like the banknotes, with an elastic band. Loretta stared at it for a moment, struggling with her conscience. Reading a dead woman's correspondence—wasn't there something distasteful about that? Loretta told herself she had done it before, in the course of research, although it was hardly a fair analogy. These were *private* letters, not those of a public or semi-public figure. On the other hand, they might well throw some light on the mystery of Sandra's death, and wasn't that sufficient justification for examining them? It wasn't as if it was sheer nosiness—

Loretta picked up the bundle and twisted off the elastic band. Her eyes lit up when she saw that the first letter to Sandra, which wasn't in an envelope, was dated September; perhaps she could now solve the mystery of Sandra's whereabouts immediately before her move to London. But a quick flip through the correspondence produced only two envelopes, one blank and the other addressed to Sandra in Notting Hill. The postmark was so smudged that it gave no clue as to when Sandra took up residence there, though it did at least provide Loretta with the address of her flat. Sandra had lived at 35 Norfolk Gardens, W10; the name of the road rang a faint bell, and Loretta remembered that one of the lecturers in her department had lived briefly in Suffolk Gardens—she had been to dinner there a couple of times. Both roads, she thought, ran between Ladbroke Grove and Portobello Road. She gave up her attempt to read the postmark and went back to the top letter, smoothing it out and reading a few lines before passing on to the next.

It, and the next four or five, were from Sandra's children,

Felix and Lizzie. The boy's letters were short and perfunctory, dutiful accounts of rugby matches, debates, and the usual paraphernalia of public-school life. Loretta learned that he was a pupil at Rokeham, an expensive establishment on the Welsh border with a reputation for athletic prowess rather than academic achievement. His sister was also at boarding-school, one near Plymouth which Loretta hadn't heard of, but her letters were composed with a great deal more vivacity. There was nothing to suggest anything out of the ordinary in either child's correspondence, and Loretta began to think the letters had no bearing on Sandra's disappearance and death. She came to the blank envelope, which turned out to contain a set of printed membership cards: "In The Pink—Luxury Health and Fitness Centre," she read, wondering in that case why the cards were pale blue. Perhaps it was some sort of joke? They were unused, and each had a space for the member's name, number and expiry date. The club's address was somewhere in South London, with a postcode Loretta couldn't put an area to. Nor could she imagine why Sandra was carrying the cards around with her, until it occurred to her that perhaps she had been hoping to recruit her friends to the club. Loretta pulled a face, thankful that Sandra hadn't tried to talk her into joining, and returned the cards to the envelope.

There were more letters from the children, written in the late autumn, and a complaining note had entered Lizzie's. Why hadn't Sandra answered her last letter—it was *two and a half weeks* since she'd written. Later she thanked her mother for a postcard but said it didn't make up for not having a *proper* letter. *And* why hadn't Sandra come home at half-term? Had she had another row with Daddy? Loretta raised her eyebrows at this point, and read on with interest. Tom Neil had taken his daughter and a friend of hers called Emma to lunch at the Old Mill in Winchester, but this had apparently failed to placate her. Felix hadn't come home at half-term, either, Lizzie wrote, he'd gone to stay with one of his *repulsive* friends . . .

If Sandra had fallen behind in writing to Felix, his letters betrayed no sign of it. He had scored three tries and one conversion in an inter-house rugby match; he had made a sort of metal thing for hanging coats on in Mr. Porcas's metalwork class. Loretta thought he sounded a very unimaginative young man. But the last letter from Lizzie, in December, was a genuine cry of anguish:

WHY aren't you coming on holiday? You promised you would, and I haven't seen you since AUGUST. You NEVER come to see me at school any more. Daddy says you're too busy at work but I don't believe him. Emma says you and Daddy are going to get divorced, and then I'll have to stay at school in the holidays like that Italian girl whose father is a prince or something. You won't get divorced, will you? Emma's mum doesn't let her dad into the house any more, she has to wait for him outside when he comes to take her to McDonald's. She says your parents getting divorced is AWFUL.

There was more in this vein, but it didn't add anything to what Loretta had already learned and she folded up the letter. Poor kid, she thought wryly, no wonder she'd been suspicious on the phone. She wondered how old Lizzie was—the impression she had was fourteen or fifteen, though boarding-school children were sometimes precocious. She'd certainly been sharp enough to pick up the fact that something was wrong between her parents—she hadn't believed Tom Neil's excuse for Sandra missing the family holiday, either. It occurred to Loretta that the rows between Sandra and her husband might account for Sandra's volatile mood at Christmas, though she was still no wiser about the source of the money . . . She shook her head and turned to the final piece of correspondence, the envelope with the unreadable postmark and the Norfolk Gardens address. She felt inside and pulled out a postcard, staring in surprise at a rather tasteless soft-focus photograph of a naked woman lying on a bed. The model was facing away from the camera, and filmy white curtains blew into the room from an open window. Loretta turned it over and read the handwritten message, her eyes opening wide as she did so:

> Saturday night was great [underlined]—can't wait to do it again! Apart from the hotel—too bloody stuffy! How about that place in Brighton you told me about? Hope you like the picture—guess who it reminds me of!

There was no signature, just three words which made an extraordinary initial impact on Loretta: ''Your loving son!'' The idea that the note was from Felix Neil lasted only a few seconds; it was obvious that Sandra had spent a night at a hotel with the writer, and Loretta dismissed out of hand the idea that she had had an affair with her own son. In any case, she quickly realized the handwriting was different. She cast around for other explanations for the phrase, and decided the most plausible was that the unknown lover was, or looked, considerably younger than Sandra, and had been taken for her son—perhaps by the hotel they'd stayed at. Loretta felt a stab of pity—such a mistake couldn't have done much for Sandra's self-esteem. It was followed by anger as she thought of John Tracey's engagement to a woman half his age and the double standard which sanctioned relationships between men and much younger women but treated the reverse situation as a joke. Loretta read the message again, turning it over to look with distaste at the reclining nude on the other side. Presumably the last line was intended to suggest a resemblance between the model and Sandra. She couldn't see it, but then she'd never encountered Sandra without her clothes. She was thrusting the card back in its envelope when it occurred to her that it might be an important clue. Ghilardi had wanted to know whether Sandra had a lover, and here was the evidence . . . All the same, it was of limited use: Loretta had no idea of his name or where he lived, and the only inference that could be drawn from the message was that he was young or had a youthful appearance. She bundled up the letters and returned them to the bottom of the suitcase, following them with Sandra's folded clothes. The cat had got tired of playing with the single earring and she picked it up from the floor, tucking it in with the clothes and wondering what had happened to its partner. Soon everything was in place except the purple dress and the bundles of banknotes. Loretta hesitated and then, not knowing what else to do, grasped the cash with both hands and dumped it on top. She arranged the folds of the dress over it and closed the lid, feeling a momentary sense of relief as great as if she'd solved all the problems raised by her investigation of the luggage.

She hadn't, of course, and she sat thoughtfully on the edge of the sofa, her chin resting on her right hand. The cat had gone to sleep in the empty holdall, and she leaned across and lifted him out, ignoring his mew of protest. She ought to try Ghilardi again, especially now she'd found evidence that Sandra was having an affair, but she couldn't see any way round the problem of the money. If she admitted to knowing what was in the suitcase, wasn't it inevitable that a degree of suspicion would fall on her? She locked the suitcase, put the key back in the toe of the suede shoe, and began repacking the holdall. She carried out these actions automatically, so much so that the ringing of the telephone made her jump. Her immediate reaction was one of panic, a conviction that Tom Neil was returning her call before she'd had a chance to think, but then she glanced at her watch and saw it was only twenty past five; there was every chance that it wasn't him at all. She crossed the room and picked up the phone, so keyed up that she didn't immediately recognize Robert's voice.

"You sound very odd. Is everything all right?"

"Yes, I—yes. I was miles away, sorry." She'd been intending to ring Robert that evening and suggest driving up to see him the weekend after next; she'd be too tired to make the journey this Saturday, two days after term started. Dragging her mind away from the problem of Sandra, she said in her brightest voice: "So—how have you been? Busy?"

"That's what I'm ringing about. I have to be in London tonight, there's a problem over a contract—it needs a signature and apparently they won't accept a fax, so I've got to

135

come to town. My solicitor's going to wait for me . . . I thought perhaps we could have dinner? I'm sorry it's short notice—it's only just happened.''

''Tonight?'' Loretta thought quickly. If she was out for the evening, she could turn the answering-machine on—avoid speaking to Tom Neil with a clear conscience. And, she told herself hastily, she hadn't seen Robert for a while . . .

''Yes, why not? Have you got anywhere in mind?''

''How about that little Greek place at the bottom of Charlotte Street? It's quite near my solicitor's office.''

''I know—the one that does the wonderful puddings.''

''That's right. Is eight-thirty too late for you? It'll take me an hour and a half to get to London, then I've got the meeting—''

''It's fine. See you then.''

Loretta put down the phone and looked across the room at Sandra's bags. She summoned up courage and decided to give Ghilardi another try. It might get her into trouble, but she couldn't in all honesty hand over the luggage to Neil without telling the police what was inside. She dialled the number of Lymington police station, which she now knew by heart, and was put through CID. This time the phone was answered; Ghilardi had called in briefly a few minutes ago, she was told, but had now left for the day.

Loretta got up and went into the kitchen, remembering she hadn't got round to making the cup of tea she'd wanted over an hour ago. She switched on the kettle and checked her watch again, feeling restless. She wasn't due to meet Robert for hours, but Ghilardi was beyond reach—

It occurred to her that she might be able to get his home number from directory inquiries. Ghilardi was hardly a common name—it was a stroke of luck that the case hadn't been assigned to a detective called Smith or Brown. She went to the wall-phone and made the call, spelling the name carefully to the operator.

''Sorry, love—the only number we've got for that name's ex-directory.''

''Oh, but . . . Thank you.''

She sighed and put down the phone. The kettle had boiled and she spooned Earl Grey tea into the pot, standing with her hands on the back of a kitchen chair while she waited for it to brew. What now? She had found two and a half thousand pounds in cash, a postcard which seemed to indicate that Sandra had had a lover, letters which suggested a falling-out with Tom Neil—and for the moment there was nothing she could do about any of it.

Unless . . . Her eyes lit up as the thought came to her. She had the address of Sandra's flat in Notting Hill—35 Norfolk Gardens was engraved on her memory. It couldn't do any harm to go and have a look at the place. She wouldn't be able to get inside, she realized that, but the neighbours might know something. That was how the police went about things—house-to-house inquiries, she remembered the phrase from her talk with Ghilardi the day before. It was easier for them, of course—Loretta shrugged off this objection, glad to have something to do. She strained her tea into a mug and carried it upstairs to the bathroom, where she washed her face and cleaned her teeth. Then, feeling she ought to make a bit of an effort for Robert, she changed into a pair of black leggings and a blue jumper with appliqué silk flowers. Downstairs again she fed Bertie, switched on the answering-machine, and went out to face the rush-hour traffic.

There was nowhere to park in Norfolk Gardens, so Loretta drove round into the next street, the one where her friend used to live. She put the car in a space just vacated by a battered yellow 2CV, and a couple of minutes later walked up the path to 35 Norfolk Gardens, a tall, wide house whose stucco looked freshly painted. She could see several bells by the front door and wondered which one was Sandra's; she had a vague notion, no more, that Sandra had mentioned a basement. A glance down and to the left proved that her memory was faulty; there was a light on in the basement window, and when Loretta stepped back to get a better look she had a clear view of a young Asian woman in jeans standing behind an ironing-board. She moved hastily forward under the protection of the porch before she could be seen.

The street lights in Norfolk Gardens were very bright and Loretta was able to read the names next to the bells without any trouble. Someone called Weir lived on the ground floor, and Bissett at the top of the house. The space next to the middle bell was blank, and Loretta assumed that she'd located Sandra's flat. Her finger hovered near the bell marked Weir; hadn't her intention been to talk to Sandra's neighbours? She took a deep breath and pressed. A second later there was a crackle as the entryphone came to life.

"Who is it?" A woman's voice.

"Hello—you don't know me, I was hoping to speak to you about Sandra Neil," Loretta said rapidly, terrified of losing her nerve.

More crackles. "Who?"

"Sandra Neil!" This time she bellowed.

"Oh."

There was a buzzing noise, and Loretta realized that the front door lock had been released. She pushed it open, astonished by the ease with which she'd gained entry to the house, and stepped gingerly into a dark hallway.

"Over here."

A light snapped on and Loretta saw a young woman with sleek dark hair peering at her through a slightly open door to the left of the stairs. She took a few uncertain steps towards her, regretting she hadn't had time to prepare her story, and heard the rattle of a chain. The door opened wide.

"Sorry about that," the woman said. "The chain, I mean. You can't be too careful round here—you know, because of the rapist. Come in."

Loretta hesitated, then followed the woman into the flat and waited while she closed the front door. Ms. Weir, if that was her name, was strikingly bronzed and dressed in a stylish blue suit which showed her tan off to perfection.

"Not that you'd expect him to ring the bell," she continued chattily, leading the way into a small front room with a deep pile carpet and heavy curtains which fell into folds on

138

the floor. "Have a seat." She motioned to an armchair and Loretta sat down, wondering where to start.

"It's just with living alone—Des, that's my boyfriend, he doesn't like me being here at all, but it's not as if I'm on the lower ground. It's basements he goes for, so it's worse for Shashi, she's the Indian lady downstairs, but you can't pick and choose, can you? They say there's more than one of them, and sometimes you hear he's been caught, but . . ." She shrugged. "Have a drink?"

"Oh no, don't go to any trouble—"

"It's no trouble, I was having one anyway—Campari and soda." She held up a glass. "Go on."

"No, really. I only came because of Sandra—"

"Wants her post, does she? I thought she might've been round while I was away—I only got back yesterday. You a friend of hers?" She crossed one leg over the other, critically inspecting her black court shoes.

"Yes." Loretta only just managed to get the word out; it had not occurred to her that Sandra's neighbours might not know she was dead. She was wondering how to break the news, at the same time puzzling over the reference to Sandra's post.

"Two and a half weeks in the sun—I didn't want to come back, I can tell you." The woman suddenly got to her feet, her eyes narrowing. "Now where did I . . . I know. If you hang on, I'll get it."

She hurried out of the room, reappearing a moment later with a handful of letters. "Found herself a place yet, has she?" she asked, unselfconsciously leafing through the mail as she sat down.

"A place?" Loretta repeated in a cautious tone.

"Yes." The girl looked up. "I mean, that flat she moved to's only temporary, isn't it? I thought she was trying to get one nearer her job. That's why she didn't redirect . . ."

"Oh, er, yes," Loretta agreed, trying to hide her amazement. The woman seemed to be implying—had Sandra lived *here*? If so, when had she—

"Actually, a lot of these seem to be, what d'you call them,

139

circulars," the girl said, finally holding them out to Loretta. "Hope she wasn't expecting a lot of Christmas presies!"

Loretta took the letters from the woman's outstretched hand, the gaudy envelope on top immediately confirming her impression that Sandra had lived in this very flat. "Mrs. S. Neil," she read silently, "Ground floor flat, 35 Norfolk Gardens."

She swallowed. "How long have you been here now?" she asked, trying to sound casual. She needed to tread a fine line between finding out as much as she could, and admitting that everything she knew about Sandra was being turned on its head. If she gave herself away, the woman might demand the letters back. The thought made Loretta tighten her grip on them.

"Mmm—let's think. Beginning of August? I think that's when it was. I'm not very good at—I'm just trying to remember when my flat-mate got married. That's why I had to move from my last place, her husband was moving in . . . I was dead lucky, I was on my way back to the office and I must've got the *Standard* before anyone else. She had dozens of calls—well, she would, wouldn't she, it's such a nice flat and so close to the tube—"

"Yes. Yes, it is." Loretta looked round the room, hardly taking it in.

"And it's very convenient—I only work round the corner."

"I—I'm trying to remember," Loretta persisted bravely. "How long was Sandra here?"

The woman shrugged her shoulders. "I dunno when she bought it. Quite a while, I should think, she certainly knew the area . . . I was only thinking, I don't mind keeping her post, but if she'd got a proper place I could send it on . . ." She looked at Loretta interrogatively.

"Oh, I think her arrangements are a bit—fluid at the moment," Loretta managed to get out. She stood up, anxious to leave before the woman asked any more questions about Sandra's whereabouts. Part of her brain was still processing what she'd just learned—that instead of moving to Notting

140

Hill at Christmas, as she'd told Loretta, Sandra had moved out of it months before. So the story about the flood . . .

"I like your jumper." Loretta's denim jacket had fallen open, and the woman was admiring the colourful silk flowers on it.

"Thank you." Loretta headed for the door.

"Come far, have you?" Ms. Weir seemed reluctant to let her go.

"Islington." Loretta paused, then said in a rush: "I don't suppose—you didn't have trouble with the pipes over Christmas?" She gazed round the room as if she was expecting to see water gush down the walls, suddenly hoping she'd misunderstood . . .

"The pipes?" The woman looked blank.

"Yes, I just thought—it's been so cold, there's been a lot of bursts," she said feebly.

"Like I said, I only got home last night and everything was all right then," the girl said, puzzled.

"That's—that's good to know."

"Why—is Sandra worried? Did she send you to check up?" She sounded hostile. "The place's fine—you can have a look round if you want. I'm not stopping you."

"No, I'm sure . . . Where did you go on holiday?" Loretta changed the subject, anxious to escape without antagonizing Sandra's tenant. She put out her hand to open the front door of the flat.

The woman immediately cheered up. "The West Indies. I'm in the travel business—it's one of the perks. Time share mainly—wait, I'll give you my card." She darted back inside the room they'd just left and returned, holding something out to Loretta. "Here you are. I don't know if you've ever thought of investing in property abroad?" Suddenly the girl fixed Loretta with a perky, professional smile. "We have extensive contacts in—"

"No, thank you, really," Loretta insisted, backing out of the flat. "I've got no money—I work in the public sector . . ." She grinned nervously, waving the envelopes. "Thanks for these. I'll see myself out."

141

She glanced back at the house as she hurried down the path, and slowed her pace when she thought she saw a curtain twitch on the ground floor. In Suffolk Gardens she unlocked the door of her car and slid behind the wheel with a sigh, leaning back against the head-rest while she tried to gather her thoughts. She realized she was clutching something in her left hand and put the envelopes down to look at it. It was the business card, and she held it up to the street light to read it. "Miss Janet Weir, foreign property consultant," it said in embossed letters. Above the words was a stylized sunburst in brilliant reds and yellows; below, the address and telephone number of a travel company in Ladbroke Grove. Loretta stuffed the card in her jacket pocket, thinking it might be useful to have the woman's phone number, and looked at her watch. If she set off now, she would have plenty of time to find a parking space near Charlotte Street; she started the engine and turned the steering-wheel hard to the right, observing as she did so that she'd been left very little room to manoeuvre by the bad-mannered driver of the red Golf parked in front of her.

An hour or so later she was sitting alone in a Greek restaurant in Charlotte Street, returning Sandra's latest batch of correspondence to her shoulder-bag. It was nearly nine; Robert was late, and Loretta had no compunction about using the time to go through the letters. Unfortunately Janet Weir had been right; the post consisted mostly of circulars and appeals—a set of charity Christmas cards, an entry form for a competition promising £250,000 as the prize, a bingo card from a national newspaper ("Win! Win! Win! Mrs. P. L. Lucas of Halifax did and YOU could be next!"), and an invitation to subscribe to *Which?* magazine. There were also several Christmas cards, including one each from Felix and Lizzie. The deception, which was what it must be, about where Sandra lived, seemed to encompass her children; for all Loretta knew it extended to Tom Neil as well, and he had been telling the truth as he knew it at the inquest. Now she really did have something to tell Derek Ghilardi, and she

142

wasted five minutes fruitlessly trying to think of ways to winkle his ex-directory number out of British Telecom before resigning herself to speaking to him tomorrow. What she couldn't begin to imagine was the reason for the deception; *why* Sandra had gone to so much trouble to mislead her family about her address. And how had she kept it up? Loretta saw a possible explanation in Lizzie's anxiety about the state of her parents' marriage, wondering if they were on sufficiently poor terms for Tom Neil not to want to ring his wife. But hadn't he mentioned speaking to her by phone on the subject of the holiday? Maybe *she* had contacted *him*. At this point Loretta had finished her second glass of retsina and poured a third.

There were two more items of post which added a little to her growing store of information about Sandra, but each raised more questions than it answered. The first was a tasteless greeting card with a drunken Father Christmas on the front. Inside was the printed promise—Loretta shuddered as she read it—that "Santa's got a big one for you!" The writing on the card was familiar, though it took her a moment to make the connection. Then she realized it resembled the scrawl on the postcard she'd found in Sandra's luggage that afternoon; if she was right in thinking the sender was one and the same person, it seemed that his first name was Paul. This time the message was even shorter—"Long time no see?" The envelope in which the card had arrived was postmarked Exeter.

The other communication which interested her was a letter from Sandra's bank in Notting Hill Gate. It was dated 12 December, but the envelope had been sent by second-class post and Loretta guessed it might not have arrived at the flat until after Christmas. The assistant manager thanked Sandra for depositing £2,120 in her account at the end of November, but pointed out that her overdraft still exceeded its limit by £1,000. Until she deposited that sum, he would be unable to revert to honouring her cheques. Loretta frowned as she read the letter, puzzled by Sandra's lack of funds on paper and the abundance of cash in her suitcase. How had Sandra come by the money? Why was it in cash? And why had she turned up on Loretta's doorstep with a completely bogus story about burst pipes? Thinking about the money made her uneasy, and Loretta picked up the Christmas card from "Paul." The scribbled message seemed to indicate a break in the relationship; did that make it more or less likely that he was the cause of Sandra's trip to Hampshire? If "Paul" lived in Exeter, perhaps Hardimans Deep was a convenient meeting-point. Regretting her poor geography, Loretta had helped herself to a little more retsina, glancing at her watch and wondering where Robert had got to.

Now, with the letters safely in her bag, she decided she could go without food no longer. She summoned the waiter and ordered aubergine salad and pitta bread as her first course. "And I'd like the *afelia* next, and some mineral water, please."

She sat back and drew patterns on the table in the damp patch where the waiter had spilled a drop of retsina while pouring her first glass. She had intended to confide in Robert, to try out her various theories—though they hardly deserved so grand a title—on him. Everything she had learned suggested that Sandra had been leading a—a double life, that was the phrase that came into Loretta's head. No wonder Sandra had behaved oddly at Christmas, though Loretta hadn't suspected anything on this scale; how could she? It was impossible to believe that the deception had nothing to do with Sandra's death, but the problem was to make the right connections . . . Loretta was beginning to feel tired and a little bad-tempered; Robert might at least have phoned the restaurant to warn her he was going to be as late as this. She brightened as the waiter returned with her first course and fell on it hungrily, remembering she hadn't eaten since breakfast. She was wiping her plate clean when Robert appeared.

"Loretta—sorry, it took longer than I expected. Oh, you didn't wait." He looked at her empty plate.

"I was hungry. You're almost an hour late."

"An hour? God, it's even later than I thought. I'm sorry,

144

you know what these meetings with lawyers are like. There were problems with the contract . . ." He pulled out a chair and sat down opposite her.

"What did you have?"

"What did I—oh, *melitzanosalata*."

"Was it good?"

"Yes."

They sat in silence for a moment.

"Is it all right if I—" He lifted the wine bottle.

"Help yourself." Loretta noticed for the first time that the bottle was half empty; she had drunk it without noticing, and it explained the slight buzzing in her head.

"I think I'll skip the first course," she heard Robert saying. "Excuse me—" He raised his voice. "Is the *kleftico* on tonight? Good—and another glass of mineral water. So, Loretta—it seems ages since I've seen you. What have you been doing?"

Loretta opened her mouth to tell him about Sandra and closed it again. It was too complicated; he didn't even know she'd been to the inquest. She cast around for something else to talk about, and remembered her book.

"I had a letter from Vixen yesterday. They like the book."

"Great," said Robert, drawing the word out. "Let's drink to that." He held up his glass and after a moment Loretta followed suit. "To Edith Wharton—and Loretta Lawson." He chinked his glass against hers, then drank from it. Loretta did likewise, beginning to feel anxious about driving home. Perhaps by the time they left . . .

"What else?"

"Oh—I've started work on a new course, a new set of tutorials."

"On?"

"On crime fiction." A sudden burst of enthusiasm seemed to clear her head. "I have this idea that a lot of women find the idea of writing a novel—*the* novel—terrifying so they write crime fiction instead. The rules make them feel safe. I think that's why it's such a female form, in this country at any rate. Which makes it the perfect way to examine women's ideas about fiction—'' She pulled her chair closer to the table, warming to her theme. "I went to the London Library today, I wanted to have a look at Baroness Orczy . . . What's the matter?" She was puzzled by the look on Robert's face.

"We-ell." Robert held out his hands, palms upwards, and shrugged. "It's nothing to do with me, but . . . I'm curious, that's all. What has Agatha Christie got to do with an English Literature course?"

"It won't just be Agatha Christie. The point is to look at the development of the form, as one would with, say, the nineteenth-century novel."

"You're not comparing Agatha Christie to the Brontës?" Robert leaned back in his chair, an amused look on his face.

"Why do you keep going on about Agatha Christie? There are dozens of other women who write detective stories, most of them a good deal better . . . It sounds to me like you're defending the canon—the idea that you can draw a line and say this is literature and everything else is rubbish."

"Isn't that the case? Surely your job is to make sure your students . . ."

"I think I know what my job is," Loretta interrupted him angrily. She was about to say more when the waiter placed a plate of *afelia* in front of her. "Oh—thanks." She glanced down at the chunks of meat and coriander seeds, no longer sure she felt like eating. When she looked up, Robert was eyeing his lamb with an equal lack of enthusiasm. She said: "Let's drop it, the food's going to get cold."

She saw a distant look in his eyes, and he responded with a polite nod. "As you like."

They ate in silence, then had a desultory conversation about something Robert had heard on the Radio Four news as he drove to London. Loretta refused the waiter's offer of coffee, saying truthfully that she was tired, and was relieved when Robert told her she needn't wait for him. She took out her purse and put fifteen pounds in notes on the table, resisting his half-hearted attempt to return it to her. Then she stood up and threw her denim jacket over her shoulders.

"Well, goodnight."

146

"Goodnight."

They stared at each other for a moment, then Loretta moved out from behind the table and went to the door. The waiter leapt to open it, and she left the restaurant without a backward glance. Outside on the pavement she was aware of a catch in her throat; she swallowed, and hurried in the direction of her car. All at once she realized it would be risky to drive home in her present agitated state, not to mention the fact that she was probably over the breathalyser limit. She remembered she had parked the car in a meter bay; if she got back to it reasonably early in the morning, it was unlikely to have been towed away. She turned up the collar of her jacket, thrust her hands into the pockets, and turned into a side street, heading for Tottenham Court Road and a taxi.

10

THE ANSWERING-MACHINE WAS FLASHING when Loretta arrived home and she pressed the playback button wearily. The first message was from Andrew Walker, a history lecturer from college, who wanted to pass on some gossip about a mutual enemy of theirs in the bursar's office. He would be at his cottage in Charlbury next day, he said, and in the history department on Friday. Loretta shook her head, wondering how Andrew had managed to avoid being in London on the first day of term. She waited for the next message, expecting Tom Neil's voice, but it didn't come. Instead she heard the machine rewind, and looked at it in surprise. Maybe Neil had phoned but decided against leaving a message? Since acquiring the answering-machine a few weeks before Christmas Loretta had discovered that this was a disappointingly frequent occurrence, regardless of how she phrased the out-going message. She decided she needed to record it again, this time with a direct plea to callers not to ring off without announcing themselves, and made a mental note to do it at the weekend.

She scooped up Bertie from an armchair and left the room, turning off the light. She went slowly up the stairs, the cat cradled in her arms, and deposited him on the bed. He blinked, flexed his front paws a couple of times, and went back to sleep. It occurred to her that he at least would not miss Robert, whose visits to the flat tended to coincide with the cat's exclusion from the bedroom, and she wondered if she would come to regret their chilly parting. She was too tired to worry about it now, she thought, glancing at the clock on the bedside table and seeing it was nearly midnight. Where would Robert spend the night? She felt a momentary pang of guilt, then remembered he had come to London by car and could just as easily drive back again. And of course there was his club . . . Loretta began pulling her jumper over her head, slipping her shoes off at the same time.

A few minutes later, her clothes folded neatly over a chair, she was in bed. The room was at the back of the house, undisturbed by street lights and traffic noise from Liverpool Road, and she lay in the darkness with her hands clasped on the pillow behind her head. Her eyes were beginning to adjust to the gloom and she fixed them on the outline of the lampshade, its deep fringe casting a curiously elongated shadow on the ceiling. For the second night running she didn't feel the least bit sleepy, in spite of the ache behind her eyes which would probably be a lot worse in the morning. Her mind returned restlessly to the scene in the Greek restaurant, picking over the sequence of events from the moment of Robert's arrival in an attempt to pinpoint when things went wrong. At the time the row had seemed to come out of the blue, without warning, but now Loretta wasn't so sure. She realized she hadn't been looking forward to seeing him, and wondered if she'd subconsciously chosen a subject that was bound to provoke an argument. She ought to have known by now that Robert's views were both entrenched and surprisingly conventional.

The last word brought her up short. Someone else had used it of Robert . . . Loretta suddenly remembered a conversation with Sandra just after Christmas. At the time she had been irritated by Sandra's unsolicited opinion on the incongruity of her relationship with Robert, but perhaps it had struck a chord? If so, Loretta wasn't yet sure whether she was grateful or angry about the result, and her conflicting feelings on this issue stirred up others. Sandra had used her, she thought, visualizing the woman's arrival at the flat on

Christmas Eve. Where had she come from, and why? She pictured Sandra in the hall, unbuttoning her raincoat with her luggage at her feet. It wasn't a far step to thinking of the suitcase lying open on the drawing-room floor that afternoon, the bundles of money sitting on top of Sandra's crumpled clothes. The scene changed again, images coming into her head almost randomly now: Janet Weir beckoning from the door of the Notting Hill flat; Sandra walking into Loretta's kitchen in the lilac kimono she used as a dressing-gown; the naked woman on the postcard from Sandra's lover. Suddenly Robert was standing just inside the bedroom door, and when Loretta looked more closely he was carrying Sandra's body in his arms. "Where would you like it?" he asked, advancing on the bed, and Loretta heard a scream—

She jerked into a sitting position, staring wildly round the empty room, and it took her a moment to realize that the scream which had woken her was her own. She lay back against the pillow, her heart pounding as the dream receded, then sat up and reached for the glass of water on the bedside table. She took a couple of sips, noticing that it was now ten minutes to one; she *must* get some rest—she had to be up early to move her car nearer the college, and she had a lecture at ten followed by a two-hour tutorial. The head of the English department, Bernard Shilling, had called a meeting after lunch, an event which Loretta considered a complete waste of time but couldn't afford to miss. As the government's education cuts bit deeper, Shilling seemed to regard it as his duty to give his staff regular pep talks. The elements were familiar, and consisted of numerous platitudes about "these difficult times," combined with veiled threats about the consequences for any member of the department foolish enough to take part in the public protests organized by the AUT . . . Loretta sighed, realizing she had allowed herself to be sidetracked by a new set of worries. She'd be tied up until at least three-thirty, and when was she going to find time to call Derek Ghilardi? In desperation she put out a hand and touched the cat, allowing herself to be comforted by his sleepy purr and the softness of his coat. Then she turned over

150

onto her side, drew up her legs, and sternly commanded herself to go to sleep.

The next day was as busy as Loretta had anticipated, and she returned from college in the late afternoon somewhat out of sorts; she still hadn't succeeded in speaking to Ghilardi, who had been in a meeting when she snatched time to phone him, but she had collected a parking-ticket in spite of returning to her car at nine-fifteen. She stopped at Sainsbury's on her way home, then parked the car and walked the last few yards to her flat with a shopping bag in each hand. The weather was cold, though not bitterly so, and she debated with herself as to whether she had the energy to light a fire in the drawing-room. She had no plans to go out; her scheme for the evening was an early supper followed by a couple of hours of marking, making a start on the essays she'd collected that morning.

Someone was sitting on the step in front of Loretta's house. The hunched, child-like figure in a duffel coat was leaning against the railings, arms clasped round knees and white face staring glumly ahead. On drawing level Loretta saw it was a girl, eleven or twelve years old, with long brown hair pulled back in a pony tail.

"Hello," she said in surprise, wondering if the visitor was waiting for Shahin. If so, perhaps she ought to invite her in. She could hardly leave her sitting on the doorstep in the gathering dusk. "Have you—"

"Are you Loretta?" The girl sprang to her feet, and immediately seemed older. "I'm Lizzie."

"Lizzie?"

"Lizzie Neil—you talked to me last night. Can we go inside? I'm freezing, I've been waiting *hours*."

"Have you?" Loretta gazed at the girl, taken aback by this unexpected visitation. "Did your father—is he here?" She glanced hurriedly up and down the street, half expecting Tom Neil to materialize from behind a lamppost.

"Of *course* not," Lizzie said scornfully. "Look, I'm jolly cold, so if you don't mind . . ."

"Um, yes, of course. Just let me find my keys." Loretta lowered one of the carrier bags to the ground and fumbled in her shoulder-bag. "Here we are."

She unlocked the street door and led the way inside. "It's at the top, I'm afraid." She began climbing the stairs, wondering why she was apologizing to Lizzie Neil. She hadn't asked her to turn up like this, and she couldn't imagine what the girl wanted. Surely Neil hadn't sent her to collect her mother's luggage on her own?

"Come in," she called over her shoulder. "You'd better take off your coat."

She hung up her own, shaking it first to get rid of the creases it had acquired on the journey home.

"Is that real?" Lizzie asked in a disapproving voice, hanging her duffel coat on the next-door hook.

"Good God no," said Loretta. She stared at the bright red fake fur. "Have you ever seen an animal this colour?"

"It might be dyed," Lizzie said dismissively, transferring her attention to the hall and gazing round it with a slight frown on her face.

"Well it isn't," Loretta said firmly. "Now, would you like a hot drink? How long have you been sitting on the step?"

Lizzie didn't need to consult her watch. "Two and a quarter hours last time I looked. That was just before you came." She thrust her hands into the pockets of a new pair of jeans and looked down at her baseball boots. "I would have got here earlier but I got lost on the Underground—I've never been to London on my own before. Is this your cat?" She knelt to stroke Bertie, who had just appeared at the bottom of the stairs.

"Yes, he's called Bertie. He's Burmese."

"Why do you keep a cat in a flat? It isn't very big." She peered past Loretta into the kitchen with the air of a prospective purchaser who is unimpressed by what she sees. Lizzie's resemblance to her mother was unsettling, Loretta thought, and it wasn't confined to her appearance.

"He's quite happy," she said tartly.

"Where does he—"

152

"He's got a litter tray." Loretta tried to make it clear from her tone that the subject was closed. "Would you like some tea?"

"Yes please. Have you got Earl Grey? Tea, I mean, not tea-bags."

"Um—yes." Loretta thought Lizzie was treating her like a canteen assistant and decided to assert herself. "You go in there and I'll bring it through," she said, pointing in the direction of the drawing-room.

Lizzie shrugged. "OK."

Five minutes later, when Loretta arrived with a tray, she found Lizzie playing with Bertie.

"I like your cat," she announced, making circles in the air with a biro. Bertie was watching closely; suddenly he shot out a paw and knocked the pen to the floor. Lizzie laughed, a surprisingly girlish sound.

"Milk? Sugar?"

"No sugar." Lizzie took the mug and trickled milk into it like a connoisseur.

Loretta took her mug to the sofa, sat down and fixed the girl with a direct look. "Lizzie, I'm not sure why you're here—"

"I'm here about Mum," Lizzie said impatiently, turning to look at Loretta. "You said she stayed with you at Christmas—I wanted to see what your house was like. I didn't know it was a flat until I saw the bell. It doesn't say in the phone book." She looked as disapproving as she had in the hall.

Loretta swallowed the urge to apologize for the meagreness of her living quarters. "Well, this is it," she said instead, gesturing round the room. "Your mother slept in here, where I'm sitting—this sofa turns into a bed. There's only one bedroom," she added, feeling like the urban poor.

"That's what I don't understand," said Lizzie. "You haven't really got room—why didn't she come home if she couldn't stay at her flat?"

Loretta moved in her seat, looking down so that Lizzie

couldn't see her face. "Well, I suppose she wanted to stay in London—she had lots of friends here—"

"You're not just saying that?"

Loretta looked up, startled.

"I mean, I'm not saying you're lying, exactly," Lizzie continued. "You probably think it's for my own good—like Daddy." She rolled her eyes up towards the ceiling. "But I don't think I believe you."

"You don't?" Loretta repeated faintly.

"She'd left him, hadn't she? That's why she didn't come home—they were going to get a divorce."

"Oh, I don't think—" Loretta bit her lip, not knowing what to say. Lizzie's guess about the state of her parents' relationship was as good as hers, and she was anxious not to upset her. "That is—she didn't mention it to me," she said truthfully. She saw that Lizzie was waiting for her to say more, and decided to stick with the story Sandra had told her, or an edited version of it.

"All she said was she'd had a flood, and you were all away in Switzerland. So of course I said she could come here—"

"But she could have come home," Lizzie objected again. "She could have been there when we got back. I hadn't seen her since *August*." Her voice quavered, but then she seemed to recover.

"Maybe she didn't want to be on her own—people don't, sometimes," Loretta said helplessly. She tried another tack. "Lizzie, does your father know you're here?"

The girl rolled her eyes up again, saying nothing.

"What did he—you did give him my message?"

Lizzie leaned forward and lifted Bertie on to her lap, avoiding Loretta's gaze.

Loretta frowned. "Why didn't you tell him?"

"Why should I?" Her voice was sulky. "He doesn't tell *me* anything. He said I was too young to go to the inquest—"

"How old are you?"

"Thirteen. Fourteen next month. That's old enough—a

154

girl in my class had to go to court and give evidence about a man who stole her pony, and she's younger than me.''

"I'm sure he meant it for the best.''

"I'm not." Lizzie stared at her defiantly. "It's all his fault.''

"How is it his fault?''

"He was horrible to her and she wanted to get a divorce. If he hadn't been so horrible she'd have come on holiday and she wouldn't have gone to that stupid place.''

Loretta shook her head. "Lizzie, how do you know these things? Surely you were at school—''

"Not in the holidays—the summer holidays. Mum was only home for two weeks and they had terrible rows. I heard them after I was in bed, they were shouting in the kitchen. One night I got up and sat on the top step—I heard Mum crying and I wanted to go down but I was scared.''

"What were they—'' Loretta stopped, ashamed of even thinking of trying to get information from a bereaved teen-ager, but Lizzie ignored her.

"I *hate* him!'' she exclaimed, her eyes growing red. She began to cry, feeling in the pocket of her jeans and drawing out a grubby handkerchief. Loretta hesitated, not knowing whether she should go and comfort her, and decided against it. She was hardly acquainted with the girl, but had seen enough to guess that such attention from a stranger would be unwelcome.

"Drink your tea,'' she said gently. "Are you cold? I think I'll light a fire.''

She got up and busied herself in front of the grate, leaving Lizzie to recover in her own good time. She took a firelighter from an open cardboard box, covered it with sticks and put a match to it. Behind her Lizzie's sobs were subsiding, and when Loretta got to her feet the girl was obediently sipping her tea.

"Better?''

Lizzie nodded, keeping her head averted.

Loretta returned to the sofa, troubled by the responsibility of having the girl in her flat. At some point she would have

155

to ring Tom Neil, and she wondered if she should do it in the kitchen, behind Lizzie's back. She didn't like the idea, but was afraid the girl might bolt into the night if she suggested contacting her father.

"That's Mum's suitcase!" Lizzie's voice, still thick with tears, interrupted this train of thought.

"Yes, didn't I say? I'm sure—she left it here. That's why I rang your father . . ."

"What're you going to do with it?" Lizzie's tone was accusing.

"Nothing! In fact I think I'd better—" A thought had just struck her. She could hardly inform Tom Neil of his daughter's whereabouts without mentioning Sandra's bags, but she still hadn't spoken to Ghilardi . . . She wrestled with this problem for a few seconds, then admitted that events had defeated her. "I'd better ring your father," she said, in as low-key a way as she could manage. "Don't you think—he'll be worried when he finds you gone, won't he?"

Lizzie gave an angry shrug, but said nothing and made no move for the door.

"Will he be at home?"

Lizzie pulled back her cuff and looked at her watch, an outsize one with a thick strap and a large round face. "No, he'll be at his stupid warehouse," she said sulkily. "That's all he cares about, his stupid wine."

Loretta crossed to the phone and picked it up. "What's the number?"

Lizzie reeled it off, and Loretta dialled.

"Got any biscuits?" Lizzie demanded suddenly.

"In the kitchen. In a tin, next to the tea caddy." Loretta watched anxiously as Lizzie left the room, and relaxed when she heard her moving about in the kitchen.

"Mr. Neil? My name's Loretta Lawson—I'm ringing from London. I've got your daughter here." It sounded rather bald, but Loretta didn't know how else to put it.

"My daughter? Lizzie? I'm afraid I don't understand." Neil's tone was brusque, uncomprehending.

Loretta explained briefly about Sandra's arrival at Christmas. "What would you like me to do?" she finished, suddenly alarmed by the thought that Neil might expect her to drive Lizzie all the way to Winchester. There and back in one evening—Loretta's heart sank.

There was silence for a moment, then Neil said crisply: "Put her on, please."

Loretta looked at the receiver, thinking that the whole family seemed to be in the habit of giving orders, but said nothing. "Lizzie," she called. "Your father wants a word."

The girl came back into the room and took the phone unenthusiastically, nibbling a chocolate digestive biscuit. Loretta heard only half of the ensuing conversation, but it was obviously acrimonious.

"I only wanted to see where she lived."

"I didn't—"

"Dunno."

"Dunno."

"All right. I-do-not-know."

"I can get the tra—"

"Come *on*, Dad . . . *All* right."

Lizzie handed the phone back to Loretta with an exaggerated sigh. "He's coming to get me. Sorry." She wandered out of the room, apparently in search of another biscuit.

"Miss—er?"

"Lawson. Loretta Lawson." She didn't like being called Miss, but couldn't summon up the energy to correct him.

"Miss Lawson. I've told Lizzie I'm coming to collect her. If I leave now I should be in London by—what? Half past seven? I'm sorry to put you to all this trouble."

"That's all right." Loretta couldn't think of anything else to say. "Shall I give you the address?"

"Please." Neil wrote it down. "See you in an hour and a half," he said briskly, and the line went dead.

Lizzie reappeared, still looking sulky. "I could have got the train," she said. "It's a waste of the ticket. And he'll make me go back to school," she added, throwing herself into the armchair she'd previously occupied.

"To school? Shouldn't you be there now?" It had only

157

just occurred to Loretta that term must have started at least a week before.

"Yes," said Lizzie carelessly, swinging her arms over the sides of the chair with a reckless disregard for Loretta's furniture. "I'm allowed to go back late—I'm supposed to stay at home till I get over it. Felix, that's my brother, he's gone back already. He isn't sensitive."

Loretta stared glumly at her charge, wondering how to entertain her until Tom Neil arrived. She hadn't much experience of teenage girls, and this one seemed particularly difficult to deal with. It wasn't that she didn't feel sorry for Lizzie, it was just that her mood was clearly unpredictable. Her mind wandered back to Neil, and it occurred to her that he might recognize her from the inquest. She doubted it; he had been so distressed that he probably hadn't taken in much about the other people in the court-room.

"Sorry?" She looked at Lizzie.

"I was just saying—I don't want to be rude but have you got anything I could eat? I'm starving."

"Yes, I—when did you last have something?" Loretta felt guilty, thinking this should have occurred to her without prompting.

"On the train. It was *repulsive*." Lizzie pulled a face, once again reminding Loretta of Sandra.

She thought about the food she'd bought in Sainsbury's, the fresh pasta and the *lollo rosso* lettuce, and doubted whether either would interest Lizzie. Then she brightened.

"How about a pizza? There's a place round the corner—it's only five minutes' walk." Time would pass more quickly in a restaurant, she thought, and they'd get back just in time for Tom Neil's arrival.

Lizzie's eyes narrowed. "All right—but I haven't got much money."

"Leave that to me." Loretta thought fleetingly of the cash in Sandra's suitcase, and wondered what would happen to it. "Ready? The bathroom's upstairs if you—"

"No thanks." Lizzie got to her feet. "Where's my—oh, I remember, I hung it up." She went into the hall.

Loretta turned on the answering-machine and moved a small brass fireguard in front of the fire. As an afterthought, she reached over and added a couple more logs.

"Can we go now?" Lizzie's voice sounded from the hall.

"Coming," called Loretta, amazed by the girl's self-assurance. Had she behaved like this at Lizzie's age? She didn't think so; she suspected it was one of the results of private education, of which she heartily disapproved. With a backward glance at the fire to check that the logs had caught, she followed Lizzie into the hall and lifted down her coat.

"Hello, can you hear me?" Tom Neil's voice was distorted by the entryphone.

"Yes, come up." Loretta pressed the button to release the street door. "It's your father," she told Lizzie, who was looking grumpy in the doorway of the drawing-room.

She opened the front door of the flat and waited for Tom Neil to appear, listening to his footsteps grow louder as he mounted the stairs. She wrinkled her nose, wondering if he would expect to be offered a drink. She hoped not; Lizzie's spirits, which had improved considerably with the consumption of a deep-pan pizza and two glasses of Coca-Cola, had deteriorated as soon as the prospect of seeing her father drew near. Loretta stepped forward on to the landing, a rather forced smile on her face.

"Hi," she said, as Neil rounded the bend. He was wearing a Burberry—just like Sandra, she thought.

"You made good time. We've only just—" She stopped, astonished by the look on his face.

"You!" he said accusingly. "You were at the inquest!" He paused on the stairs, and she felt a wave of anger and suspicion cross the space between them.

"Yes . . ." she said, unconsciously taking a step back. "It was the least I could do," she said, plucking the cliché from the air. "With missing the funeral," she added by way of explanation.

Neil was staring at her. "You mean you're not—I was under the impression you were from the press."

"Oh *no*." Suddenly Loretta understood the reason for his hostility. She could see why bereaved relatives might resent the presence of reporters, scribbling away and turning their grief into copy. "I sat in the wrong place and everyone assumed . . ." She realized she was babbling, and turned to Lizzie, who was now behind her.

"I suppose you're going to tell me off," the girl said, hanging back near the kitchen.

"Lizzie—" Neil's voice softened. He hesitated at the top of the stairs. "I thought you'd gone shopping with Jenny's mother," he said, gently accusing.

"Yes, well, I had to say something, didn't I?" Lizzie retorted. "Anyway, you'd have had to come to London some time to collect Mum's bags. Wouldn't he?" She looked at Loretta for support.

"I'm sorry, Miss Lawson, you've been put to a lot of trouble," Neil said smoothly. "I had no idea Sandra had been staying here." He advanced into the hall, and Loretta saw he was wearing a suit under his raincoat. "Now you've told me, I suppose I ought to go and have a look at the damage. Do you know how bad the flood was?"

"I—" Loretta goggled at the thought of Neil turning up in Norfolk Gardens and encountering his wife's tenant. "I don't—'

"Well—" Neil was looking at his watch and appeared not to have noticed her consternation. "I think it'll have to wait. I'm going to take this young lady back to school first thing tomorrow."

"I *told* you so," Lizzie wailed.

"And I'd like her in bed at a reasonable hour," he finished, ignoring the outburst. "You said—my wife's bags?" He looked at Loretta politely, all hostility gone.

"I'll get them." Loretta turned and went into the drawing-room, hearing a muted exchange between father and daughter as she did so. "Here they are," she said, returning.

"Let me." Neil hurried forward. "This is the lot?"
She nodded.

"You don't hap—" Whatever he had been about to say,

Neil stopped, apparently thinking better of it. "Lizzie, your coat."

Loretta watched the girl heave on her duffel coat, a mutinous look on her face. "Bye, Lizzie," she said, suddenly wishing they'd got on better.

"Bye," said Lizzie, dragging her feet as she went to the top of the stairs. "Oh—" She turned. "Thanks for taking me to the restaurant."

"You've been to a restaurant?" Neil asked, surprised. He started feeling in his pockets. "I must owe you some money, Miss Lawson—"

Loretta shook her head violently. "It was only a pizza."

"If you're sure . . ."

"Really."

"Well—goodbye." Neil held out his right hand.

Loretta shook it, impressed by the firmness of his grip. He released her hand and lifted the bags. She watched him follow his daughter down the stairs, screwing up her face as she watched the suitcase disappear round the bend. She couldn't help feeling as if she'd handed over an unexploded bomb, and she wondered what Neil would do when he finally discovered the cash. Well, she wasn't going to admit anything, even if he phoned her—but why should he? There was no reason for him to suspect she'd looked inside . . . Loretta closed the front door and leaned against it for a few seconds, as if she feared the Neils were coming back. When the phone rang at half past nine she was struggling with a letter to John Tracey, having abandoned all hope of making inroads on her marking before the weekend.

"I must admit I was rather surprised by your news," she had written, thinking this was something of an understatement. "But now I've got used to the idea I just want to say I hope you'll both be very happy."

The letter was proving difficult, and Loretta was glad of the interruption until it occurred to her that the caller might be Robert. Surely not; it must be obvious by now that they were unsuited in all ways but one . . . She balanced her pen on the writing-pad and got up to answer it.

161

"Hello?"

"Hi, this is Sally. How are you?"

"Sally!" Loretta's hand flew guiltily to her forehead. She had completely forgotten her promise to ring if she found out any more about Sandra's death—hadn't even told Sally about the inquest, in fact.

"I can't talk for long," Sally informed her. "Felicity's got some sort of stomach bug—I've only just managed to get her down. But I wanted to tell you about Sandra—"

"About Sandra?" Surely Sally was ringing to get information, not give it? Loretta sank into a chair, confused.

"I don't suppose you saw the report of the inquest? I don't usually read the *Telegraph*, either—someone happened to leave yesterday's in my office."

"The *Telegraph*?"

"Yes. I had a look in the *Guardian* but they didn't seem to have it. There wasn't very much, just a couple of paragraphs. It was mainly about the time of the crash—it happened on New Year's Eve, apparently, or just after, so the story was whether she died this year or last. Did you manage to speak to Tom Neil?"

Loretta hesitated, wondering where to start. "Well, I—"

"Hang on—I think I can hear Fliss—" Sally was silent for a few seconds, listening. Loretta's mind went back to the man next to her on the press bench at the inquest, and she guessed he had supplied the story to the *Daily Telegraph*. Tom Neil was right, she thought with distaste, journalists of that sort were vultures.

"No, I think it's all right—God, they don't warn you about this sort of thing in ante-natal classes. Listen, Loretta, I'd better be quick—I was at a meeting today, a sort of mini-conference on developments in managing drug dependency. I know one of the speakers, he's quite well-known in his field, and I got talking to him in the lunch break.

"The point is that he's the director of a project in Holland Park, a centre that's trying out a multi-agency approach to working with drug-dependent people who've come into contact with the courts. It's been going for eighteen months and it's getting excellent results, a very low rate of recidivism.''

Loretta eyes widened; she was unused to social work jargon.

"And it turns out Sandra used to work for him.'' Sally announced, unable to disguise her triumph at this discovery. "That's where she went when she left Westminster. But she didn't stay long—at first he said something about a relationship with a client, and then he backtracked like anything and said she left over a policy disagreement. I got the distinct impression there was more to it than that—that she might have even been asked to leave. It explains the business of the health club, doesn't it? I always thought it was strange, but if she left under a cloud—and getting involved with a client is a pretty big cloud, I can tell you—it's be just about impossible for her to get a job in social work again.''

"When did all this happen?'' asked Loretta.

"Um—last summer, I think. Can that be right? Yes, I'm pretty sure—it was set up in the summer of '86, I remember reading about it at the time, and he said something about her going after a year—I don't know what she can have been thinking of—''

"But what was she doing in between?'' Loretta wondered aloud. "If she left last summer, I mean, and the health club job didn't start till this month—''

"Maybe she signed on,'' Sally suggested. "Though it's hard to imagine Sandra signing on the dole.''

"Certainly is,'' Loretta agreed, trying to get her thoughts in order. Sandra had rented her flat in Norfolk Gardens to Janet Weir in August, perhaps because she could no longer afford to live in it. If she had been unemployed, it would also explain how she'd got into the financial mess revealed by the letter from her bank. It didn't cast any light on the cash in the suitcase, though, or the £2,000 she'd paid into her account at the end of November.

"Gosh, Sally,'' Loretta exclaimed, "it gets more and more—''

"Oh *no*,'' Sally wailed. "She's woken up *again*. Sorry,

Loretta, I'll have to go and see to her. Poor little mite, I'm sure it's something in the water—I'll ring if I find out any more. Bye."

"Wait—" Loretta heard the phone go down at Sally's end and was left staring at the receiver. She sighed, bit her lip and returned it to its cradle. She hadn't even had a chance to fix another time to talk, and this new piece of information . . .

She got up and went slowly back to her place on the sofa. Had Sandra eventually found a short-term, well-paid job outside London, concealing it from her family because— because she was ashamed of the circumstances in which she'd left the drug project? That was the most plausible explanation of her pretence that she was still living in Notting Hill. But what sort of job could it have been? It wasn't as if women could go off and work on an oil rig, for instance . . .

Loretta picked up her letter to John Tracey, thinking that a few months ago she'd have been able to confide in him. She re-read what she'd written before Sally's call, wondering why her congratulations on his engagement sounded so half-hearted. She added another sentence, writing that she was touched to be invited to the wedding, and of course she was longing to meet Soulla. The funny thing was that it was all true, yet the letter seemed stilted and formal. Loretta began a new paragraph, explaining the divorce procedure and informing Tracey that she was enclosing forms which needed his signature.

"It seems fairly straightforward," she finished. "Let me know your plans and I'll keep you posted from this end. I really do hope you'll both be very happy, and we can still be friends. Much love from Loretta."

She was folding the letter when something occurred to her and she smoothed it out to add a short PS: "Any idea where our marriage certificate is? I can't find it anywhere."

She slid the letter into a large envelope, along with the forms from the County Court, and was licking the flap when Bertie strolled into the room. He immediately jumped on to her knee, butting her hands with his head until she took the hint and put the envelope beside her on the sofa.

"At least I've got you, Bertie," she said, bending her head and burying it in the soft fur of his neck.

11

LORETTA HAD JUST WALKED INTO HER OF-
fice next morning, a styrofoam cup containing tea in one
hand, when the department secretary put her head round the
door to say that Susie Lathlean from Vixen Press had already
called twice. Loretta felt a moment's apprehension, wondering if Susie had changed her mind about the book—surely
not, after her enthusiastic letter earlier in the week—or wanted
lots of changes.

Susie had good news, however. The manuscript had now
been read by another Vixen editor, who liked it as much as
she did, and the company wanted to include the book on its
spring list for the following year, 1989. Susie said nothing
about the title and Loretta didn't mention it either, anxious
not to introduce a jarring note into such an exhilarating conversation. She glowed with excitement as she discussed illustrations with Susie; although she had contributed chapters
to various critical anthologies this was her first full-length
book, and she was thrilled to think it would be published in
little over a year.

"One last thing," said Susie, when Loretta had agreed to
compile a list of photographs and where they might be found.
"Have you got an agent?"

"An agent?"

"Obviously not," Susie sounded relieved. "No problem—we prefer to negotiate direct with the author if we can.

We've got a standard contract covering rights and so on, and I'll come back to you on money—the managing director's away till next week. Well, Loretta, we're all absolutely delighted to be publishing you.''

''Thanks very much.''

Loretta put down the phone, a slight frown on her face. She had been so delighted about completing the book that she hadn't give a moment's thought to money—or to the mysterious ''rights'' Susie had mentioned. Perhaps she did need a literary agent, but she had no idea how to go about acquiring one. She thought for a moment, pondering the question of who might be able to advise her. The most prolific author in the English department was Henry Hedger, whose Popular Profiles series of short, gossipy biographies was rumoured to be, as someone in the college had jealously put it, ''a nice little earner.'' Loretta suspected that many readers of Dickens, Wilkie Collins and George Eliot owed much of their ''knowledge'' of these authors to Henry's racy little volumes. She didn't like him much, and they had frequently clashed over questions of department policy, but on this subject he was almost certain her best bet. Loretta finished her tea and stood up, intending to go and knock on Henry's door, but at that moment the phone rang.

''Hello?''

''Good morning. Am I speaking to Dr. Laura Lawson?'' A male voice, breezy and confident.

Loretta eye's narrowed. ''Um—yes, you are—but it's *Loretta* Lawson, actually.''

''Funny—it's got Laura Lawson here—Laura Anne, date of birth nineteen-eight-fifty-three.''

''That's right, that's me—it's just I don't use either of those names . . . haven't for years. Look, if you tell me who you are, I'll see if I can help.''

''Hang on, let's get this straight. Your name's Laura Anne Lawson but you use something else?''

Loretta raised her eyes to the ceiling. ''Yes, I've just told you—everyone calls me Loretta.''

''Why's that then?''

"Because—" Loretta searched for words. "Because that's the name I use—What is all this? How do you know my date of birth?" It occurred to her that some organization she belonged to, perhaps one of her credit cards, must have sold her details to a double glazing firm. "If you're trying to sell me something I can tell you right now I'm not interested." They had a nerve, she thought, ringing her at work.

There was a moment's silence. "The name's Farr, madam. Detective Sergeant Steve Farr, Lymington CID."

"Oh."

"I've been going through your statement, the one you gave on January the twelfth concerning Mrs. Neil. You talked to my colleague, Mr. Ghilardi, am I right?"

"Ye-es . . ."

"It says here," the voice went on, "that Mrs. Neil was resident at your flat from December the twenty-fourth to December the thirty-first last year, when you came home to find her gone."

"Well, 'resident' is putting it a bit strong. She slept on my sofa, that's all."

"But I'm right in thinking you knew her well?"

"If you've read my statement, you'll know I hadn't seen her for years," Loretta said shortly. "I was doing her a favour, I wouldn't say she was a close friend."

"I'm sorry, you're quite right," said Farr, and read from her statement. " 'I had not seen Mrs. Neil for some years and was surprised when she rang me on Christmas Eve . . .' You had a lot to catch up on, then—had a bit of a chin-wag, am I right?"

Loretta's brows drew together. "I wouldn't say—we chatted, yes, but it was mostly small talk. We couldn't help bumping into each other—it's a small flat."

"And you talked about—what? What sort of thing?"

"As I said, nothing in particular. I wasn't there all that much. I was at my office—"

"What, at Christmas?" He sounded sceptical.

"Between Christmas and New Year. I was finishing a book. Look, Mr. Farr, I don't know what this is about—"

"Just routine, Miss—I'm sorry, *Dr.* Lawson. I'll only take up a couple more minutes of your time. Now, when you were having these chats with Mrs. Neil about nothing in particular—the name Fleming come up at all? Bob Fleming?"

"Fleming? No, I'm sure not. Is it important?"

He ignored the question. "Quite sure? She didn't say—oh, if a bloke called Fleming rings up, can you tell him I'm not here?"

"Heavens, no." Loretta hadn't the least idea what the detective was talking about.

"OK. No mention of Fleming." Loretta had the impression he was writing down her answers. "A couple more things, then I'll let you get back to work. Did Mrs. Neil—she brought things with her, I suppose? Clothes, make-up, that sort of thing? Some sort of bag, maybe more than one?"

Loretta was suddenly wary. Had the police found out about the cash in Sandra's luggage? If so, should she mention it first? She had been putting off ringing Ghilardi while she mulled over how much to tell him, now the bags were no longer in her possession. If they already knew about the money, however, perhaps she didn't need to say anything—

"Dr. Lawson?"

"I'm sorry, I didn't hear . . ."

"I asked you whether Mrs. Neil had a bag with her."

"Oh yes." Loretta came to a decision. "She had a suitcase, a blue one, and a biggish holdall."

"And did she act as if—did you get the impression she was . . . protective about them? Didn't like you going near them?"

"Protective?" Loretta stalled. They did know about the cash; Tom Neil must have told them as soon as he opened the suitcase. "No, I wouldn't have said so. She kept them at the end of the sofa, and I can't say I took much notice . . ." She hesitated, wondering what Farr would expect her to say if she genuinely didn't understand what lay behind his questions. "You still haven't told me what this is about."

"Don't worry, Dr. Lawson, it's all routine. You've no idea how many pointless questions we have to ask every day

169

of the week. That's police work for you. My wife says I never switch off—but you don't want to waste time hearing what my wife says. These bags—sorry, a bag and a suitcase, I think you said? Where are they now?''

"Where—" Loretta was momentarily taken aback. Then it occurred to her that Farr was playing some silly game, cross-checking her story with Tom Neil's. "I gave them to her husband—Sandra's husband—last night. He came about half past seven, quarter to eight.'' That would tie in with what Neil had told them, she thought with satisfaction.

"Took you quite some time to get round to it, didn't it, Dr. Lawson?''

"I—I forgot. The accident was a terrible shock, and I suppose I didn't think . . .''

"And that's all she had—one bag and one blue suitcase?''
"Yes.''

"So there's nothing belonging to Mrs. Neil in your flat now?''

"Nothing.''

"She didn't—just checking—she didn't ask you to look after anything for her?''

"Such as?'' Loretta didn't know what he was getting at.

"Mmm—anything at all.'' Farr was evasive.

"If you mean did she present me with a diamond necklace and ask me to guard it with my life, the answer is no,'' Loretta snapped. Why was Farr asking all these questions? Surely he wasn't implying—he didn't think there was *more* cash stowed away in Loretta's flat?

"I'm sorry, could you—''

"I said you don't seem very happy about answering my questions, Miss—Dr. Lawson.''

"I—'' Her throat was dry. "What do you expect? You haven't given me a clue what all this is about—''

"That's not my job, Dr. Lawson. It's not my job to go round telling people what it's all about.''

"Maybe not, but—''

"Anyway, I think we can leave it there—for the moment. Oh, sorry, there is one more thing. Always is, isn't there? It says here Mrs. Neil told you she'd been away from London for a while. Did she say where? Who she was working for?''

"No, I'm sure she didn't." Loretta was relieved by the change of subject. She had begun to think Farr wasn't interested in tracing down the source of the cash.

"Doesn't sound like she told you much at all," Farr observed, and let the remark hang in the air.

"I agreed to put her up for a few nights—we didn't play *Twenty Questions*."

"*Twenty Questions*! Now that does take me back. Animal, vegetable or mineral. Well, Dr. Lawson, I'm sure you've got better things to do than listen to me going on about prehistoric radio programmes." His tone changed abruptly. "Not planning any trips, are you? I may need to get another statement."

Loretta bridled. "Look," she said indignantly, "it says in my statement I'm a university lecturer. Yesterday was the first day of the spring term. I have five hours of lectures each week, plus six of tutorials. I also have—"

"Thanks very much, Dr. Lawson. I'll be in touch." The line went dead.

Loretta was left staring angrily at the phone. Who was Steve Farr, and why had he rung her instead of Ghilardi? On Tuesday, only three days ago, the case had been officially closed; now she was being interrogated by a detective sergeant. Her first instinct was to ring Ghilardi at once and ask him what had happened, but it occurred to her that someone else might answer the CID phone—going on past form this was almost certain to happen, she might even get Farr himself—and she didn't want to let him know she was rattled.

Rattled? Loretta shook her head. What was she thinking of? She hadn't done anything wrong, apart from succumbing to curiosity, and that from the best of motives. She played with the on-off switch of her computer terminal, watching the screen alternately light up and go grey. She realized that Farr had set out to make her feel guilty; that was his technique. Unlike Ghilardi—she gave the switch a final jab, turning the machine off, and told herself she wasn't going to let

171

Farr wreck her morning. What had she been doing before his call?

Oh yes, she had been on her way to consult Henry Hedger about literary agents. It took her a moment to remember why she needed advice on this subject, and when she did she was amazed at the ease with which Farr's insinuations had driven the morning's good news out of her head. She was about to be a published author, to join the ranks of that select body she had so long admired from outside, and that was more important than worrying about what some policeman in Hampshire did or didn't believe about her. Loretta got to her feet, slid out from behind her desk, and walked purposefully to the door.

Three-quarters of an hour later she returned to her office in a much more cheerful frame of mind, having been regaled by Henry with all the latest literary gossip. Her stock had risen considerably, she perceived, as soon as she'd told him about her book, and he'd given her dire warnings not to sign anything before speaking to a literary agent.

"What rights are they asking for?" he'd demanded. "Hang on to everything except British and Commonwealth—whatever you do, don't sign away North America."

"I'm not sure—I don't think it's going to be a bestseller," Loretta had said rather timidly, still unsettled by the phone call.

Henry held up a hand. "You never know—look at Ackroyd. And he wasn't even allowed to quote. Yours got much sex in it?"

"Well, there's quite a lot about the way her sexuality informed her writing—"

"Oh, *sexuality* isn't any good." Henry shook his head. "I mean *sex*—did she have affairs? I can't say I know much about her. American literature—" He gave a dismissive wave.

"She did have an affair, as a matter of fact," Loretta said guardedly, thinking of Morton Fullerton. "And she was divorced, which was fairly unusual . . ."

"Better and better. Let me have a word with my agent—" Henry was already punching numbers into his phone.

"But—"

"Is Zizzy in? It's Henry Hedger. Could you get her to call me back at the office? Thanks." He wrote a name and number on a piece of paper and handed it to Loretta. "There you are. Zizzy's very good. Tall and blonde—bit of a firebreather, as a matter of fact. I'm terrified of her, but so are most of the publishers she deals with. You'll like her—birds of a feather and all that." He winked. "Better not ring till I've spoken to her—it's personal introductions that count in this game."

"Thank you very much," Loretta had said, getting to her feet in a daze. How would Vixen react when she told them she'd acquired an agent? Always assuming the curiously named Zizzy Fox was prepared to take her on—though Henry had seemed very confident on her behalf. It was certainly the case that she didn't know the first thing about rights and contracts; Henry had spluttered in disbelief when she admitted she couldn't even tell him whether Vixen planned to publish the book in hardback or soft cover . . .

Loretta was sitting in her office, staring at Zizzy's phone number, when there was a knock at the door. She looked up and called "Come in!"

"Loretta—is this a bad time?"

It was Sarah Guzelian, an American who had come to work in the department at the beginning of the autumn term on a year's exchange from Columbia.

"No. Have a seat." Loretta was always glad to see Sarah. "I've just been talking to Henry about my book—he wanted to know if there's any sex in it!" She smiled, expecting the anecdote to raise a laugh, but Sarah was looking sombre. "Is everything all right?"

Sarah didn't answer immediately, but leaned back in her chair, running her hands through her short grey hair. Then she thrust them into the pockets of her trousers.

"Loretta, I'm gonna be upfront about this. Are you in some kind of trouble?"

173

"I hope not," said Loretta, looking puzzled. Her immediate thought, so ridiculous that she dismissed it, was that Sarah knew about the call from Detective Sergeant Farr. She'd be believing in telepathy next, she told herself. "What sort of trouble?" she added, folding her arms and leaning back in her chair. "Something to do with the department?"

Sarah shook her head vehemently. "No—real trouble. The police."

"The *police*?" Loretta's mouth fell open.

"I just had a call from this guy down in Hampshire, seems he's some kind of a detective—"

"*You*'ve had a call?" Loretta was flabbergasted. "I don't understand—is this—" She had been going to ask if it was a joke, but saw from Sarah's face that it wasn't.

"Hey, don't get excited. I didn't tell him a *thing*. I guess this is some kind of a political . . . Do you have anything like the ACLU over here?"

"The—oh, civil liberties. Yes, we call it the NCCL . . ."

"Maybe you should give them a call. I mean—Christ, calling up people you work with?"

Loretta took a deep breath. "What did he want to know?"

Sarah responded with an angry shake of the head. "We didn't get into that. Soon as he said who he was I told him nothing doing. I'm sure as hell no—what's the word you use? A sneak?"

Loretta nodded glumly. Presumably Farr had been checking up on her, trying to find out whether she was an honest witness. Sarah had acted from the best of motives, jumping to the conclusion that the call was connected with Loretta's well-known anti-nuclear activities. If only she'd co-operated, Loretta thought ruefully; had told the detective Loretta was a model citizen—

"This has really shaken me up, I can tell you, Loretta," she heard Sarah say, and roused herself from her unpleasant reverie to ask another question.

"But how did he—I don't understand how he got your name."

174

"Oh—he called up the department office. Bernard was out and Mrs. Whittaker buzzed him through."

"Mrs. Whittaker?" Loretta repeated the secretary's name. "What did he—was his name Farr?"

"Yeah. Know the guy?"

"I've spoken to him." Loretta fell silent again, trying to work out what was in Farr's mind. Why go to this trouble unless he really did suspect her of something, presumably of pocketing cash from Sandra's suitcase? And how could she ever prove otherwise?

"Loretta, you OK?" Sarah was looking more worried by the minute.

"Yes, yes," she said distractedly.

"You *are* in some kind of trouble, right?"

"No, I—" Loretta suddenly wished Sarah would leave the room so she could ring Ghilardi. "I suppose they have to make these inquiries," she added, belatedly trying to make light of the call. "It's nothing sinister—just something to do with a car accident . . ." She tailed off, realizing the police would hardly check on the *bona fides* of a witness to a straightforward car crash. Sarah was looking unconvinced and she tried a new tack, abruptly changing the subject.

"Actually, Sarah," she said with forced brightness, "as you're here—"

"Yeah?"

"There is something I want to talk to you about. Remember we had a discussion last term about a new course, a set of tutorials on crime fiction?"

Sarah was looking at her oddly, as though she had seen through this diversionary tactic, but she nodded.

"I've been doing some thinking, and it would help me a lot if we could have a chat. You know the American stuff much better than I do . . ."

"Sure." Now Sarah seemed puzzled. "I don't have anything for the next half hour—"

"I didn't mean now," Loretta said hastily, thinking about Ghilardi. "But I'm working on a reading-list—" She glanced covertly at her watch: twenty past eleven. It would be just her luck if Ghilardi had already gone out.

"Maybe if you give me an idea who's on it I can come back with some more names . . ."

"Dorothy Sayers," Loretta said quickly. "Margery Allingham. Possibly Ngaio Marsh—"

"I guess I'm more familiar with the later stuff. If it's Americans you're after, how about Sara Paretsky?"

"I've got her. She's wonderful."

"Amanda Cross?"

"Oh—maybe." The conversation was having a calming effect on Loretta, and she elaborated. "I'm not so sure about academic mysteries. I tried one by Joan Smith the other day and she got all the details wrong . . ."

Sarah looked blank. "Oh yeah? She British? Maybe I should look out for her . . . I know Carolyn, of course."

"Oh—of course." Loretta realized she would have to tread carefully; she had forgotten that Carolyn Heilbrun, author of the Amanda Cross novels, was a professor at Columbia. "I tell you what," she suggested, "you might even want to teach one or two of the sessions yourself. Why don't we talk about it next week?"

"Sure. We need a bit of time, I guess. You free Monday night? For dinner?" At last Sarah stood up and prepared to go.

"Yes—I've got a lecture at five and that's it. D'you want to meet here?"

"OK." The American woman paused as though she was about to say something, then appeared to think better of it and opened the door.

"Oh, and Sarah—thanks."

Sarah shrugged, waved and went out. Loretta seized the phone and dialled the number of Lymington police station. The switchboard put her through to CID and she demanded rather breathlessly to speak to Derek Ghilardi.

"Hang on a minute." It was a male voice but not, she thought, Steve Farr's. The man must have put his hand over the receiver for the next words she heard were muffled.

176

"Anyone seen Dirty Del? There's a bird here wants to speak to him."

Loretta's eyes widened; she didn't know whether she was more offended by Ghilardi's nickname or by being referred to as a "bird." Either way, her impression that the detective was the odd man out at the police station was reinforced. The man came back on the line, chuckling at some joke she hadn't heard. "Hang on, love," he said, irritating her even more. "Someone's gone to get him. Who is it?"

She hesitated, then identified herself reluctantly. "Over here, Del," she heard him call. "Loretta Lawson." He sang out her name as though she were a nightclub turn.

"Hello, is that Derek Ghilardi?"

"Ye-es." He sounded cautious.

"What on earth's going on? I've had someone called Farr on the phone to me, and—"

"That's right, inquiries are continuing," Ghilardi said in a formal voice.

"But—"

"I don't think you need worry about that, you'll be contacted if we need anything else. Thanks for ringing."

"Wait a minute—" Loretta was left gasping with indignation; she slammed down the receiver so hard that for a moment she thought she'd broken the phone. She was relieved to hear the ringing tone when she picked up the receiver, and put it back gently this time. She was aware of a painful pressure behind her eyes, as though she was about to get a headache, and she massaged her temples with her right hand as she thought about what had just happened. What had got into Ghilardi? Was she so much a suspect that he wasn't even permitted to speak to her? The phone rang and she snatched it up.

"Loretta? Derek Ghilardi again. Sorry about that, it was a bit difficult—"

"What's going on?" wailed Loretta, not allowing him to finish.

"I can't talk now—sorry. But there's nothing to worry

177

about. I'll try and ring you tonight, OK? What's your number?"

"I gave it—"

"I know, but give it me again. 01 . . ."

Loretta filled in the remaining seven digits.

"Will you be at home this evening?"

"Yes—"

"I'll explain then. Bye."

Loretta bit her lip, disconcerted by this turn of events. How could she help worrying? Her headache was beginning to get into its stride, thudding away somewhere behind her eyes, and she pulled open a drawer of her desk in search of paracetamol. Painful memories were returning, vivid recollections of the summer before last, the only previous occasion on which she'd had any protracted dealings with the police. She'd been questioned for hours, and at the end of it she hadn't been believed . . . She found the tablets and got up to fetch some water from the tiny kitchen at the end of the corridor. She had got as far as the door when the phone sounded again, and she went back to answer it.

"Loretta Lawson? This is Zizzy Fox. Henry tells me you've written a *wonderful* book about Edith Wharton. Why don't we have lunch and talk about it?"

Loretta arrived home just before seven that evening, and was removing her coat in the hall when she heard the phone. She hurried into the drawing-room before it could be intercepted by the answering-machine.

"Yes?" she cried, willing it to be Derek Ghilardi.

"Oh—Dr. Lawson there, love?" A chirpy male voice with a strong South London accent; it meant nothing to her.

"Ye-es," she said cautiously.

"Good-o, got you first time. I left it a bit so's you'd have finished surgery."

"Surgery?"

"Yeah—you're a doctor, aren't you?"

"Not that sort of doctor," said Loretta, seeing his mistake. "I've got a PhD, not a medical degree. Where did you get my number?"

"In the book, aren't you? What you a doctor of, then?"

"English Literature. Look, if it's a GP you want, I think you'd better try the Yellow Pages. They're under physicians, I think—"

"Oh—my mistake. Always happening, is it? People wanting you to look at their bunions and all?"

"No, as a matter of fact. As I say, I think your best bet is Yellow Pag—"

"Nah, it's you I want. Fleming's the name—heard of me, have you? Bob Fleming?"

Loretta frowned, aware of a flicker of recognition. She had heard the name recently.

Quite suddenly it came back to her: "Oh!"

"That's the girl! Sandra talk about me, did she?"

"Yes—no. I mean—" Loretta hesitated, "I'm not sure," she finished lamely. What had Steve Farr said? Something about Sandra not wanting to speak to a man called Fleming, no more than that—

"Oh dear, oh *dear*. Memory playing up, is it?"

"What is all this?" Loretta demanded, not liking Fleming's tone. "If you don't tell me what this is about," she told him firmly, "I'm going to put the phone down."

"Hang about, hang about—keep your hair on. All I'm after is a little chat."

"A little chat about what?"

"About *Sandra*," he said patiently, as though it was obvious. "You know—our mutual friend." He chuckled.

"What about her?"

"Not on the *phone*. You can't have a proper natter on the phone. Come round to your place, shall I?"

"No!" Loretta said wildly. "I mean, no. I've got friends coming to dinner," she improvised.

"Oh—pity. Don't want to spoil your evening, do I? How about in the morning then? Half ten?"

"No, you can't come here—I don't know anything about you."

179

"Oh dear—that's not very nice, is it? And me a friend of Sandra's."

"We seem to be going around in circles," Loretta pointed out. "Why don't you just tell me—"

"Look, like I said, I don't wanna talk about it on the phone. All right, you don't want me coming round to your place. Fair enough. I'll meet you anywhere you like—name your place. Can't say fairer than that, can I? Got a local, have you?"

"A local? I don't go to pubs much . . ."

"All right, make it an *art gallery* for all I care." He put on a posh voice for the middle two words, mocking her.

Loretta hesitated. The telephone directory contained her address as well as her phone number; if she refused to see him, what was there to prevent Fleming from turning up on the doorstep? No harm could come to her in a public place, and she had to admit she was curious . . .

"You still there, love? I can't stand here all night watching my hair grow."

"I'm thinking," Loretta said truthfully. Not a pub, she didn't feel comfortable in pubs, and certainly not a restaurant—she didn't want to spend more time with Fleming than she had to.

"I know," she said suddenly, her mind throwing up the perfect place. "There's a little café—the Superior Snack Bar in Holloway Road." The place was always busy, and the owners knew her by sight. "It's opposite North London Poly."

"North London what?"

"The polytechnic—Oh, never mind. Do you know this area?" It occurred to her that she had no idea where Fleming was calling from.

"Nah. But I'll find it."

"It's between Holloway Road Underground station and Highbury Corner, on the right as you're coming towards Islington."

"OK. Tomorrow morning, half ten?"

"Eleven." The time was immaterial to Loretta, but she wanted to assert herself.

"Good girl. See you."

Loretta put the phone down and drifted into the hall, retrieving her coat from the floor where she'd dropped it earlier. What had she got herself into? She was aware of a combination of excitement and nervousness, a sense of being on the verge of further discoveries about Sandra and a fluttering in her stomach at the prospect of meeting Fleming on her own. He claimed he had found her number in the phone book, but how did he know about her connection with Sandra? Suddenly a thought occurred to Loretta and she hurried into the kitchen to ring Shahin, her downstairs neighbour.

"It's Loretta . . . yes, I'm well. And you? I wanted to ask you something—I'm probably being silly, but it's just possible someone might turn up tonight who I don't want to see. If he tries your entryphone . . . No, I didn't think you would. Thanks . . . Oh no, nothing's wrong, really."

Loretta put the phone down, satisfied to have taken this sensible precaution against Bob Fleming's going back on his word. She glanced at her watch: twenty-five past seven. Should she start supper or wait for Ghilardi to ring? When she agreed to the rendezvous at the snack bar she had done it with the detective's promise at the back of her mind; the Lymington police obviously knew something about Fleming, and she felt sure Ghilardi would warn her if she was making a dreadful mistake.

She decided to get on with supper, taking the frying-pan out of a cupboard and pouring in sufficient oil to moisten the bottom. She peeled and crushed several cloves of garlic, browned them in the pan with a chopped onion and a sprinkling of dried chillies, and put a pan of water on to boil. Half an hour later she sat down to a plate of *penne all'arrabbiata*, sprinkling the spicy tomato sauce liberally with *pecorino* cheese. Afterwards she picked up her glass of wine and carried it into the drawing-room, leaving it on the table next to the phone while she set up the video recorder. It was a while since she'd watched a film, and she decided to indulge herself

181

with a third or fourth viewing of *Rebecca*. She was soon absorbed in it, Bertie asleep on her lap, and it was only towards the end of the film that she began to feel restless, aware that time was passing and Ghilardi still hadn't called. The film finished and she watched the beginning of *News at Ten*; nothing much had happened in the world and she switched off the television.

What was Ghilardi playing at? Loretta wandered into the kitchen, refilled her glass, and returned to the drawing-room. She stared at the phone, her unease increasing as she faced the prospect of meeting Bob Fleming without knowing a single fact about him. Suddenly the idea came into her head that he was a moneylender, the source of the banknotes in Sandra's suitcase. Her brow darkened as she remembered a recent *World In Action* programme on this very subject, exposing the crooks who loaned money to the unemployed at spiralling interest rates and threatened them when they got into debt. If Sandra *had* been on the dole she might have run out of money quite quickly . . . Loretta shivered, remembering that one of the men featured in the programme made a habit of breaking people's legs—

She seized the phone and dialled Lymington police station. She allowed it to ring a couple of times, frowning as she worked out what she was going to say, then put out her left hand and severed the connection. As soon as the dialling tone came back she tried a London number instead.

"Sally?" Loretta realized she sounded panic-stricken and modified her tone. "It's Loretta. I'm sorry to ring so late but I think I may be in trouble . . ."

She lifted the phone and walked about the room, bringing Sally up to date on her discoveries about Sandra.

"A moneylender?" Sally exclaimed when Loretta had finished. "And you've agreed to meet him? You must be mad, Loretta—you don't know what these people are like! One of my clients ended up in hospital—"

"I don't *know* he's a moneylender," Loretta interrupted, acknowledging she'd overstated her case. "I just thought—I couldn't think of any other connection between him and Sandra, and there was all that mon—'' She stopped, remembering Sally didn't know about the cash. She'd been too embarrassed to admit to her search of Sandra's belongings. ''She told me she was short of money, I suppose that's why it occurred to me . . .''

''Oh, I see—you're just guessing,'' said Sally, sounding relieved. ''But surely, Loretta, there could be lots of reasons? What did he sound like, this bloke?''

''Oldish. South London accent.''

''That doesn't make him a crook, does it?'' Sally's voice was reproving. ''Lots of perfectly honest people live in South London.''

''No, of course not,'' Loretta agreed hastily, anxious to clear up the misunderstanding. ''It's nothing to do with his accent, it's the way he— Oh, I can't explain.''

''Could be an ex-client, have you thought of that? Not from her last job, necessarily—I think the Holland Park project deals mainly with younger people. She worked for Westminster for quite a long time—could be somebody she knew from back then. Did she do any private counselling, do you know?''

''Gosh, I've no idea.'' Bob Fleming hadn't struck Loretta as the sort of person who'd have much time for psychotherapy.

''On the other hand—maybe you should tell the police. Just to be on the safe side. They do have their uses, you know.''

''I thought of that.'' Loretta paused.

''But?''

''Well, as you say, I haven't got any evidence . . . All he wants is to talk to me, or so he says.''

''And you're curious.''

''Yes.''

''Curiosity killed the cat, remember. Where did you say you were meeting him? In some caff?''

Loretta told her.

''At least you had the sense to choose a public place. What time?''

"Eleven."

"Hmmm—I think I'd better come with you."

"Oh, Sally, would you?" Loretta felt a surge of relief. "It's not far from you, six or seven minutes' walk, I should think."

"I'll have to bring Felicity, of course. Peter's working in the morning."

"Felicity?" Loretta guiltily realized she had forgotten Sally's baby. "Oh, in that case I couldn't possibly—"

"No, it's all right, she won't be any trouble," Sally assured Loretta, misinterpreting her misgivings. "She'll probably sleep, she usually has a nap in the mornings. Tell you what, Loretta—why don't we get there early and have some breakfast? I haven't been to a caff for *ages*."

Loretta blinked, startled by Sally's sudden display of levity. Anyone would think they were arranging an outing—

"Egg and chips with lots of brown sauce, that's what I fancy," Sally went on. "Shall we say half past ten? Is that early enough?"

"Yes, I suppose . . ."

"Great. Goodnight, Loretta."

"Oh—goodnight." She heard Sally put the phone down.

12

THE WAITRESS HAD JUST CLEARED AWAY
their plates next morning when Sally leaned across the table
and whispered to Loretta.

"Think this is him?"

Loretta turned. A short man with black, slicked-back hair
was standing inside the door, a copy of the *Sun* sticking
jauntily out of the pocket of his sheepskin coat. The jacket
emphasized the width of his shoulders, and his crooked nose
gave him the look of an ex-boxer—or worse, Loretta thought,
remembering her theorizing the previous evening about loan
sharks and broken legs.

"Crikey—I hope not," she said *sotto voce*, looking back
at Sally in alarm.

"It *is* him," Sally insisted. "He's looking for someone,
you can tell." Her hand went out to the handle of Felicity's
pushchair.

Loretta turned to face the door again, and she had to admit
that Sally was right. The man was scanning the occupants of
the café, and his face was growing darker by the minute.

"*Do* something," whispered Sally.

Loretta's own inclination was to lie low, using Sally and
the baby sleeping beside them as cover; Fleming was expecting her to be alone. But her friend's injunction, combined with the fear that this gorilla-like person might turn up
at her flat if she ducked out of the meeting, impelled her to

act. She stood up, nervously clearing her throat to gain his attention.

"Ah, Mr. Fleming?"

The man's head swivelled to stare at her. "Yeah?"

Loretta had no difficulty in recognizing the voice. Any lingering hope that there'd been a mistake, that this was some innocent local with nothing more sinister on his mind than tucking into a Superior Mixed Grill, was swept away. She saw his eyes slide suspiciously past her to Sally and the baby, then back again. She braced herself for an explosion: instead, to her astonishment, his mouth opened, an uncertain smile appeared on his lips, and he took a couple of steps in her direction.

"You Dr. Lawson?"

"Yes."

"How d'you do? Glad to meet you!" He surged forward, beaming, and extended his right hand.

Loretta had no choice but to offer hers in return; a thick gold ring bit into her fingers, and she winced at his grip.

"Had me worried there, you did," he said, releasing her. "Though you'd changed your mind. Who's your friend?" He nodded at Sally, conveying the impression he was just as pleased to see her as he was Loretta.

"This is Sally. She knew Sandra, too."

"Oh yeah—Sandra." He looked serious for a moment, then brightened. He pulled out the chair next to Loretta. "Mind if I—?"

"No, of course . . ."

He sat down. "Sally, Laura, and—who's this little fella?" He pointed to the pushchair.

Loretta frowned. Somewhere in her brain a connection was made, but she wasn't yet fully conscious of it. "It's not Lau—" she began, but Sally interrupted.

"She's a girl," she said with the vigour of affronted motherhood. "She's called Felicity." The baby stirred in her sleep, perhaps in response to her mother's use of her name, and let out a faint whimper.

"She is? Why you put her in that, then?" Fleming indicated Felicity's blue romper suit. "Don't you know the old saying? Blue for a boy, pink for a girl—" He registered Sally's expression and chuckled. "Suppose you young people don't go in for that sort of thing any more," he conceded. "You married, girl?" he asked, glancing at Sally's left hand where it still rested on the handle of the pushchair.

"No. Are you?"

"Me? *Course* I am. Been married to the same woman for thirty-two years, haven't I? Lovely woman, she is, wouldn't change her for the world . . . here, love." This was addressed to the waitress, a teenager with olive skin and short dark hair whom Loretta knew to be the daughter of the owners. As she obeyed his summons, Fleming threw out a question: "You girls want anything else?"

"No thanks," they said in unison.

"Suit yourself—and I was gonna treat you." He looked up at the waitress. "A nice cup of tea, love, with two sugars. She an Eyetie?" he asked in a scarcely lower voice as the girl disappeared into the kitchen.

"Her parents are Italian, yes," Loretta said, frowning at the pejorative.

"It's all right, love, I got nothing against the Eyeties," Fleming assured her without malice. "Make a bloody awful cup of tea, that's all. What's the nosh like here?" He seemed in no hurry to address the subject of the meeting.

"Mr. Fleming—" Loretta began.

"Bob, love—we're all friends here, aren't we?"

She ignored the remark, distrustful of his *bonhomie*. She hadn't forgotten the scowl she had seen on his face when he thought she had stood him up.

"You wanted to talk about Sandra," she said without preamble, and waited for his reaction.

At once his expression changed; she was aware of intense feeling in his face, though she wasn't certain what it was. His eyes, though, were cunning.

"You're right there, girl," he said, dropping his jocular manner. "Now don't get me wrong, I know she was a mate of yours. Liked her myself, I did.

"Yeah, I did," he went on, nodding as though someone had contradicted him. "But that don't change the fact she took me for a proper ride." His eyes glittered.

"What do you mean?" Loretta asked, doing her best to disguise her foreboding. "I don't even—you haven't said how you knew her."

"Worked for me, didn't she? Didn't she tell you?" He was watching her closely, and Loretta was relieved to be able to tell the truth.

"No." She shook her head vehemently. "I'm sure she never mentioned you."

"Oh. Funny, that."

"Where?" asked Sally, coming to Loretta's rescue. "Where did she work for you?"

"At the club," Fleming said, frowning at these questions.

"At the—" Loretta's forehead wrinkled as she tried to imagine Sandra in the sort of club she associated with Fleming—almost certainly some dive in Soho, she thought. "Doing what?" she asked.

"Manageress," Fleming said, feeling inside his jacket. "I put her in charge—trusted her, I did. Here, have a butcher's at this." He brought out a leaflet and handed it to Loretta.

"In The Pink," she read aloud. "Oh! You mean—" She stopped and went on reading. "South London's premier health and fitness centre. Sauna, gym, jacuzzi, weight training—our experienced instructors will devise your very own programme, tailored to your individual needs." There was a line drawing of a woman in a stripey leotard, her outstretched leg pointing to the club's address and a telephone number for making bookings. The leaflet was pale pink and Loretta suddenly remembered the blue membership cards in Sandra's suitcase.

"Wait a minute," she said. "She wasn't supposed to start this job till after Christmas. I don't see how—"

"After Christmas? That what she told you? Nah—July she came. Keep it—you never know . . ." He waved away the leaflet, which Loretta was attempting to return to him. "Yeah,

188

July she started. It's all in the records. I couldn't get her to move into the flat straightaway, there was a bit of argy-bargy about that—had to find someone for her place first, she said. August it was by the time she moved in—place was standing empty for weeks.''

"The flat?''

"Goes with the job, see. I like my managers on the premises where they can keep an eye on things. Leastways I do usually, but I made a big mistake with Sandra—had her fingers in the till, didn't she?''

"She what?'' Sally looked aghast.

Loretta bit her lip, hardly shocked at all. She hadn't been far out—the cash in the suitcase did belong to Fleming, and probably the money Sandra had paid into her bank account as well. She looked at him covertly, observing his air of flash affluence: the expensive coat, the signet ring which had crushed her fingers, the Rolex watch. She doubted if the amount Sandra had stolen was large by his standards, but she guessed it would be a matter of pride with him to get it back. Sandra had been on the run—and quite suddenly she wondered where Fleming had been on the night of the car crash. No, not Fleming himself, more likely one of his associates . . . She shivered.

"Not very warm in here, is it?'' she said quickly, and began pulling on her denim jacket. To her relief the waitress appeared with Fleming's tea and there was a natural lull in the conversation while he tasted it.

"Ugh.'' He pulled a face and reached for the sugar bowl. "Like I said—these Eyeties don't know how to make a decent cuppa.'' He added two heaped teaspoons and stirred noisily.

"How much did she . . . ?'' Loretta prompted, thinking she might as well know the worst.

"Who knows?'' Fleming scowled. "Five grand, maybe.'' Loretta could see that even the thought of it made him angry.

"Five thousand?'' Sally said incredulously.

"Thereabouts. By the time you add in what she was creaming off from the juice bar—''

At another time the peculiar image conjured up by this metaphor would have made Loretta smile. Now she said: "How d'you mean, add in?"

"Only the icing on the cake, that was. Mainly it come from the membership cards fiddle."

He saw their blank looks and launched into a lengthy explanation, the crux of which was that Sandra had falsified the club's records, offering a discount for cash on the annual fee of £200 to a small number of would-be members, and pocketing the money. The scam had been discovered by accident, two days before Christmas, when a woman who claimed to have lost her membership card couldn't be found on the list in the drawer of Sandra's desk. Had she not been careless, leaving her office unlocked while she slipped out to the bank, it was quite likely that the fiddle would have continued for some time.

"What did she say when you—I presume you told her she'd been found out?" asked Loretta.

"Never got the chance. Christmas Eve it was, by the time Sharon got hold of me. I goes straight down to the club and she's already scarpered. She was very matey with some of the instructors, Sandra, so maybe they tipped her off. Next thing I know is the wife's sister gets on the blower and says have we seen about Sandra in the *Daily Telegraph*. Her old man's a dentist," he added obscurely, perhaps to explain his sister-in-law's choice of newspaper.

"I had no idea," Loretta said quietly, thinking back to the evening of Sandra's arrival at her flat. Even when she found Sandra in tears, it had never occurred to her . . . Loretta realized she had at no point doubted Fleming's story, that it fitted all too well with the extraordinary picture of Sandra which had been emerging since the inquest.

"What's that, love?" Fleming glanced at his watch and smiled at her encouragingly, his good humour returning for no obvious reason.

"I was just wondering," Loretta said, taking the bull by the horns, "what all this has to do with me."

Fleming held up his hands. "Obvious, innit? I want my

190

money. Don't get me wrong, I'm not accusing you—but I gotta ask, haven't I? Mind if I smoke?" he asked unexpectedly, looking down and fumbling inside his jacket.

"Yes," Sally said flatly.

He brought his hand out empty, and there was a tense silence. Loretta wondered what reaction he expected from her.

"You're wasting your time," she said eventually, preparing herself for veiled threats. "I haven't got it."

"Not saying you have, am I? She might've left it at your place without you knowing, in her handbag or something."

"She took her handbag with her. She did leave a couple of bags behind—a holdall and a suitcase. I phoned her husband and he collected them last week."

"Oh." Fleming sounded disappointed. "That's it, then." The hand with the signet ring lay on the table, and he regarded it in silence.

Loretta's eyes narrowed; she hadn't expected him to give up as easily as this. She had an urge to say more, to protest her innocence, but repressed it, waiting to see what he would do next. Fleming withdrew his hand from the table and felt in one of his pockets, bringing out two twenty-pence pieces and placing them in front of him.

"For the cuppa," he said, and glanced at his watch. "Is that the time? Time I was off." He pushed back his chair and stood up, nodding to each of them in turn. "Nice to meet you, Sally, Laura."

Loretta opened her mouth but he was already heading for the door. He went out without a backward glance, leaving the two women staring after him in astonishment.

"What did you make of that?" Sally demanded, turning to Loretta.

She shrugged, saying nothing.

"But do you—d'you think he was telling the truth?"

"I suppose so."

"But it's—it's incredible. I can't imagine—how on earth did Sandra get mixed up with him?"

"He may have advertised the job somewhere," Loretta

suggested, remembering that Sandra had used the *Evening Standard* to find a tenant for her flat. Perhaps she'd also looked at the sits vac columns.

"Yes, but she must've been desperate . . ."

"Well, if she was sacked from her last job . . . You did say she left under some sort of cloud. She probably didn't have any references."

"Even so—Sandra's the last person . . . You really think she stole all that money?"

"I don't suppose he paid her much," Loretta pointed out, "especially with the flat thrown in."

Suddenly Sally's expression changed from unease to alarm. "God, Loretta, you don't think—"

Loretta sighed and held out her hands. "I doubt if he personally—I imagine he has other people . . ."

Abruptly Sally bent to wipe a dribble of saliva away from Felicity's lower lip. "I thought she might be awake by now," she said in a distracted voice. She screwed the paper handkerchief she had been using into a ball and dropped it into her bag.

"But how did he—who told him about Sandra staying with you?"

Loretta said: "I think I can guess."

Sally waited.

"Did you notice he called me Laura? Twice, when he arrived and at the end . . ."

"Oh yes, so he did." Sally frowned, not seeing the significance.

"Nobody knows—I haven't used it for years. Except when I was giving my statement last week. It says Laura Anne Lawson at the top. That policeman, the one who rang me at work, he asked for Laura Lawson."

"You don't think—"

"It's too much of a coincidence, surely?"

Sally screwed up her face in thought. "I don't know, it doesn't seem all that likely . . ."

"I'm surprised to hear you defending the police."

"I'm not. But Fleming's here in London and this detective

you're talking about is down in Hampshire. I can't see—well, let's not argue. What are you going to do now?''

Loretta shook her head. "I've no idea."

"What about the other detective, the nice one?"

"Ghilardi. He still hasn't phoned. Maybe I'll try the station again . . .''

Sally was looking at her watch. "Loretta, I've got to go. I promised to take Fliss round to Peter's mother's—I'm sorry."

Loretta's shoulders drooped, but she said: "Don't worry. Thanks for coming. Is it all right if I ring you later, when I've had time to think?"

"Of course. I'll be in this evening." Sally stood up and released the brake on Felicity's pushchair. "Oh, the bill—"

"Leave it, I'll see to it." Loretta began looking inside her shoulder-bag for her purse.

Still Sally hesitated. "Loretta—you will be careful, won't you?"

"Of course." Loretta looked up and smiled, though she didn't feel very cheerful.

"If I don't hear from you I'll ring," Sally continued, a worried look on her face. She bent and kissed Loretta's cheek, then manoeuvred the pushchair between tables to the door. An elderly man got up and opened it for her. Sally paused on the threshold and looked back over her shoulder.

"Bye, Loretta."

"Bye." Loretta watched Sally disappear into the street, suddenly aware of an uncomfortable prickling sensation at the back of her neck.

It took Loretta twenty minutes to walk home from the Superior Snack Bar, and she was fitting her key into the lock of the street door when she heard a faint miaow. It sounded like Bertie, and she turned her head, puzzled. How could he have got out into Liverpool Road? The noise came again; this time to her immense relief, clearly from *inside* the house.

"Bertie?" She bent to peer through the letter-box and was

rewarded by a loud wail from the cat, who jumped up and rested his paws on the door in an attempt to reach her.

"It's all right, I'm coming," she said, wrinkling her brow and wondering how he'd got into the hall. She turned the key and pushed open the door, herding him inside with her foot as he began to display an unhealthy interest in the outside world. She closed the door behind her and gave the light switch a hard push, glancing up the stairs. They stretched emptily in front of her, and she could hear nothing except the ecstatic purring of the cat as he rubbed himself against her calves. Still perplexed, she went to the front door of the downstairs flat, rapping on it with her knuckles.

"Shahin?"

As far as she knew Shahin had never used her key to the upstairs flat, and Loretta couldn't imagine what might have taken her up there this morning. In any case, Shahin was fond of Bertie, it seemed unlikely she would have been so careless—

"Shahin?" Loretta knocked more loudly, her stomach tightening. There was silence inside the flat and after a moment she turned away, noticing that the woman's mail was still lying undisturbed on top of the meter cupboard. She'd put it there on her way to meet Sally, observing that the top letter was from Shahin's relatives in Iran—a rare event as the postal service in that country had been brought almost to a standstill by the war with Iraq. Loretta wondered if she had gone away for the weekend.

"Come on, Bertie." She scooped him up and began climbing the stairs. Had she inadvertently let him out of the flat herself when she set off for the Superior Snack Bar? She didn't think so; she hadn't been in a hurry, and she had a fairly clear memory of leaving him curled up on the kitchen table. But that meant—she shook her head, rejecting the only other explanation that came to mind. He must have slipped past when she wasn't looking; she would have to be more careful in future. As she reached the bend Bertie struggled violently and leapt from her arms, hurtling down the stairs the way they had come. He was determined to make the most of his new-found freedom, Loretta thought, glancing uneasily upwards before continuing her climb.

She had just reached her front door when the light went out, plunging her into darkness. She groped for the time-switch, little shivers running up and down her spine, and breathed a sigh of relief when she could see again. Inserting the key into the lock, she pushed the door inwards and took a couple of cautious steps across the threshold. Inside she waited and listened, receiving a welcome impression of emptiness which slowly calmed her thudding heart. Tiptoeing to the door of the kitchen, she peered inside and was reassured by the sight of that morning's *Guardian* lying on the table, her breakfast plate and the teapot on the draining-board exactly where she'd left them.

In the drawing-room the answering-machine was flashing but Loretta was too preoccupied to play back her messages. She checked that nothing had been taken—the stereo system was intact, and a valuable Turkish rug was in its usual place in front of the fire. Her fears gradually subsiding, she went back into the hall and was about to go upstairs when she heard the pounding of paws behind her. Bertie shot past into the kitchen, performed a skidding turn round the legs of the table and disappeared through the front door before she had a chance to stop him. Loretta had relaxed enough to smile at these antics, but she was still uneasy as she made her way upstairs, peering into the bathroom, utility room and bedroom in turn. Nothing seemed to be missing; her one valuable piece of jewellery, a pair of amethyst ear-rings which had been a birthday present from John Tracey years before, was lying on the dressing-table where any half-competent thief would have seen it. Loretta felt almost dizzy with relief, and was on the verge of leaving the room when she noticed a hollow in the otherwise flat surface of the quilt. She moved to straighten it, putting out a hand without conscious thought, and then froze in mid-air. Her mind went back several hours to the moment of getting out of bed, and she pictured herself grasping the quilt with both hands, as she did every morning, and giving it a good shake. Then she'd had a bath, returning to the room to take her red corduroy skirt from the wardrobe . . . She remembered slipping it over her head, sitting down to fasten her black ankle boots, standing up and smoothing out the indentation in the cover—

Someone *had* been in the room. Loretta breathed in sharply, realizing she had begun to shake. She felt an urge to run, to get out of the flat as fast as she could, and she was at the door before she got a grip on herself. She stopped, forcing herself to look back, and tried to think logically. Could she have been mistaken? She stared at the hollow in the quilt, the rounded shape of a human bottom—it was so slight a clue to hang a theory on. The she remembered the cat's escape from the flat—either event meant nothing on its own, but together . . .

She took the stairs two a time, coming to a halt in the hall as she realized the pointlessness of her flight. The intruder was gone, she'd checked the entire flat—her eyes came to rest on the front door, on the untouched lock which had provided no protection at all. It was a Yale—child's play to a professional, she'd heard, and she'd been meaning to change it since the recent spate of burglaries in the area . . . Loretta started as she heard a throaty sound from the stairwell, pushing her hair back from her face as she belatedly recognized Bertie's voice. She peered into the shadows, failing to spot him until a second noise gave him away, crouched three steps down and hard against the right-hand wall.

"Here, Bertie," she called in a small voice. The cat gathered himself into a tense ball, as though they were playing some kind of game, and raced past her into the flat. Loretta saw how the intruder, or intruders, had overlooked him; the grey animal was almost invisible in poor light. But what had they been after in the flat? Nothing had been taken—

Loretta wheeled round and hurried into the drawing-room. She pulled open the door of the pine cupboard, reaching inside to the shelf on which she'd placed the letters she'd collected from Sandra's flat in Notting Hill. They weren't there. She straightened up, the blood rushing to her face. She recalled the ease with which Bob Fleming had accepted her denial of any knowledge of the missing cash, her sense when he left the café that she hadn't heard the last of him, and realized she'd been tricked. Fleming had never intended to come to the flat, his phone call the previous evening had been carefully staged to frighten her into meeting him elsewhere, giving his associates time to get in and search—no wonder he'd scowled when he thought she'd failed to keep the appointment, Loretta thought grimly. She folded her arms tightly across her chest, not knowing whether she was more frightened or angry: what if she'd changed her mind, had been alone in the building when the intruder slipped inside?

She shut the cupboard door, harder than she intended so it rocked against the wall, and hurried to the phone. So agitated was she that her first attempt at dialling produced a wrong number, a grumpy man who asked her why she didn't ring 999 if she was so anxious to speak to the police. Loretta got him off the line and tried again, taking more care this time. A tired male voice answered the CID phone, and Loretta demanded to speak to Derek Ghilardi.

"Speaking."

"Oh!" The reply brought her up short; she hadn't expected to get hold of him so easily. "I—it's Loretta Lawson. You were supposed to ring—"

"You didn't get my message? Your answering-machine must be on the blink."

"I haven't had a chance to—I've been burgled!"

"Burgled?"

"Well—searched. I've just come home and the cat was in the hall, and when I looked for Sandra's letters they've been taken—"

"Hang on. What letters?"

"The ones from her flat," Loretta said without thinking. "He got me out of here and someone got in and looked for the money—they didn't find it, so maybe he took them out of spite, or maybe he didn't have time to read them, he couldn't know how soon I'd come back—"

"Sorry, Loretta, I've been up all night—can you go a bit slower?"

Loretta raised her eyes to the ceiling, taking in nothing except the fact that Ghilardi didn't seem to be listening properly. It didn't even occur to her to wonder why he hadn't had any sleep.

"*Fleming*, that's who I'm talking about," she pressed on. "Bob Fleming."

"This is the bloke who says your friend worked for him, right? The one who turned up here the other day?"

"Yes! So you do know—"

"Only at second-hand. I was going to tell you—I know I said I'd phone last night but all hell broke loose . . ." He paused, sounding utterly weary. "You've only just caught me, I'm going off duty any minute." There was a noise as though he was stifling a yawn.

"Sorry, Loretta. The thing is, it's not my case any more. I was out seeing someone when this bloke Fleming turned up. Steve Farr talked to him—you know who I mean. He was coming in as you went out."

Ghilardi sounded slightly embarrassed. Loretta had been listening impatiently, on the verge of interrupting him, but this last sentence brought her up short. She recalled the tall, sandy-haired man who had passed her in the corridor at Lymington police station, the sly look on his face.

"Hmm!" she exclaimed, wondering why she hadn't made the connection before.

"Yes—" Ghilardi was taken aback.

"Do you realize what he did? It's him who gave Fleming my name—this is all his fault, my flat being—"

"He did what?" Ghilardi was suddenly alert.

"He gave Fleming my name!" Loretta repeated angrily. She took a deep breath and explained.

"Well, well, well," Ghilardi remarked when she'd finished. He sounded almost pleased.

"Is that all you can say?"

"No, wait a minute—this might come in very handy. It wouldn't be the first time—"

"Oh, you do believe me, then?"

"I don't say he wrote your name on a bit of paper and

198

handed it over. He did have the file out, though . . . You're obviously upset—are you thinking about making a formal complaint?''

"A complaint?'' It hadn't occurred to her, and she was astonished that Ghilardi, of all people, should suggest it.

"I don't mean you should go through with it,'' he added hastily, lowering his voice. "But it'd give me a lever . . . He's always pulling tricks like this, it's bloody annoying.''

"I'm sorry, I don't follow—''

"Muscling in on other people's cases,'' Ghilardi explained. "After he talked to this Fleming bloke he got all excited . . . Had a word with the boss—'Derek's pretty tied up with the Owen murder, hasn't got the time, blah blah blah.' If I can put the wind up him, say you want to make a complaint but I think I can talk you out of it—you with me?''

"Yes,'' Loretta said eagerly. "You'd be back on the case—you could find out where Fleming was on New Year's Eve?''

"Steve may have done that already—I don't know without looking at the file.''

"Tell him what you like,'' Loretta said recklessly. "He was pretty rude on the phone yesterday—he very nearly accused me of being a *thief*.''

"Take no notice. He's a bit of a—a chauvinist, actually. Likes giving women a hard time.''

"Oh—'' Loretta was momentarily taken aback by Ghilardi's analysis of his colleague's behaviour. "But you see what I'm getting at—if Fleming's going to all this trouble to find his money—''

"I'll have to get the file,'' Ghilardi said again. He sounded exhausted. "Look, there's nothing I can do at the moment—Steve's not in today, and the boss is tied up. Your flat in much of a mess?''

"No, they seem to have picked the locks or something. I'll have to get them changed.''

"Sounds like a good idea. You said something about some letters—''

"Oh yes.'' Loretta blushed. "I went to Sandra's flat—the one in Notting Hill. She rented it out ages ago, when she

199

went to work for Fleming. I was going to tell you all this but you were so hard to get hold of . . . The woman there gave me some letters, I didn't know what to do—'' She swallowed. ''They weren't all that interesting, to be honest, mostly Christmas Cards. But there was one from her bank, about her overdraft, she was definitely in financial trouble— I suppose the manager could give you a copy. And a Christmas card from—well, I got the impression he was a—a boyfriend.'' She had been about to say lover, but changed her mind at the last moment. ''Someone called Paul. But I don't suppose it matters much, now we know about Fleming . . .'' She had the impression Ghilardi was no longer paying attention, and thought she ought to bide her time, wait until he was less tired. ''Shall I ring you on Monday?''

''Yeah, or I'll ring you. Have you been on to the local boys?''

''Who?''

''The police.''

''No, I didn't think—''

''You'd better give them a ring. Give them my name if they want the background.''

''Oh—all right.'' The idea of the Islington police tramping through her flat, of telling the story all over again, was not very welcome to Loretta.

''I'm going to get some sleep,'' Ghilardi told her. ''You're probably pretty safe—whoever it was is unlikely to come back again. D'you think the money was in your flat, by the way? Hidden somewhere, I mean?''

''Of cour—I doubt it,'' Loretta amended.

''Right. Bye, Loretta—Oh, I've got your book.'' His voice was suddenly perkier.

''My book?''

''Yeah, you left it behind. By some bloke called Blake. I'll have to get it back to you.''

''Oh, it doesn't matter.'' Loretta had been vaguely aware that the Nicholas Blake novel was missing, but assumed she'd dropped it in her car or left it at the office. Now she remembered Ghilardi picking it up in the interview room.

"Maybe I could drop it by, next time I'm in London?" she heard him say.

"Don't go to any trouble, I can always get another copy—"

"No trouble. Islington, you live, don't you? Know any good Italian restaurants?"

"Well, yes—" Loretta couldn't help sounding surprised.

"Maybe I could buy you dinner some time. Unless you're coming down this way—then I could take you to my dad's place. You did say you liked Italian food?"

"Yes . . ."

"It's a date. Don't forget to call the police. Bye, Loretta."

"Bye."

She put down the phone, in a state of some confusion. Ghilardi seemed as interested in her as he was in finding out what had happened to Sandra. Her doubts multiplied: was that why he'd spent so long talking to her after the inquest? She remembered the way he'd approached her in court, her initial assumption that he was trying to chat her up. Loretta suddenly felt tired; she let her head fall back and flexed her shoulders. Was it important? She wanted to know the truth about Sandra's death, and she'd much rather Ghilardi was in charge of the inquiry than Steve Farr. Just thinking about the sergeant made her cross.

Her gaze fell on the answering-machine and she realized she still hadn't played back her messages. She activated it and waited.

"Hi, Derek Ghilardi calling. It's—yeah, it's half past eleven on Saturday morning. I'll call back." His voice was casual, more like that of a friend than a policeman, and Loretta's impression that he had a personal interest in her was reinforced. She shook her head, unable to cope with this unexpected development, and waited to see if there was another message.

"Hello—" She was startled to hear Robert's voice issuing from the machine. "Loretta—I was just wondering how you are . . ." His voice was hesitant, quite unlike him. "I'll call again."

There were no more messages and the tape began to rewind. Loretta pulled a face, suddenly reminded of the nightmare from which she'd woken in panic on Wednesday night. It was as she feared, Robert was trying to revive the relationship. His promise to ring back was sufficiently alarming for her to reach out and turn on the answering-machine. Thus protected against further calls, she considered Ghilardi's advice to phone the local police. What was the point? No doubt the intruder had worn gloves, and they might well be sceptical about her claim that a search had taken place at all: there were no splintered locks, just the cat's presence on the stairs, the hollow in the quilt, the missing letters—and the latter would take some explaining. Loretta decided to leave things as they were, and reached for the Yellow Pages to look for a locksmith.

She found one in Holloway Road and had a long conversation with a helpful man about which type of lock would be the most suitable, both for her front door and for the street door she shared with Shahin. She was about to ask him to send someone round that afternoon when she remembered that her neighbour was away.

"Oh—I'd better wait till she comes back," she said regretfully, thinking it was hardly fair to change the locks without consulting her.

She put the phone down and looked at her watch, surprised to see it was only half past one; she felt as if she'd already lived through a complete day. She got up and looked for her shoulder-bag, thinking she would go to Woolworth's in Chapel Market and buy a sturdy bolt for her front door. It would make her feel a bit safer while she was inside the flat, and with any luck Shahin would be back on Monday. She found the bag on the floor in the hall, where she'd dumped it; checking that her purse and keys were inside, she closed the front door carefully behind her and went down the stairs.

13

THE FOLLOWING MORNING LORETTA DREW back the shiny new bolt on her front door and slipped downstairs to pick up the *Sunday Herald*. She scanned the front page as she returned to her flat, and her eye was caught by a headline: "Two held in Christmas card killing." The brief story underneath reported that two men had been charged with the murder of seventeen-year-old Yvonne Owen, a student whose body had been found on the outskirts of Lymington just before Christmas. *Two* men, Loretta thought, appalled, and pushed away the horrible image this information conjured up. She recalled Ghilardi's description of the murder as particularly nasty, but she hadn't known any of the details—had hardly thought about it, so preoccupied was she with Sandra's death. It certainly explained why Ghilardi had been up all Friday night; he might even have been interrogating the suspects. Loretta wondered what sort of men they were, why they'd done it, and shuddered. Then she reminded herself that they hadn't been tried yet, reading on and discovering that they were due to appear in court in Lymington on Monday. Would Ghilardi have to be present? She couldn't bear the thought of a further delay before inquiries into Bob Fleming got under way. But perhaps Ghilardi was right, and Steve Farr had already initiated them . . . She tutted with impatience, irritated by the revelation that, against

203

her expectations, office politics seemed to affect the police as much as any other organization.

"In, Bertie. I'll feed you in a moment."

His appetite whetted by the outing of the previous day, the cat was now trying to get out of the flat at every opportunity. Shooing him inside, Loretta went into the kitchen, scraped the last third of a tin of cat food into a dish, and put it on the floor. She filled the kettle and, while she waited for it to boil, glanced over the rest of the *Herald* front page, learning that the AIDS toll had risen again, and that severe weather in Scotland was expected to move south, paralysing major roads in the north of England—

The phone rang and Loretta looked up in surprise. It wasn't even nine o'clock, and she wasn't expecting any calls.

"Hello," she said warily, wondering if the early morning nuisance caller who had plagued her for a few weeks the previous autumn had come back.

"Loretta? Where have you *been*?"

"Oh, *Sally*." Loretta was relieved. "I tried ringing you last night but you hadn't got back. I was feeling a bit—I decided to go to the pictures, on the spur of the moment really, and it was quite late when I came home . . ." Loretta remembered that Sally didn't know about the search of her flat, and she reached for a kitchen chair to make herself comfortable.

"You left your answering-machine off," Sally announced before Loretta could begin. "I rang and rang—I was so worried, and there's something I've been dying to tell you. I've found out how Sandra met Bob Fleming."

"You have?" Loretta was only mildly interested; that part of the story seemed like ancient history to her now.

"Don't you want to know?" Sally sounded disappointed.

"Of course—"

This half-hearted assurance was enough. "Well, I wasn't convinced she'd answered an advert or something—I just couldn't imagine her applying for that sort of job. I was sure there must be something else . . . I couldn't think of any way of finding out, so in the end I rang the unit, more or less on spec. Eventually I got hold of Frank, the bloke I was telling you about—the one who runs it. They wouldn't give me his home number but I said it was urgent and they got him to ring me back . . . He didn't want to say anything, but I kept on—I had to tell him what it was about, I'm sorry. I didn't mention your name or anything—''

"It wouldn't matter if you had, I'm sure he doesn't know me from Adam." Loretta couldn't help smiling at Sally's ingrained habit of caution.

"Oh." Sally sounded surprised. "Anyway, what he said in the end was—Sandra *was* asked to leave because of a relationship with a client. We'd already guessed that, of course, that's not what I—

"This is the new bit," she went on, unable to hide her excitement. "I found out his name—the client. And it's *Fleming*.''

She paused for effect. Loretta's eyes opened wide, and Sally now had her full attention.

"Fleming? You don't mean Sandra was having an affair with Bob Fleming?" Loretta asked incredulously.

"No, silly; his *son*.''

"Good God." Loretta's mind scrolled back like a computer, retrieving bits of information which might connect with Sally's revelation. She pictured the suggestive postcard in Sandra's luggage, the Christmas card with the leering Santa.

"Is his name Paul?" she asked suddenly.

"Oh, I think—I don't remember," Sally said, crestfallen. "It might've been. It was the Fleming bit that—Why'd you ask?''

"The Christmas card—I told you about it; the one sent to Norfolk Gardens. It was signed Paul.''

"Oh, but why would he send it there? I mean, if she was working for his dad—I presume he got her the job in the first place. He'd be bound to know she'd moved—''

"I see what you mean," Loretta said slowly. "Unless . . . unless his dad didn't know about them having an affair. I got the impression—I had a feeling he was quite young, whoever

205

wrote the card—'' she was thinking more about the postcard than the Christmas card, but she couldn't tell Sally that ''—and I don't suppose Fleming would be very pleased at the idea . . . His son being seduced by an older woman, I mean. He would see it like that, don't you think?''

"God, yes," Sally agreed. "All that guff about being married to the same woman for thirty years. When it comes to sex, crooks are the most moralistic . . ."

"So maybe they thought it was safer to use her old address. We don't know how often Fleming goes to the club, or whether she had a separate letter-box . . ."

"Gosh, do you think he found out?" Sally asked suddenly. "I mean, it gives him an extra motive—"

"I was thinking that, too."

"Just as well you didn't turn up at that caff on your own," Sally exclaimed.

"Oh, I was quite safe—that was just a ruse," Loretta said without thinking. "I don't—"

"What d'you mean, a ruse?"

"Of course, I haven't had a chance . . ." Loretta described what had happened at her flat the previous day.

"You mean you stayed there on your own last night?" Sally asked, aghast. "You should have come here—I could have made you a bed on the sofa."

"It's all right, Sally, I don't think they'll be back—neither does Ghilardi. To be honest, I didn't even call the local police."

"You're mad! Sandra's *dead*, Loretta, you seem to have forgotten that—"

"I know, but I haven't got what they want—what Fleming wants."

"But he might be a—a *murderer*."

"I think that's going a bit far . . . It's quite possible he was there on New Year's Eve, I agree, or he sent someone after her—" Loretta, who had been quite comfortable on her own in the building, suddenly felt uneasy.

"Someone who attacked her—someone she was so frightened of she crashed her car—"

206

Loretta sighed. "I don't think there's any point . . . Did you find out anything else from—from Frank?" she asked, changing the subject.

"Anything—no. Look Loretta, I don't think you should be there on your own. Is your neighbour at home? Downstairs, I mean?"

"I—I'm pretty sure she's gone away for the weekend."

Sally gave an exasperated sigh. "That makes it—why don't you come round for lunch and we'll talk about it?"

"Thanks, Sally, but I can't. It's my sister's birthday on Tuesday and I've got to go to Camden Market and look for a present—it's my last chance. And I've got masses of marking to do. Everything's all right, really. I've talked to the police in Lymington, they'll be on to Fleming tomorrow—"

"What about this evening, then? Fliss'll be in bed, we can have a proper chat."

"We-ell—"

"*Please*, Loretta. Come about eight. It won't be anything special, just some pasta, but—but it'll make me feel better," Sally finished honestly.

"All right." Loretta gave in. "D'you want me to bring anything?" She had been planning a rather pleasant supper, and she could at least make the pudding—

"No, leave it to me." Sally said firmly. "See you at eight."

Loretta put down the phone, pulling a face. She was perfectly safe in the flat, Sally was being wildly over-protective . . . She boiled the kettle again, made a cup of tea, and took it back to bed, snuggling up under the quilt with her arms free to hold the paper. It was getting colder, she thought, goose pimples appearing on her bare skin. Either that, or the conversation with Sally had unsettled her.

Half an hour later she got out of bed, put on her warmest clothes and, in a somewhat disgruntled frame of mind, left the flat for her trip to Camden.

Loretta ran downstairs at ten past nine the following morning, afraid she was going to be late for her ten o'clock lecture. The post had arrived and she scooped up three letters, two for herself and one for Shahin. The latter she added to the pile of envelopes on the meter cupboard, then glanced at the others. She recognized her mother's handwriting on one of them and stuffed it into her shoulder-bag; it was probably a plea not to forget Jenny's birthday, and her sister's present was sitting in her bag, waiting to be posted. The second letter, a largeish brown envelope with an Oxford postmark, had her puzzled for a moment until she realized it was from Robert. The envelope was thick, as though it contained several sheets of paper, and Loretta's face fell. Robert hadn't phoned since Saturday, and she had been hoping that he'd thought better of it. To be fair, the letter had been posted on Friday, and he might now be regretting . . . She didn't have time to deal with it now, she thought, checking her watch; she should be running through her ideas on the interplay of tragedy and comedy in the novels of Elizabeth Bowen, not dithering in the hall over a letter from an ex-lover. She slid the envelope into her bag, next to the letter from her mother, and let herself out into the street.

After the majority of her students had filed out, she lingered in the lecture theatre for ten minutes or so, talking to one of her brightest third-years about *The Death of the Heart*, and got back to her office to find a message on her desk to call Mr. Gillard. She stared at it for a moment, then recognized it as Mrs. Whittaker's attempt at Ghilardi. She picked up the phone, dialled Lymington police station, and got the engaged tone. Loretta looked at her watch, deciding she'd try again in five minutes, then remembered that Martha Campbell, a second-year who seemed to be having a lot of problems with her set work, had an appointment to bring in a much overdue essay at eleven-thirty. There was a knock on the door and the girl appeared, slightly early and with a sheepish grin on her face.

"Don't tell me," cried Loretta, correctly reading her expression. "What's the excuse this time? Martha, we really can't go on like this—"

"I'm sorry, Dr. Lawson. I was going to do it over the weekend, honestly I was, but I got arrested—"

"*Arrested?*"

"Yes—I thought you'd approve." She looked hurt. "It was at the South African embassy, the twenty-four hour picket . . ."

Loretta dropped her head into her hands, completely disarmed. It was, she had to admit, the most novel excuse she'd ever heard.

"We weren't doing anything," Martha was assuring her, "just standing on the pavement, but this policeman appeared and said we were causing an obstruction . . . I pointed out people could get by, and the next thing I knew I was in this police van—"

Loretta lifted her head. "And you didn't think to mention you had an essay to write on consciousness and the death of the self in *The Waves*?" She held up her hand. "All right, that was a joke. Did they charge you?"

"No. In the end they just let us go."

"All right. You've got till Friday. This is your last chance. I mean it. That essay has got to be on my desk at ten o'clock, or—"

"Thank you, Dr. Lawson, it will be, I promise."

Martha scuttled towards the door, disappearing through it before Loretta could specify what course of action she would take if the essay failed to materialize. It was just as well, for she hated invoking formal procedures against even the most slovenly of her students. She reached for the phone to try Ghilardi again. She was told he'd nipped out for five minutes, so she left her name and number and put down the phone. She stared restlessly round the room, and her eye fell on her shoulder-bag, reminding her that she hadn't yet opened the morning's post. She went over to the bag, unenthusiastically drawing out the envelope from Robert, and slid her finger under the flap at the back. Inside she felt something glossy, and when she upended the envelope a bundle of photographs fell out. There was a note on top, held in place by an elastic

209

band, and she read: "Thought you'd like so see these. Keep them—I've got copies of the ones I want. Robert."

It was so short and to the point that Loretta was almost disappointed. She removed the elastic band, gazing at a picture of herself in her red coat on Hampstead Heath. She remembered the occasion; she and Robert had gone for a walk there one Sunday afternoon before Christmas. There were two more from the same day, then a photograph of herself and Robert peering tipsily at the camera over an impressive collection of wine and Perrier bottles. She stared at it, wondering when and where it had been taken, and it was the gold dress which eventually jogged her memory: Christmas Eve, in a restaurant on Islington Green. They had been getting on well that night, she thought with a tiny pang of regret—as well as they'd ever done, which wasn't saying much. She passed on to the next picture, squinting at a print which had somehow got in upside-down.

"Oh!" She'd turned it round and Sandra was smiling up at her, a champagne glass held high in one hand. Loretta recognized the background as her own kitchen, and realized that the picture had been taken on Christmas Day. Poor Sandra—she looked so cheerful, even if her expression had been assumed for the camera, and only a week later . . .

Loretta shivered violently and shuffled the picture to the back. Now she was looking at herself and Sandra sitting side by side on the grey sofa in her drawing-room; now one of herself by the fireplace; now a close-up of Sandra's face, this time topped by a paper hat which came down almost to the top of her glasses. Loretta stared at the picture, which was far from flattering; the silly hat emphasized the length of Sandra's face, making her look horsey, and her eyes were unnaturally large behind her glasses. Loretta couldn't imagine why Sandra had allowed Robert to take it, presumably she hadn't realized what she looked like. Suddenly something about the photo caught Loretta's attention; she held it up, observing it closely. The phone rang and she groped for it, her eyes still fixed on the image in front of her.

"Hello?"

"Loretta? Is that you? It's Derek Ghilardi."

Loretta put down the picture. "You got my message?"

"Yes, and you'll be pleased to know it worked."

"You mean—"

"Steve saw sense, yes. And you'll be interested to know I've just had a call back from a DS in Balham who knows all about Bob Fleming."

"He does?"

"Yep. They've had their eye on him for some time. Seems he hasn't put a foot wrong since he finished a stretch for armed robbery seven or eight years ago, but they've got a file as thick as a telephone directory . . . He's clever—he's got two or three straight firms as a front, including the health club and a bathroom business—"

"A *bathroom* business?" Loretta sounded incredulous.

"Yeah, you know—they come round to your house and draw the thing, fit it, the lot. Very good way of laundering dirty money—sorry, no pun intended. They do the job cheap, file false invoices for twice the amount—very useful little number."

"But what do you think he's—what's his real business?"

"He's a fence. He's given up the dirty work himself, lets other people take the risk. He's got some pretty nasty friends—they think he works on and off for the Cook brothers." The name meant nothing to Loretta. "Anyway, this DS is going round to have a word—see how Mr. Fleming claims to have spent New Year's Eve."

"Won't he have an alibi?" Loretta inquired.

"Bound to, but you've got to start somewhere. Come on, Loretta, this is progress. This time on Tuesday we'd never even heard of Bob Fleming."

"I suppose . . ." Loretta felt suddenly despondent, sure that the mystery surrounding Sandra's death would never be cleared up.

Ghilardi, by contrast, was in an ebullient mood. "I'm on the trail of Fleming's money," he told her. "Not that I give a toss whether he gets it back, I just want to get a clear picture. Thanks for your tip about the bank—I've put in a

211

request to the manager to have a look at her account. She may have paid the lot in, you never know. It wasn't in her luggage, by the way, I've checked with the husband—"

"*What?*"

"Yeah, spoke to him this morning. There's nothing in her bags but clothes—"

"He's lying!"

"How d'you mean?" Ghilardi's voice had sharpened.

"I—" Loretta bit her lip, then blurted out the truth.

Ghilardi heard her out in silence. He said reproachfully: "You might have told us all this before, Loretta."

"I didn't know he was going to lie, did I? And I did try to tell you, but you were never in—"

"Steve Farr would have your guts for garters, you know that? I've got his notes here, you said—"

"He only asked if she'd left anything behind, he didn't say anything about what was in them!"

"Yeah, but you must've known what he was after."

"I—I'm sorry," she said in a low voice. "You do believe me, don't you?"

Ghilardi sighed heavily. "Yeah, I suppose—thousands wouldn't. You academics," he added unexpectedly. "Thinking you know what's best . . . Let's get this straight. You say there was how much in this suitcase?"

"Nearly two and a half thousand pounds," Loretta said. "I've got it written down somewhere—"

"That'll do for now. And you're sure you put it back?"

"Of *course.*"

"Don't get excited. I'm just trying to—where did you put it exactly?"

"In the case—Oh, I see. Almost on top, I think I put a dress over it . . ."

"So if he just lifted the lid, he wouldn't necessarily see it?"

Loretta frowned. "I suppose not, but surely he'd have a proper look?"

"He wasn't very co-operative in the first place—said the

whole idea was preposterous. I'll have to get back to him. Anything else you haven't told me, Loretta?''

"No—" She felt like a naughty schoolgirl. She remembered the photograph of Sandra, lying on the desk in front of her, and she picked it up eagerly, glad to have a reason to change the subject. "There is one thing—something I've only just thought of," she added quickly. "I've been looking at some photos, a friend took them at Christmas—"

"And?" Ghilardi said impatiently.

"Well, she's wearing glasses in all of them. Those pictures you showed me—I don't remember seeing them."

"She was in a car crash," the detective pointed out. "Things get thrown around—"

"Oh—you mean they were in the wreckage?" Loretta asked, relieved.

Ghilardi didn't answer directly. "What're you getting at?"

"Just—well, if they weren't in the car—" She didn't want to spell out what she'd imagined—a blow to Sandra's face, her glasses breaking, the woman being dragged to the car . . .

"I'll check," Ghilardi told her without enthusiasm. "There'll be an inventory. You sure she always wore them? What about contact lenses?"

"Not while she was staying here," Loretta said confidently. "We shared a bathroom."

"I'll check," Ghilardi said again. "Now, about this money. I'll go back to Neil, but I'm probably going to have to get another statement from you. Unless he changes his story there may be trouble."

"You don't believe me!" Loretta felt betrayed.

Ghilardi sighed again. "I do, actually. Why'd you have to spring this on me, just when everything was shaping up so nicely?"

Loretta assumed the question was rhetorical, and treated it as such.

"You going to be there all day?"

"Yes," she said meekly, her mind racing. Should she contact a solicitor? She'd never employed one, except for conveyancing, and she hadn't a clue where to start.

213

"OK—leave it with me. I'll be in touch. Bye."

Loretta put the phone down without answering, a tight feeling in her chest. What the hell was Tom Neil up to? Maybe Ghilardi was right, maybe he'd just glanced inside the suitcase . . . She certainly hoped so. It occurred to her to ring him herself, to urge him to have a more thorough look inside the suitcase, and she was reaching for the phone when she realized it would only make things worse. It was acting on her own initiative that had got her into this situation; she had no choice but to trust Ghilardi.

She was leaning back in her chair, trying to persuade herself that she had nothing to fear, when an unpleasant thought came into her head. Perhaps Tom Neil *wanted* to get her into trouble. He had been pretty unfriendly when he arrived at her flat—

Loretta jumped, someone was knocking on her door. "Come in," she croaked, then cleared her throat and said it again, louder.

"Loretta, hi." It was Sarah Guzelian. "You still on for tonight?"

"Tonight?" Loretta's mind went blank, then she remembered her arrangement to eat with Sarah and discuss the crime fiction seminars. Crime fiction: she was struck by the irony.

"Yes—yes, of course."

"You're through around six, right?"

"Yes." She realized with alarm that she had another lecture at five o'clock.

"I'll come by your office, OK?"

"OK."

Sarah looked at her oddly. "See you later."

"Bye," Loretta said to the closing door. She swivelled her head to look at the blank computer screen, staring at it as though the machine contained all the answers in the world and would spill them out if only she knew which keys to press.

14

THERE WERE FLURRIES OF SNOW ON THE pavement as Loretta got out of a taxi in Liverpool Road just after midnight. The temperature had been dropping all evening and it looked as though the weather forecast had been correct in predicting the imminent arrival of severe weather from the north.

"Reckon we're getting our white Christmas late this year," the taxi driver said cheerfully, feeling in a leather pouch for change of Loretta's ten-pound note. "You'll be skating to work tomorrow. Doesn't bother me—I'll be in bed," he added, registering Loretta's look of surprise. "Ta, love." He took the fifty-pence piece she offered him as a tip, waved, and drove off.

Loretta turned and headed for the street door, keys in hand. She hadn't intended to return so late, but Sarah had surprised her by suggesting they go to a screening of an old Visconti film before eating. Loretta relaxed in the cinema, largely because she was away from a phone and it was pointless to worry about if and when Ghilardi would ring. It had taken a superhuman effort on her part not to call him, especially as the afternoon wore on with no word. She'd invented various excuses to pick up the phone—she'd forgotten to tell Ghilardi about Sandra's relationship with Paul Fleming, that was one of them—but somehow she managed to stick to her resolution. When Sarah arrived at twenty past six Loretta could tell from her colleague's quizzical expression that she knew something was wrong, but she didn't mention it, probably remembering Friday's rebuff. By the time the lights came up in the cinema Loretta was feeling more like her normal self, and she was even able to hold her own in a lively discussion of trends in crime fiction over dinner in Charlotte Street, in a different Greek restaurant from the one in which she'd argued with Robert. She had parted from Sarah with regret, watching her through the back window of the taxi until she disappeared into Warren Street tube station. The American woman, who had taken self-defence classes in New York, refused to be intimidated into paying for expensive cab rides while the Underground system was still running.

Loretta let herself into the building, noticing out of the corner of her eye that Shahin still hadn't collected her post. She closed the door, wondering when her neighbour would come back; she didn't want to wait too long before changing the locks. Such chores tended to be forgotten if they weren't dealt with quickly. Perhaps she should pin a note to Shahin's door—Loretta yawned and began climbing the stairs, unbuttoning her heavy coat. The stairwell was still warm, even though the radiator in the hall turned itself off around eleven, and she was aware of a delicious sensation of languor. Even if the answering-machine was flashing she would ignore it, leave it until morning.

Loretta reached the top of the stairs and as she inserted her key into the front door the stair light went out. She didn't bother to reach for the switch, just gave the door a gentle push and stepped into the moonlit hall.

"What—"

A shadow moved and pain exploded in the left side of her head. Lights flashed before her eyes in spider-web patterns, and she staggered forwards, her head seeming to expand until she was no longer conscious of her surroundings. She collided with something and lost her balance, falling to the floor where she lay immobile, aware of nothing but pain and the firework darkness in her head. Then there was a shift, and a sort of clouded consciousness began to return. Loretta groaned and tried to raise herself on her left elbow, a strange sensation in her head as though it was slowly shrinking to its normal size. She was starting to take in things outside herself: moonlight streaming through the open kitchen door, a small table lying across her legs and a man—a man *whimpering* behind her.

She tried to turn her head and cried out, dizzy with sudden pain. Struggling to a sitting position, she knew she was in danger, that she had to get past the crying man, but a spasm of weakness passed through her and she remained where she was. Now the pain was coming in waves, and she put up a hand to the left side of her head, remembering she had been wearing a beret . . . It was gone, and her hair was a sticky mess.

The whimpering noise was subsiding. Fearing a fresh attack, Loretta put both hands on the floor, trying to get into a kneeling position. Her fingers touched something reedy which snapped and crumbled, and it took her a moment to identify the dried flowers which had been standing in a vase on the table she'd knocked over. She brushed them aside, gave up the attempt to get to her feet and began crawling towards the open front door.

"No!"

The door slammed, followed by the bolt, and then someone was clutching at her back, trying to haul her away. Loretta screamed and struggled, sickened by whisky fumes and the touch of her attacker.

"Don't—I'm trying to *help* you!" The man's voice was high-pitched, hysterical.

Loretta gathered her strength and threw off the enfolding arms, staggering to her feet, but the effort was too much and she would have fallen had her assailant not clasped her from behind. They staggered grotesquely across the hall, Loretta's head hurting so fiercely she was overcome by nausea. She retched, temporarily losing her capacity to focus on anything but physical sensations, and brought her hand up to her mouth. A warm, watery liquid ran through her fingers.

"Come—in here—" The man's voice again, close to her

right ear. She felt his arms groping for her waist, impeded by the bulkiness of her fake fur coat, and then she was being dragged across the hall towards the drawing-room.

"*Let me—*" was all she got out before a gush of vomit silenced her. She heard an exclamation of disgust and the man's hand moved round to grasp the handle of the drawing-room door. Loretta resisted with all her strength but was propelled into the room, raising her hands ineffectually to her head in terror of further blows. He pushed her towards the sofa, and she fell on to it with a protracted moan, closing her eyes as if she could escape this nightmare . . . Then she opened them and saw her attacker for the first time—

"You!"

The yellow light of a street lamp streamed through the uncurtained windows, illuminating Tom Neil's haggard features with a ghastly glare.

"Shut up!" he said savagely, backing away from her. "*Shut up.*"

One hand groped behind him for a chair; the other was holding something which Loretta recognized with a shock as a hammer. A *hammer*—how much damage had he done? Her hand went to her head and hovered there, afraid of what she would find if she touched the wound. She saw Neil sit down abruptly and put the weapon on the floor by his foot. He seized a whisky bottle and a glass from the table beside him; the bottle was already open, and his hands were shaking so much that it clinked repeatedly against the rim of the glass, making a noise like chattering teeth.

"What—I don't—" Tears were trickling down Loretta's face but she was hardly aware of them.

"*Shut up!*"

Neil drained the glass and even in her enfeebled state she could see that he would soon be senseless if he carried on at this rate. She leaned back against the sofa, the pain in her head now a dull ache, and became aware of the sour smell of bile. She touched the front of her coat and found a sticky mess of regurgitated food which she tried to brush away, giving up when she realized she was only spreading it over a wider area. The room was hot and she felt faint, but didn't dare remove the coat—it might offer her some protection, she thought, glancing down at the hammer.

"Oh!" She let out a small cry, then her body sagged with relief as she recognized the weight against her calves as Bertie. Where had he appeared from? A new fear assailed her and she pulled him up on to her lap, running her hands over his fur.

"I haven't touched him," Neil said roughly, slurring his words: "touched" came out as "tushed." "What do you think I am?"

Loretta hugged the cat and said nothing, taking a little comfort from his presence. He sniffed her coat, turned round, and settled down on her lap.

"You want some of this?" Neil grabbed the bottle and held it up.

Loretta shook her head and immediately regretted it. She put up her hand and felt a trail of blood from the wound in her head to her left cheek. She located a crumpled paper handkerchief in the pocket of her coat and dabbed surreptitiously at the blood on her face. She was trying to remember the little she knew about head wounds, though the attempt at rational thought was like groping for dim shapes through fog. She thought she'd blacked out, which seemed a bad sign.

"Sure you don't want it?" Neil was back at the bottle.

"Yes."

"You'll be all right," he said unexpectedly, tilting the bottle and drinking from it. This time he put it down on the floor, next to the hammer, and Loretta was afraid he'd knock it over, spoiling her hopes of waiting until he drank himself stupid. She didn't dare speak, however.

"Don't look at me like that!"

She closed her eyes, wondering what he expected of her, and tried to make her features neutral; not an easy task, given the pain in her head.

"This is all your fault—*your* fault." Neil was angry. "You know that?"

She shook her head very slowly.

"Like *her*—"

Loretta didn't catch the rest of the sentence. Neil was muttering to himself, and as she watched, his head sank on to his chest. She tensed; perhaps he was already lapsing into an alcoholic stupor. She sat very still, willing him to black out.

Time passed. The room was quiet, and unevenly lit by the light of the street lamps. Every now and then a bus rumbled by and Neil lifted his head, mumbling under his breath. Loretta heard car doors slam in the street outside, people shouting goodnight to one another, and the knowledge that help was so close, yet beyond her reach, was almost too much to bear. At some point she inched her arm forwards out of the sleeve of her coat, turning it so she could see the face of her watch. Twenty-five past one—over an hour since she got out of the taxi in Liverpool Road. The events of the evening— the film, the pleasant meal—had begun to seem unreal, part of a distant and unreachable past. Tears rolled down her face and dripped on to the cat; Loretta wiped his fur with her hand and he purred.

On the other side of the room Neil stirred, opened his eyes and looked straight at her, then closed them just as abruptly. Loretta put her hand to her head and felt crumbly, congealed blood in her hair. The wound seemed to have stopped bleeding, but she still didn't dare touch it. She was gripped by a sudden feat of a haemorrhage, a secret welling of blood inside her skull which would lead inexorably to unconsciousness. There was no time, she couldn't just sit here . . .

She peered across the room. Neil hadn't moved for five, maybe even ten minutes. Loretta held the cat tightly and edged forwards in her seat. She was getting stealthily to her feet when Neil started, said something unintelligble, and kicked the hammer in his sleep. Loretta froze, then relaxed as she detected no further movement from him. Should she try and get the hammer? Five or six paces across the room— it was too dangerous. The cat was already waking, starting to squirm in her arms. She moved sideways, heading for the slightly open door.

"Don't go."

He had spoken in a relatively normal voice, and Loretta was so surprised that she stood rooted to the spot. Neil shifted in his seat, looked up at her, and added: "I'm sorry."

"*Sorry?*" It came out before she had time to think.

He was getting to his feet and she shrank back. "Don't—"

Neil put out a hand and said pleadingly: "Let me have a look at your head."

"No!" She looked toward the door.

"I've told you—I'm sorry. I want to help."

Bertie struggled and jumped from her arms, trotting from the room. Loretta felt a slight sense of relief—at least he was out of the way of this maniac—

"Have you got a first-aid kit? For God's sake sit down, why don't you?"

The hammer was still at Neil's feet. Loretta sat down. He followed her gaze to the floor and with a sudden movement kicked the hammer towards her. It made a grating noise on the wooden boards, coming to a halt inches from her feet. She stared at it, recognizing it as her own, from the tool-box in the utility room.

"You see. I'm not going to hurt you. It's over." He sounded irritated. "You must have something—TCP, a cloth—"

"There's some TCP in the bathroom." Loretta could hardly believe the conversation was taking place.

"Stay there."

He left the door ajar. Loretta heard him run up the stairs, and the sound of the bathroom cabinet being opened; she was still calculating whether she had time to reach the front door and draw back the bolt when he reappeared.

"Turn your head."

She did as she was told and felt a piercing pain which made her cry out as he applied a damp cloth to the site of the wound.

"*Keep still.*" The pressure ceased and he unscrewed the bottle of TCP, pouring it on to the cloth. Loretta clutched

221

the arm of the sofa, gritting her teeth as the antiseptic stung the wound.

"You'll be all right," he said a second time. He dropped the cloth to the floor and returned to his seat on the other side of the room. "Thank God," he added in a low voice, but Loretta hardly heard him; she was looking down, horrified by the stains on the cloth. So much blood . . .

"Don't look." Neil took a deep breath, held it, then let it out in a long sigh. "Whatever you think, I didn't come here to . . ."

"To hit me with a hammer? You must be mad." Loretta looked up, speaking in a low, angry voice. Her head was clearing at last, perhaps with the shock of the antiseptic.

Neil said: "I've suffered. I have suffered."

"What's that supposed to mean?"

He looked away, turning his head towards the window. "Have you ever loved somebody? Really loved them—so you'd do anything for them?"

Loretta didn't say anything, more and more convinced he was deranged.

"I loved my wife," he said, still not looking at her. "You have to understand—it's the key . . . From the moment I set eyes on her—she was only sixteen. She was so—it doesn't change anything, death, you know. You still—"

"But you killed her," Loretta interrupted him. "Didn't you? That's why you're here. You broke her glasses and made her get into the car. Did you have a hammer that night as well?"

"No," Neil said wonderingly, turning back to her. "It wasn't *like* that. I didn't mean to hit her, I lost my temper—it's not—I went after her, I tried to stop her . . ."

"I don't believe you." Loretta suddenly felt brave. "You say you loved her—"

"I didn't—you've got to understand." He was pleading with her again. "I know that's what they'll think, the police . . . I should've put them in the car, it would've looked like they'd broken in the crash—I didn't think . . .

"She was alive, you know—when I got to the car. She

222

looked at me, she was making a noise . . . I couldn't—there was nothing I could do." He shuddered. "I wanted to die, do you realize that? Can't you see what I've been through? What it's cost me to . . . ?"

"What *you've* been through?"

Neil looked down at his hands. "It was the first time I'd seen her since—something came over me, I couldn't stop . . . I put up with so *much*. I took it—the other men, I knew about—that was her other life, as long as she kept it . . ." He lifted his head. "You think that's pathetic, don't you? But it was the price, what I had to—I didn't want to lose her. Think of it as a sickness, an obsession," he said with unusual clarity. "Does that make it better?"

Loretta said nothing.

"But then she got her hooks into Felix—"

"*Felix?*"

"Shocked, are you? Her own *son*. I knew there was somebody last summer, she was restless, she stopped—" He broke off, shaking his head. "I didn't guess. How could I? She took him to a hotel, can you believe—He left his tie . . . a parcel came, I shouldn't have opened it—but I'm not so sick I didn't know what to do," he finished defiantly.

"You mean you accused her—" Loretta began incredulously, thinking of Paul Fleming.

"I told her I wanted a divorce," Neil said, not answering the question. "I cut off her allowance, told her to stay away from the kids. She kept ringing me, I told her to keep away . . . She was on the phone on New Year's Eve, as soon's I got back. She said all right, I could have the divorce, but she had to see me. I thought—I actually thought she might be sorry." He paused. "And do you know what she wanted? Money. *Money* in return for the divorce. I couldn't . . . I didn't mean to hit her." He dropped his head into his hands.

"When I saw her in the car, I wanted to die . . ." He was mumbling, Loretta had to strain to hear him. "Only the children—"

Suddenly he sat bolt upright in his seat and stared at Loretta. "I didn't mean to. It was an accident. You understand? I *loved* her."

Loretta nodded slowly. There was silence for a moment.

"Could you make some tea?"

"Some tea?" Loretta was so astonished she repeated the words as if she had not understood them.

"Yes. Go on, see if you can stand up," His voice was gentle, encouraging.

"I—all right." Loretta wondered if it was some sort of trick. She rose slowly to her feet, swayed, then edged towards the door. Neil slumped forward with his elbows on his knees, staring at the floor. She reached for the door handle and turned it awkwardly, pulling the door inwards without ever turning her back on Neil. Then she slid round it, wondering whether she dared close it as she prepared for her flight down the stairs.

"Shut the door." Neil's voice, still calm, came from inside the room.

Loretta obeyed, then tiptoed towards the front door. She put out a hand to the bolt, heard a noise in the drawing-room and froze. She had left the hammer behind, was he about to come after her? She waited, straining to hear what was happening; Neil was moving about, there was no doubt about that. Then—silence. Loretta stood very still, holding her breath. A minute passed, then two. She eased the bolt back, now more puzzled than afraid. Why hadn't he called out, asked what was happening to the tea? The tea—it was a ludicrous request. Loretta went back to the drawing-room door, listened, then threw it open. She paused on the threshold, took a couple of steps inside—

Tom Neil was no longer in the room. Loretta's mouth fell open and she glanced behind her into the hall, still afraid of a trick. It was only when she turned back that it struck her that one of the sash windows had been thrown up and the curtains were blowing inwards in great gusts of cold air. He's escaped, she thought incredulously—climbed down the drainpipe that runs parallel to the window-frame. She hur-

224

ried across the room to the telephone, slowing as the pain started up again in her head, and dialled 999.

"The police," she said urgently when the operator asked what service she required. "And an ambulance . . ."

She heard a squeal of brakes outside in the road and put the phone down on the table. Going to the open window, she saw that a car had come to a swerving halt a few yards up the road from her flat. The driver was getting out, leaving his engine running and the car door open. His passenger followed, shouting unintelligibly, and there was more braking and hooting as a van travelling in the opposite direction performed an emergency stop. The two men from the first car were running towards her, and Loretta's first, irrational thought was that they were coming to her aid . . . She leaned out of the window to shout to them, then realized that they hadn't seen her, after all—were too intent on something at street level, directly below her. With a sick horror she looked down, anticipating by a split second the sight that met her eyes—Tom Neil's body impaled on the railings, two black spikes pushing up through the back of his old sports jacket in the centre of a dark, spreading stain.

"Hello?" The operator's voice sounded tinnily behind her. "Hello? Is anybody there?"

Coda

LORETTA SAT DOWN BY THE WINDOW, NOT taking off her denim jacket. She undid the scarf she had tied round her head, folding it up and placing it neatly on the table beside her. The flat was cold and airless, and there was a thin layer of dust on the surface of the table. She pulled the edges of her jacket together and reached across with a gloved hand to activate the answering-machine.

"Loretta, I've just heard the news. I'm—I can't believe it—I guessed you wouldn't be there, but the radio didn't say which hospital . . . If you get this message please ring and let me know—they said head injuries . . . This is Sally, by the way . . . *Please* ring, I'm so *worried* . . ."

"Loretta, this is Susie Lathlean from Vixen Press, calling on Tuesday. I tried to get you at work just now and they were *very* mysterious—said you wouldn't be in for a while, but wouldn't say why. Is everything all right—you haven't been sacked or anything?" She laughed nervously. "Give me a ring when you get the chance, I need to talk to you about money. Bye for now."

"Hello there, Mrs. Lawson, you don't know me—Gordon McKay from the *Sun*. I've been trying to get you at the hospital but you know what they're like . . . I'm very keen to talk to you about your ordeal—can you ring me back on this number?" He read it out. "That's a freephone number, won't cost you anything. It is a bit urgent, love."

226

"It's Susie Lathlean again. Someone's just shown me the *Standard*—I feel dreadful about my last message—I had no idea! I gather you're being kept in for observation, whatever that means . . . I didn't want to bother you at the hospital, so I thought I'd ring your machine again—we're all hoping you're all right, and if there's anything we can do—don't worry about the book, don't give it a thought till you're feeling better . . ."

"Loretta—I don't know what to say. This is Bridget, I'm back in Oxford . . . I've just seen the *Six O'Clock News*—they said head injuries . . . I'll have to try and find out the name of the hospital—I wonder if the BBC would tell me, who would I ring? Sorry, I'm not thinking straight—perhaps you won't get this message . . . Ring me if you can—lots of love."

"Loretta? It's Robert . . . I didn't really expect you to be there—I'll try and find out which hospital you're in. It's Tuesday evening, by the way."

"Jesus Christ, Loretta, what the hell's going on? I've only just heard, Bill Reevell from Foreign phoned—says some guy jumped out of your window. Jesus, what am I supposed to—maybe I should ring the airport . . . I'll try your mother. Why the hell hasn't anyone been in touch—we're not divorced *yet*, I'm still your next of kin!"

"Loretta—I've spoken to the hospital but they say you're not well enough to come to the phone . . . This is Robert again. If you do get this message, please give me a ring. It's Wednesday afternoon."

"Hello Miss Lawson, I hope you don't mind me calling you at home . . . I write for the women's page of the *Sunday Herald* . . . This is nothing to do with John Tracey, by the way . . . I'm putting together a feature on women who've been attacked in their own homes, whether it's changed their feelings about where they live and so on, and in view of what happened on Monday night . . . My name's Sylvia Raines, by the way. I'm sure you've got the *Herald* number—I'm on extension 6366."

Loretta shook her head and thought it was just as well Sylvia Raines hadn't succeeded in getting hold of her.

"Hello, this is Mrs. Beach from Lady Diana Florist's, St. Paul's Road. We've been trying to deliver some flowers to your flat but you're always out, and your neighbor doesn't seem to be there during the day, either. Could you let us know when it would be convenient to deliver? Thank you so much."

"Ah, Dr. Lawson, Shirley Potter from Connell Potter, Upper Street. Just letting you know that the young lady downstairs let us into your flat, as per your instructions, and we've measured up. I'm putting a copy of the details in the post to you, the only thing I haven't got is the rateable value. If you could get back to us as soon as possible, I've already got several people wanting to view . . . We're doing our best to weed out sightseers, but in view of the recent unfortunate incident . . . The asking price for the property is £89,950, as agreed. Thanking you."

"Mrs. Beach again, Lady Diana Florist's. If you could contact us . . ."

"This is a message for Dr. Laura Lawson from the coroner's office, St. Pancras, calling on Wednesday the twenty-seventh of January. I haven't had a reply to my letter of the twenty-second, requiring her to attend as a witness at the inquest into the death of Mr. Thomas Edward Thornton Neil next month . . . I understand there's some question of head injuries, and I'm just ringing to advise that a doctor's certificate will be necessary if Dr. Lawson is unable to attend. Thank you."

"Hallo, Loretta, you come back today, yes? This is Shahin. I am coming home at six o'clock tonight, but do not wait to collect your pussy cat. He is very well, but he misses you, I think. Bye bye."

This was the final message, and the machine began winding back. Loretta remained in the chair, staring into space, and jumped when the phone rang.

"Hello?" she said tiredly.

"Loretta? It's Derek. Sorry to trouble you. How's the head?"

Her hand went up to it automatically. "Well, it looks a bit of a mess, especially where they shaved the hair . . . I'm still getting headaches, but the hospital says I'm very lucky—I've got a thick skull, apparently. There's no fracture . . . The beret helped, of course."

"Yeah, so I heard. The papers didn't get hold of you in Oxford?"

"No. Thanks for not letting them know. I needed the rest."

"You should be all right now. These things aren't even a nine-day wonder as far as journalists are concerned," Ghilardi said in disgust. He hesitated. "Look, I'm sorry—mentioning your name when I asked about the glasses, I mean. I never thought—"

"That's all right," said Loretta, not wanting to talk about it. "Was that all—?"

"Oh—no." Ghilardi sounded relieved. "Couple of things—you want your keys back?"

"My keys? Oh, you mean the ones I gave Sandra. D'you know, it never occurred to me that he had them, I didn't even think about how he got in . . . No, we're having the locks changed tomorrow, my neighbour's fixed it up."

"Right, then. You might be interested—we tracked down the boy, the one she went to the hotel with."

"Oh, you did—Paul Fleming?"

"*Paul* Fleming? His name's Tony—no, that's not who I'm talking about."

"I don't think I—"

"Paul Elvin, that's what he's called. He went to the same school as the son, Felix, that's how she knew him. He was in the year above—he's at college now."

"Good God."

"Yeah—she met him last summer, apparently. Felix brought him home—never noticed a thing. Or so he says."

"But what about—Fleming's son, you say he's called Tony?"

"He was the previous boyfriend. She traded him in for the toy boy." Loretta frowned at the crude phrase, but Ghilardi continued, oblivious. "He's a bit nearer her age, at least—well, late twenties. Seems to have been an on-and-off sort of thing at the best of times. In fact, if he's to be believed, it was more or less over by the time she got the push. Sneaked on by another kid at the unit—you know what drug addicts are like. He felt bad about it, that's why he fixed her up at the health club. Thought he was doing her a favour."

"So—I can't quite take this in. What about—what about the tie? He—Tom Neil—" Loretta had to force herself to say the name, "he said something about a tie . . ."

Ghilardi sighed. "Felix left it in her car, end of the summer term. You know what boys are like—can't wait to get the old uniform off. This hotel, bit of a posh place—amazing she ever took him there. You have to wear a tie in the dining-room, and she remembered it was in the car. Chambermaid found it next day and they sent it back to the address she'd given—Winchester, that is. If only she'd put Balham, or Notting Hill . . . Still, that's life, isn't it?"

"I suppose . . ." Loretta thought that that was one way of looking at it.

"You've got the date of the inquest?"

"Yes, there was a message on my machine, and I think there's probably a letter in the kitchen." Loretta had dumped the post unopened on the kitchen table before playing her messages.

"I think that's it then." Ghilardi hesitated. "Except, mmm—I've still got your book."

"Oh, keep it."

"I just wondered—you going to be in London next week-end? Not tomorrow, I don't mean—next Saturday."

Loretta opened her mouth, searching for an excuse. "I—I don't think so. In fact, I'm pretty sure not . . ."

"Oh well, some other time," Ghilardi said hastily. "I'll let you . . . Bye." He put the phone down.

Loretta sat back in her chair, relieved he hadn't pressed her, and looked at her watch. Ten to four. She shivered, thinking she should turn on the central heating. The light was fading and she got up, wandering over to one of the windows and looking down into Liverpool Road. A gaggle of teenagers in school uniform was walking past, and they stopped outside her flat and pointed excitedly at the building. One of the youths, taller than the rest, suddenly lunged forward and draped himself over the railings, his long arms swinging, in a grotesque parody of the events of the week before. Loretta grimaced and drew back, thrusting her hands deep into the pockets of her denim jacket. She had expected some people to take a ghoulish interest in what had happened, but even so . . . Sighing, she picked up her keys from the table and went out of the room, turning on the light in the hall before going downstairs to collect Bertie.

About the Author

Joan Smith was born in London in 1953. She studied Latin at Reading University and then trained as a journalist on the Blackpool *Evening Gazette*. She joined the London *Sunday Times* in 1979 and has been a free-lance journalist since 1984. She reviews regularly for the *Independent*, the *Guardian*, and BBC Radio Four. The author of two previous Loretta Lawson mysteries, *A Masculine Ending* and *Why Aren't They Screaming?*, and a collection of essays, *Misogynies*, she lives in North Oxfordshire.